FICTION RIVER: FEEL THE LOVE

An Original Anthology Magazine

EDITED BY MARK LESLIE

Series Editors

KRISTINE KATHRYN RUSCH & DEAN WESLEY SMITH

FICTION
RIVER

Fiction River: Feel the Love
Copyright © 2019 by WMG Publishing
Published by WMG Publishing, in collaboration with Kobo Writing Life
Cover and layout copyright © 2019 by WMG Publishing
Editing and other written material copyright © 2019 by Mark Leslie Lefebvre
Cover art copyright © Ragsac19/Dreamstime
Cover design by Allyson Longueira/WMG Publishing
ISBN-13: 978-1-56146-074-8
ISBN-10: 1-56146-074-5

CONTENTS

FOREWORD

Just What I Needed

I've had a very strange 2018. I now live in a condo I hadn't even seen in January, in a city that I hadn't planned to move to, in a world I don't entirely recognize. I'm healthier than I was, but discouraged a lot by the news, which—to steal from Dahlia Lithwick of *Slate*—has gone from a fire hose of information to a tidal wave. In addition, this has been a hard period in other ways. I literally will not allow myself to count how many of my friends, colleagues, and acquaintances have died in the past year (with more daily, it seems).

So, while my health improved, my heart ached. And the usual respites for me, which include political discussions with friends and being a news junkie, had ceased being fun. I've had to learn how to filter, which has been harder than expected.

This past month, as I marked another passing year in my own life and I had to look at the actual number (which is shockingly large), I felt encroaching cynicism. I was having trouble finding a lot to believe in, and found it even harder to hold onto any kind of optimism about my fellow human beings (especially the ones I disagreed with).

That same month, I had to line edit this volume. Usually I find line editing annoying at best. Either I get caught up in the stories

v

and miss things (too often for my comfort), or I get annoyed at rereading when there's so much new stuff in the world. (Okay, yes. I can be a piece of work.)

This time, though. This time, I found myself looking forward to the work.

Mark Leslie's idea with this volume was to show all the different kinds of love in the world. When he decided to do this, the news was still a fire hose instead of a tidal wave, and most of us in the United States were still talking to all of our family members. Mark wasn't thinking about being uplifting. He was thinking about the kinds of stories he wanted to read, and the kind of anthology he wanted to put together.

I'll be honest: I was worried that it would be too saccharine, with too many unconvincing romances. But I've watched Mark do difficult editing tasks before with great aplomb (this volume's sister volume, *Feel The Fear,* and especially *Editor's Choice*). I did trust him to edit the volume—Dean and I wouldn't have asked him to continue to edit for us if that wasn't the case—but I had my concerns.

Oh, my, those concerns are so far gone that I can barely remember them. I had read most of the stories before, most of them at the annual anthology workshop that WMG Publishing puts together in the spring, but reading stories along with a sea of stories for other themes isn't the same as reading the stories in the order that the editor provided.

When Mark turned in the volume, I remember looking at the table of contents, and thinking I would have put the stories in a different order.

I would have been wrong.

From the first story to the last, this volume explores the ways that love not only makes us human, but makes our lives better. He has found so many different examples of love that they overwhelm the volume. Sometimes I had to reread several times to do my line editing job.

And I didn't mind one bit.

I found this volume comforting and thoughtful, uplifting and warm. My faith in humanity is restored, and I'm ready to wade into my new existence, fortified by the realization that no matter what else happens, love remains an essential and important part of the human experience.

Thanks, Mark.

—Kristine Kathryn Rusch
Las Vegas, Nevada
July 7, 2018

INTRODUCTION

Love Is

Philosophers, poets, writers, and romantics have speculated, composed, bemused, and shared perspectives on love from the beginning of recorded time.

Love is universal. It is something that humans and other animals feel and express in so many different ways, through so many different situations.

Love is complex, it is frightening, it is enlightening, it is comforting. It is confusing, it is simple, it is complex, it is pure.

Love is similar to the theme I was pursuing for *Fiction River: Feel the Fear* in that it is an emotion that reigns powerfully throughout literature and stories, almost regardless of the genre.

Love is often believed to be about romance. The perspective of romantic love is definitely a strong one in western society. Sure, you expect to read about love in a romance story. But there is also love in so many forms, shapes, sizes, and dimensions.

Love is central. It is at the core of our being. It consumes, it protects, it provides, it divides.

Love motivates.

I remember, during a World Horror Con from many years back, hearing Brian Keene talk about his recent Bram Stoker Award–

winning novel, *The Rising*. He said that it wasn't a novel about zombies; it was, at its heart, a story about the love that a father has for his son. The book he was speaking about follows a man as he fights his way across a zombie-ravaged America to get to his son. His sole motivation in this tale is his love for his boy.

As a newly minted father at the time, I was touched by Keene's words. And, though I had avoided reading zombie novels (this was even before *The Walking Dead* made zombies all kinds of flavors of popular), I picked up this novel.

Not because it was a horror novel about zombies.

But because it was about the love that a parent has for their child.

Love reigns, in all of its forms.

Love is something that we never run out of.

Love is something that, no matter how much we give, there's always more there. It is a well that can never run dry, even when, at times and for some, it might seem to be a limited resource. But we can manufacture more of it, at any time, at will.

Love is truly one of the things that, no matter how much you give to others, there is always more.

When I put the call out for the stories for *Feel the Love*, I told the writers I was looking for stories about love from across the spectrum. I knew there would be romantic love stories here, but I wanted to see if the writers could explore different aspects of love, how it is given, is received, is experienced by different people in different situations.

And they brought their game to this task. They impressed me far beyond my expectations with the unique ways that they made love central to their story, but explored a unique element of perspective of it.

I admire the way these stories explore love in ways that make me smile and laugh, but also move me and make me cry. They play upon universal fears and explore the darkness; but they also offer hope and encouragement. Ultimately, these stories make me think and reflect.

Without hyperbole, I can assure you that I love these stories.

Love is captured brilliantly by these authors on the following pages.

With Love,
Mark Leslie
Waterloo, Ontario
May 2018

THIEF

MICHAEL KOWAL

Thief represents Michael Kowal's ninth appearance in Fiction River *and is part of his popular Dream Again romance series of short stories. He also writes young adult, fantasy, and has written three novels in his John Devlin, PI hardboiled mystery series. In addition to his* Fiction River *appearances, Michael's stories have appeared in* Pulphouse Fiction Magazine. *Find out more about Michael at www.kowalkowal.com.*

There is an adeptness to the way that Michael Kowal introduces Sophia in this story as a type of thief, an elusive photographer who prefers to be unseen as she sneaks about snatching images and moments. You can sense, in a brilliantly subtle manner, the way she adores photography, and really puts herself into the moment of what she captures, or, perhaps, steals.

"I love photography and the ability it gives you to just cut out the rest of the world and only see what's in the frame," Michael says when speaking about this story. "A great way to focus on just what you think is beautiful. Even if it's not what others may feel is beautiful."

The lens by which Sophia chooses to see and share the world slowly tightens its focus on a subject she becomes fascinated with. But the story also explores what happens when the tables are turned on her and she is suddenly cast into the spotlight by someone who similarly pours their heart and soul into their own art.

The result is a delightful tale that explores a pure and raw love born from artistic vision and passion.

Sophia was a thief with a camera.

At twenty-five she was slightly overweight, nondescript, bland, had dark hair she kept pulled back and off her face, wore infinitely neutral colors, moved easily, and in the end was completely unseen.

And that was a good thing.

Because being unseen, being quiet, she could also be deadly. At least here on vacation at the Dream Again Hotel. Pinning what she wanted in the middle of her lens, and taking it. Moments, things, bits and pieces of this and that. But it was the details she loved, the smallest of things that most people would only stray past, that she focused on.

It was night as she stood atop the great winding central staircase in the main hall of the hotel. Sophia was on vacation and, for once, was happy.

The air was still around her, that far up. Five stories to be exact. And she was alone. The way she liked it.

In front of her, the great five-story curved glass wall of the hall stood protecting them all from the weather outside. But tonight it was crystal clear, the full moon out and over the Pacific Ocean, the moon gleaming back with white crystals it painted over the top of the calm ocean. But the moon didn't matter, the amazing view up there didn't matter, the only thing that mattered to her was Lawrence, sitting below in his favorite chair against the glass wall. Looking out.

The whole of Lawrence was a young man in his early thirties Sophia guessed. He was thin and reedy, her mother would probably say. But Sophia thought that his legs looked like the slow, purposeful, wonderfully long legs of an egret as it made its way through the water. Not so much being careful, as being conscious of disturbing the water. The better to observe what lay beneath.

His face was long like his legs, but angular. Not drooping, but uplifting, like he was always ready to laugh. And smile he did. Sophia didn't dare to try to catch the smile, though, because if she did try to catch it, that would mean that her lens was facing directly at him and that would just not have been good. You see, any good thief knows that she should never be seen. Half...no, all of the fun, is in the seeing, but never being seen. Until it's too late and the victim doesn't even know what's been taken.

Lawrence, an almost stranger, sat in his chair five stories below. He barely moved, with only a copy of his favorite book, *Anna Karenina*, on his lap. It was the only book Sophia had seen him with, and he seemed to enjoy it. Sometimes smiling slightly. She called it his Anna Karenina smile. It was soft, and small, and the smile was entirely intimate.

Something she'd like to see every day for the rest of her life. If she was allowed to dream.

He always had either his book with him, or a sketch pad, or both.

Sophia had seen him there at his chair the very first night they had both arrived.

She saw him checking in an hour after she had arrived. Then once he was settled, he had quickly found his chair, and stayed there most every night. She could never approach him, had spent every day the two had been there at the hotel avoiding him but at the same time, stealing bits of him with her camera.

She learned after two days, from following him, that he was a potter, working in the clay room to make cups and plates and bowls and whatever else they did there.

Sophia hated to get her hands dirty so she would never step into the studio. But she looked at him through the small rectangular window in the door. From a distance off. Just glances really. She couldn't risk being seen.

And even after a full week being in the same hotel she didn't know much about him, but he had somehow settled into her, in a most unsettling way.

Each time she found him, and photographed him, in bits and pieces, he became whole inside of her. Until he had finally become a real thing. Almost to the point where she couldn't separate him out. And honestly she didn't want to. As crazy as this whole thing was.

And it was crazy, this obsession, that wasn't really an obsession, it was just...there was something about him that she couldn't explain. Like there was something so natural about being near him. Like taking your next breath. It was that perfect.

And on nights when she let herself go there, she thought maybe even it was love. But then she quickly dismissed it. Because that was impossible.

All she really thought about, though, was the naturalness of it. Of him. And she was sad to lose that.

But the alternative to that was unthinkable.

She couldn't actually talk with him, walk up to him, so she did the only thing she knew to do—she stole bits and pieces of him, through her camera. And it was why she was up here at the top of the stairs, to capture the last of him. The whole him. As he sat in his favorite chair.

Sophia squatted down to her camera bag at her feet, took off the small telephoto lens and put on a more wide angle lens to capture everything below. So she could remember. All of it. Him.

She got up and rested her arms back on the railing, angled the camera down, and shot.

Sophia found out his name was Lawrence because she overheard it at breakfast one morning. As she sat head down, way behind him, in the corner of the hotel restaurant. The waitress had greeted him and Sophia heard that wonderful name, Lawrence, as she kept her face looking down at her sunny-side upside eggs. She didn't want him to see her. That would have been ghastly.

Completely ghastly.

She loved that word, Sophia did, because it was so dramatic. Completely unlike anything she was.

Nothing. Blank. That's pretty much the way her mother described her. And the way Sophia liked to keep it. Hidden. Camou-flaged. Tucked against a wall—you couldn't make her out against a pattern on the wallpaper.

It was an expression her mother used on her, and even though nobody used wallpaper anymore, Sophia didn't exactly like the expression. But she had taken to it. Because it allowed her to do her thing—which was capture people. Steal things. Moments. Their bits of humanity that most people would find ugly, or horrific, but that Sophia found a beauty in.

The heel of their shoe. The light, almost faint stain of butter dropped to their pant leg that they didn't even realize was there. The look in a single eye as it was lost in concentration. An eyebrow that lay there like a lounging caterpillar, or a straight-line bit of thin thread. All of it.

A hand on the handle of a car door. A knuckle. A simple, beautiful, tender fold of fabric on a waitress's light blue blouse.

A lip.

The tip of a nose.

The inside corner of an eye where a tear would come from.

Or a dollar bill left as a tip for a single cup of coffee by a person who probably couldn't even afford the price of the coffee in the first place. Because they saw humanity in the one who was about to receive it.

These are all that she stole from people. The things of beauty that they left in their wake. And that they didn't even realize.

Sophia focused the lens down, holding inside of it the entire area below, where Lawrence sat. Alone.

The weekly art exhibit at the hotel was tomorrow night and she had already picked out and submitted three photos to be included in the show. It was the first show she had ever been in, but it was open to all guests of the hotel. Their chance to show the art, and the dreams, that they had been creating for the week.

Everyone got into the show, nobody was refused, so there was zero chance of being denied. Which is why Sophia came here in the first place. For a little breath of freedom.

Sophia took another couple of shots and laughed to herself. She felt like a stalker maybe. But while she did take photos of a lot of the other guests, she always seemed to come back to Lawrence. Like you ended up in your favorite chair.

And it was so stupid, and so crazy but she couldn't help herself—she would sometimes imagine herself there next to him. Maybe even reading her own copy of *Anna Karenina*. Maybe just looking at him. Maybe even wanting to be seen.

In her very extravagant imaginings, because her mother would never call them dreams, she and Lawrence would be down walking on the wild Oregon beach below, looking for beautiful rocks, counting the grains of sand, and...holding each other. Sophia imagined she would come up just to the middle part of his shoulders, her head ready there to rest right in the middle of his chest. To hear his heart.

To feel his long arms press against her back and hold her even tighter to him. To feel...safe.

That was the extravagant imagining. But she was just Sophia, standing so far above him that he couldn't see her. Couldn't feel her, up here, looking down on him for probably the last time. Just the two of them, there in the Hall of Dreams. She, looking down, but so very far away.

Sophia took one final shot, as Lawrence turned a page, and she walked to the back of the floor, got onto the elevator, and silently whooshed herself back to her room.

Alone.

Sophia was excited, and scared, as she walked into the great hall of the hotel to the very first art show that she was in.

All the seating was cleared away, and it looked like every guest in the hotel was there. Men, women, even children but thankfully there was no sign of Lawrence. That would have scared her even more.

A Spanish guitarist played at the other end of the room, while people walked back and forth looking at all the pieces.

Just to her right on a book stand on a pedestal, was a hand-colored coloring book with a flying piano and a bear, of all things. Next to that on the floor was a broken and bent child's scooter, painted pink. Some kind of sculpture Sophia guessed, but then again, who knew? And a smile crept onto her face because that was the whole point of all of it—who knew? No one knew. You were only supposed to enjoy it. Everything.

Then Sophia saw her photos.

They were above three narrow white pedestals, but floated in the air. Frameless, they hung from thin wire from above that held them suspended over the pedestals. It was amazing. And there, in that setting, the photos were amazing.

Sophia couldn't believe it. And she also couldn't breathe...just looking at her pieces.

Nothing had ever looked so beautiful in her life. And they stood out against the black of the night out beyond the glass walls. The only other thing visible was her own reflection in the glass wall behind, backed by the night of the Pacific Ocean beyond.

The first photo on the left was of a single white shoelace, slightly dirty, and falling to the side of Lawrence's deep navy blue canvas shoe. The whiteness of the lace stood out against the blue of the shoe, the lace itself dropping as if a woman lounging. The second photo was of his left hand as he walked toward the elevator. She caught it with a telephoto lens and held the hand centered in frame as everything else in the background blurred in movement.

In the third and final photo, was a single stray piece of his hair. Caught one night while he sat in his chair, a halogen light from above rimming it in gold.

It was the most simple thing, the most mundane thing, but there was something intimate about the photo. A shared moment.

Shared by one, unfortunately.

A couple moved up in front of her photos and Sophia moved on herself. Too afraid to hear anything that they may say about it. She didn't think she could take it. Really knew, she couldn't take it.

The rest of things passed by in a whirl as Sophia moved from one piece to the next. Always surprised, always amazed, and always feeling as if her three photos fell short against all of them.

Until she found herself at the other side of the great hall and saw...

Herself.

Cast...no...sculpted in clay. From her waist up, two feet tall, in three full dimensions, with a dramatic downlight glowing on it from above, the black of the Pacific Ocean cradling it from behind.

Sophia gasped. Who did it?

She was right there, everything of her. All of it. Out for everyone to see.

On a pedestal.

Sophia turned to leave—and Lawrence stood in her way.

Tall as he was and as thin as he was, right in front of her. And a small smile spread on his long, angular face. The same smile he wore when he read *Anna Karenina*. "Hello."

It was Lawrence's voice all right, but now heard up close, and directed at her, it cut to the core of her.

She felt like a butterfly...no a moth, pinned.

"Do you like it?"

Sophia felt for an instant, a deep fearing instant, as if she were the one on the other end of the lens. How had he even seen her, and when had he done it?

He had probably seen her, spying on him. And this was some kind of trick. Some kind of thing to embarrass her. But as she turned back to look at the sculpture it was so...gorgeous. Everything about it flowed and was soft and he...he...caught her look, looking out of the corner of her eye.

He, had caught her.

And she was so embarrassed.

"It can't be that bad, can it?"

Sophia looked up at him from the corner of her eye, and he still had his Anna Karenina smile. He wasn't teasing her.

She hoped.

Then she thought of her own hundreds of photos, cutting him apart into small, insignificant pieces. They really weren't who he was, she saw that now as he stood right in front of her.

And he had captured all of her, everything flowing together beautifully. Her hands into her arms, which flowed into her shoulders, that were connected to the rest of her body as she stood there looking at it. Looking at her...self.

It was as if she were whole for the very first time in her life.

"I would watch you from the reflection in the glass. I hope you don't mind. At first I did it to just sketch you, as you were shooting me. I thought that was funny actually, then...I kept doing it because I enjoyed it. A lot. Then all the sketches led," he pointed at her, the sculpture, "to this."

Sophia looked up at him, and Lawrence's Adam's apple jumped just a bit. She loved watching the movement of the muscles to either side make that happen. Like a small miracle.

Then she lifted her eyes and when they met his, she felt a thrill reach all the way into her. And hold her, right there. And she saw that up close his eyes were really more green than hazel. She could see that now. A small bit of gold rimmed the black pupil at the center, then almost immediately brightening to the color of the light green sea.

She couldn't take him looking into her, so she looked back at the sculpture. And it was all of her.

From the back of her head to the tip of her nose. From her chin that didn't look so weak now as it sat there in beautiful, soft clay. And her neck actually looked...beautiful. How could that be?

He obviously had changed things, he had to have. But there was something growing slowly in her and maybe it was the realization that this was accurate. He even captured her hair perfectly. Including the one piece that never stayed behind her left ear.

But it wasn't just the detail of everything, it was the...it, the whole thing, the sculpture, her—had life. It was alive. And that was the thing that amazed Sophia. It captured not her, but someone else. It surely wasn't her.

It wasn't.

Couldn't be.

But it was. If she softened her eyes just a bit she could see herself breathing there.

And it took her breath away.

"Do you like it?"

"I..." Sophia couldn't find the words. "I don't know what to say."

"I think it's my best."

"I think it's amazing."

"Do you?"

Sophia looked up at Lawrence and she could feel the longing in his words. Longing she'd felt her whole life. As if he couldn't believe that. "Yes." She nodded, and looked back at the sculpture. Her. "It's amazing."

She heard, and didn't need to look back to know, Lawrence was licking his lips. He got that way when he was nervous. But what did he have to be nervous about? He was amazing.

And Sophia's head and shoulders shook involuntarily. A nervous tick, her mother used to say, but Sophia looked at it as releasing energy that had built up unexpectedly. Surprisingly And you didn't know what else to do with it.

"I had wanted to capture that."

"What?" She looked back at him.

"That." He motioned to her with a slight shrug of his shoulders, and a chin that pointed at her. Like he was too afraid of touching her. It was cute. Very cute. "That kind of...shake you do with your shoulders and head." Nervous. She was nervous. Then he smiled. "I wanted to capture that because it's you." Then he looked back at the sculpture. "But you can't exactly do that in clay, can you?"

Then he smiled. And Sophia felt her heart go to complete, melting cheese. Which wasn't so sexy at the moment, but it kind of described it. Because she loved cheese. Cheddar. The extra-sharp kind. Oh God, she was babbling. In her head. Have to stop now.

"But with your photos, you captured that. My movement."

Sophia instantly seized up, everything inside her going hard as glass. Her breath quickened and she felt that one tiny hit, any hit, from him, not liking it, or hating her for doing it, any hit from that hammer would shatter her. Completely. And she tried to hold together the pieces even before the hammer struck. It was a reflex. And it was comfortable.

"I love them. Really..." Lawrence looked at the small photos across the room. "Love them." Then he looked at her. "You're amazing. Did you know that?"

And Sophia couldn't say a thing.

He shrugged. The way he always seemed to do. "I hope you don't think it was creepy, me doing this."

It was like everything inside her had short-circuited. She couldn't laugh, she couldn't speak, she couldn't think.

"Breathe."

"What?" Sophia snapped up to look at Lawrence in the eyes. God, he was tall. So wonderfully tall.

"I said breathe." He followed that with a smile, and a crinkle in his eyes, as a small blush of red showed up on his cheeks and his shoulders slouched in the most cute way.

Then the blush in Lawrence's cheeks started a burn to full red, as his face turned toward the floor. But his eyes, his glorious, amazing, full of sparkling life eyes—kept looking right at Sophia. And he maybe couldn't keep them off her. And *that* thought thrilled Sophia. Then she knew exactly what to say. "Thank you."

And Lawrence smiled. And shrugged.

And Sophia felt something release in her that she never quite knew she was holding. She didn't know what she released exactly and didn't care, but everything seemed lighter somehow.

Then Lawrence scrunched his mouth to one side in a nervous tick that...she had never seen before.

He was standing right in front of her, and he was changing. And, Sophia guessed, that was life.

Then he smiled his Anna Karenina smile. "The title. Did you see the title?"

Lawrence's eyes flicked up to the wall behind the sculpture and Sophia spotted the simple, small white card with black text against it.

She stepped a foot closer to look:

Thief of My Heart

Sophia couldn't bear to look at the card, so instead looked at the sculpture. A perfect likeness, captured in clay. In whole.

The first feel of a tear formed at her right eye, wet, and it fell. Freely.

Then she looked at Lawrence, tear-streak lying cool across her cheek.

It started simply enough that night. But as the night wore on and the moon moved from full in the sky to disappeared over the horizon, the two ended up at the top of the great circular staircase. Watching as the darkness outside turned to the first faint light of morning.

Then Lawrence kissed her there, at the top of the stairs.

Where she used to watch him, and he would watch her back.

And as fate would have it they returned to that same spot a year later. To kiss, and celebrate their marriage.

And for every year after that as a matter of fact.

Because it always amazed them how they had each come to the shore to find each other in pieces and in parts.

And altogether, whole.

DEATH'S OTHER COUSIN

LISA SILVERTHORNE

Lisa Silverthorne has published nearly ninety short stories in the genres of fantasy, science fiction, romance and mystery, appearing in anthologies published by DAW Books, Roc Books, Prime Books, and twelve Fiction River *volumes, most recently* Hard Choices. *Lisa's first short story collection,* The Sound of Angels, *is available from Wildside Press and her two novels,* Isabel's Tears *and* Rediscovery, *are also available. To find out more about her work, go to www.lisasilverthorne.com.*

I have long been partial to stories that explore the incarnations of Death, Nightmares, Dreams, and others. So, it is no surprise that I was immediately pulled into this tale by Lisa's wry and playful narrative style. But I soon found myself compelled as the tune shifted and she pulled quite eloquently on my heartstrings.

"I tried to look for unlikely places and ways I've felt or witnessed love," Lisa says. "I wanted to explore the way we distance our hearts because we just can't risk breaking them one more time." She says that the ways we make assumptions about people based on first impressions or bad timing can lead us down the wrong paths. "But sometimes, we discover that love quietly abides in those unlikely places and it patiently waits in the smallest of spaces and the little assumptions."

E ven if you're not Death, January's still the best time to visit nursing homes, retirement centers, and the elderly. With the holiday rush over, much of the world just settles back into its familiar routine and coasts for a while. Out of habit or sheer exhaustion, I'm not sure, but either way, everything just sort of takes a deep breath and chills the fuck out, making it easier for me to make my rounds and confer with my cousins. Visit the world's oldest residents and do my thing.

So, Cousin Death asked us to meet him outside the Cedar Hill Manor retirement community. Set on a rolling meadow of thick green grass, willow trees, and wildflowers, this place looked like a grand dame in a summer parade. The sprawling, gabled Victorian rest home has ice-blue cypress siding trimmed in white with fish-scale shingles, two turrets, a slate roof, wraparound porch, and spandrels everywhere. A line of wooden rockers and Adirondack chairs overlooked the hibernating hydrangeas, velvety hollyhocks, lavender, and lilacs waiting for spring. It looked like a dream.

Hell, I wanna retire here! I'd volunteer to be the social programs director and everything. Organize outings and picnics...dreams would practically take care of themselves in this place. Only an occasional need for nightmares to even things out, keep people in line.

See, I got smart this year. This time, I negotiated a warmer start with my oldest cousin. Northern California (up from a balmy -18° C in Lavrentiya, Russia). I know, I know—those people's dreams are important, too, but I needed a change of district.

I check my watch. Almost eight p.m. Right on time. Sky's dark except for the deep magenta blush along the horizon. Sun's already set in this part of the globe, dropping like a golf ball in a sand trap (Cousin Death sucks at golf).

I pull in a big, deep breath and stretch my arms wide, taking in the crispness. The sweet, clear air. I do a little spin, working my legs and feet, holding in an urge to sing a few lines of "California Dreamin'." Air's fresher than a hundred of those pine tree air fresheners hanging in the car. Cool and refreshing, unlike that stuffy, dark gothic manor Death calls his crib (I call it a mausoleum).

Wind kicks up, blowing across the rolling meadow, rattling the branches of tall cedar trees and Douglas firs that frame the property. I let the air rush over me, grateful it isn't full of chemicals—enough to get my cousin's attention. Which isn't good for anybody these days.

Sorry for not introducing myself all proper-like. I'm Death's other cousin, Cousin Leo, and I handle dreams. No, I'm not that fat slob, Sleep. Always stretched out on somebody's sofa, sleepin' off a bribe or takin' a nap instead of helping out his cousins. Or helping mortals with insomnia—some cat too grumpy to sleep. Animals dream too, ya know.

No, I'm the taller cousin. The taller, younger, charming, and devastatingly handsome cousin that handles mortal dreams and nightmares.

That's right, dreaming is my business. Dreams are important, people! They're not just some fluffy distraction for your brain. Or wasting time until the real thinking begins.

Hey, I save lives and protect people! Like sending Little Billy some cute, fuzzy dinosaurs to dream about after his lunk-head older brother leaves up images of gunshot victims on his computer.

C'mon, the kid's only four years old!

Look! It's Cousin William (or Death as he's known in the profession), standing on the porch, looking fly in his black robe, hood arranged neatly around his shoulders. His scythe shines with fresh polish, its gnarled handle smooth as he clutches it in his right hand. And those shoes. Shiniest black leather I ever saw...damned expensive, too. Ferragamos? Berluti?

I can't hold back my frown. He looks a little thin, those mahogany brown eyes colder than I remember. His brown hair's a little shorter than usual. And straighter He's about three inches shorter than me and at least twenty pounds lighter. I wave and shuffle toward the porch.

His face brightens a little when he sees me and smiles, holding out his hand.

"Leo, Happy New Year." His voice sounds tired. No, jaded. This isn't good.

Normally, he enjoys his job. Likes bringing people over, striking down people being bastards, and showing the nice ones Act Two of their own stories. He's good at it, too. Can scare the shit out of hardened criminals, have them pissing themselves in terror, and then gently carry kids and delicate old ladies across to the next shore.

William glances around, the sky filling with stars. "Dammit, where's Fred?"

"Cousin Lamont and Cousin Kayla should be on their way," I offered. East Coasters are always late. Can't help it. Time zones are a bitch.

William shakes his head, propping his left hand on his hip. "No,

Leo, they're not. This meeting is just you and me." He grimaces. "And Fred. But he's probably passed out on a couch in Vegas."

A Russian chill brushes across my face and I shiver. A private meeting with Cousin Death? That isn't on my list of things to do today. I'm feeling really unnerved right about now. Something ain't right.

"What's up, Cousin?" I ask, stepping onto the porch, the wind cool at my back.

Damn, that scythe looks awfully sharp tonight, but William always talks straight to me.

"Leo, we have a problem," William says with a deep sigh, and leans against his scythe.

"Hey, you just say the word and I'm all over it," I say, holding out my hands. "Whatever it is, I'll fix it. Okay?"

Then William gets all quiet, sighing a couple times as he paces across the creaky porch. And it's gettin' really dark out here. Colder, too. Dammit! And Fred's out there sleeping away, napping, and having a grand ol' time.

William presses his hand to his forehead, frowning now. "They want me to retire you, Leo."

"What? Retire me? But why?" It's so much worse than I'm thinking. This is bad. Real bad.

"Your dreams are boring, Leo," says William with another sigh. He reaches out and lays a hand on my shoulder, squeezing. "They're not what mortals want anymore."

I begin to shake. Boring? Not what they want? That's a stab in the chest. I turn away from him, staring out across the meadow. Dreams are all I know. They're a part of me. How can they be...boring?

"Leo," he says in a tired voice. "You've been in this business for so long, but you've forgotten how the other side feels. How they think."

His grip on my shoulder tightens and I feel him pull in a deep breath. Winding up for the pitch.

"You've forgotten about love, Leo," says William in a soft, deadly voice. "Something that all of us dream about."

That was more than a curveball. Or a third strike. It's a hollow-point to my heart. Blowing through valves and muscle. Ripping through arteries and splattering my life force all over the celestial walls of the profession. William never misses—with scythe or words. And when he says that his other cousin has lost his touch, he means it. Leo, Death's Other Cousin of Dreams, doesn't know how to love anymore.

Shaking and out of breath, I drop down on the wooden steps, feeling heavy and useless. I half expect to see William and his scythe dribble my beating heart all over the wraparound porch. I've been at this dream thing a long time. I'm good at easing pain and fear, at building confidence, even taking braggarts down a peg or two.

But love...wow...maybe he's right?

"What happens now?" I ask him in a quiet voice.

"You've got until midnight tomorrow," says William. "Show these people how to love, Leo. Make it happen."

When I get to my feet, Cousin Death is gone. Nervous, I stare at the white door leading into the retirement home. Twenty-four or so hours isn't much time. I have my work cut out for me. But this is important. Hell, these people need something to hope for, something to dream.

Taking a deep breath, I step through the closed door (being a cousin has *some* perks) to find some students to learn about dreams. And hopefully a few teachers.

I feel lost, overwhelmed, when I enter this retirement home and I try to appear as human and as mortal as possible. Like them, I was young once. Twenty-two when I joined the business, so I let them see the real me. Jeans, gray tennis shoes, Cardinals baseball shirt, and red hoodie.

The place is huge! It smells like lemons with a hint of bleach and fried fish. A big, sprawling family room with shiny hardwood floors and lots of windows letting in the sunlight on all sides of the room

21

until those floors sparkle. Overstuffed chairs in deep blue and sofas in soft grays and greens fill the space, occupied by lots of seniors, but most of them stare into the distance, looking lost against the warm, sand-colored walls trimmed with white crown molding. Coffee tables and end tables in rich cherrywood are scattered throughout the room, unused, clear glass lamps dark but casting little sunlight rainbows across the wood floor.

It looks more like a photo shoot or a furniture store. It doesn't look lived in either. It feels kinda empty even though there's a constant stream of elderly people tottering in and out of the room, canes and walkers creaking. Some are tall and bony with pure white hair and others thick-bodied with hair speckled gray. Others roll into the room in scooters or wheelchairs and others plod in on their own. Only one or two have some younger family members in tow. And grandchildren buzzin' around like dragonflies.

I cast a little tendril of excitement through the space as I stir up memories of past dreams.

Conversations spark through the room. The people almost seem content, smiling and laughing. A stocky old woman with short white hair and soft brown eyes watches me as I sit down in a chair. Two younger kids, seven or eight, bounce around her wheelchair, chasing each other. Like grandma was just a post between them. I look closer. Their mother, about my age, motions at her kids with a cell phone smashed against her right ear. Babbling away to someone. Then I realize she's the granddaughter and her kids are the great-grandchildren.

My gaze meets the old woman's. For just a moment, I see her sadness. The corners of her mouth turn up, happy because someone has noticed her. But then she looks away, folding her age-spotted hands in her lap.

A shadow darts through the room. I glance up, frowning.

Fred. Asleep on the couch beside the woman's wheelchair. Bastard. Catching some Z's while I'm fighting to stay in the business. And grandma looks like she hasn't slept in days. I want to scream at him, make him do his job.

Instead, I get to my feet and wander over to the old woman and her granddaughter. About five feet four, the young woman has reddish brown hair and hazel eyes that gleam almost gold in the light as she stares past her grandma. She looks like she weighs about a hundred pounds. And she talks so fast into her phone that I can't keep up with the conversation. There's a thick gold ring with a ruby on her thumb. The two boys are playing tag now, running around their great-grandmother like she's a piece of fucking furniture.

And I'm the one who doesn't know how to love? These people all need a class on the subject.

I step between the darting kids, past their chattering mother, and sit down on the coffee table in front of the old woman.

"Good evening," I say, offering her a smile. "I'm Leo."

The old woman's eyes flutter open, staring at me a little wide-eyed. Like she's not used to being noticed. She smiles. "Good evening, I'm an Aries."

I laugh at her joke. "Actually, I think I'm a Scorpio."

"Are you visiting someone, Leo?" she asks, running her fingers through her white hair.

"A few people," I say, returning her smile. "Now, I've decided to visit you."

"I'm Helen," she says.

"Of Troy?" I ask. "Have those thousand ships launched yet?"

She laughs, her cheeks smudged pink now.

While her granddaughter chatters away on her phone, Helen and I talk about her life and how she came to Cedar Hill.

"Jim and I met in London in 1942. I was stationed there, part of the Women's Army Corps." She laughs and her brown eyes sparkle like something lit them from the inside. "Drove ambulances and smuggled supplies."

I grin. "Wow, you drove an ambulance?"

No foolin'! I'm totally impressed. When I was nineteen—what three years ago—I still had trouble driving a stick shift. And this woman, at nineteen, probably drove one all over England and France. While being shot at.

"Gigi drove an ambulance?" the older boy says, blue eyes wide, his gaze on his great-grandmother.

Gigi? Oh, I get it. GG, great-grandmother.

"That's how I met your great-grandfather," she says with a wink at her granddaughter, who doesn't even notice.

"Tell us, Gigi! Tell us!" shouts the younger boy, those big brown eyes as big as planets.

Both boys huddle against the coffee table, watching their great-grandmother talk about dodging machine gun fire in the ambulance. Her face flushes, eyes filling with emotion as her memories (and her past) come to life. Her body shifts, almost pulsing with energy until I half-expect her whole body to sparkle.

Her great-grandkids look mesmerized, eyes filled with wonder, every word she says touching them with excitement and curiosity.

"And I held my breath," she says, exaggerating a big breath with both hands, her voice soft and intense. "I just knew that Nazi soldier was gonna look up at any moment and see me pressed up against the side of the truck."

Helen's great-grandkids move to either side of her wheelchair, each leaning on the armrest, eyes focused on her.

"Then what happened?" asks one of the boys.

"Jim and I crawled through the grass on our bellies until we got past the guard post," Helen continues, brown eyes wide, her voice sweeping and dramatic.

"Did the Nazis see you?"

Helen shakes her head, silvery-white curls settling around her face. She's grinning from ear to ear now. "Nope. I got Jim back on his feet, letting him lean on me until we made it to the ambulance." Her gaze shifts to me. "When we got past the guard post, Jim leaned down and pressed his lips against my ear. He said that if we made it back to the field hospital in one piece, he was gonna marry me."

A shiver rushes across my skin, my eyes stinging a little. Damn allergies acting up.

"Did he propose?" I ask. Hey, even I like a happy ending. I let the cousins downstairs handle the nightmares.

But I already know the answer. It burns like a flame behind her watery brown eyes. Helen wipes back tears, nodding.

"I drove him back to the field hospital and they swarmed over him, treating wounds and broken bones." Helen reaches over and lays her left hand on top of mine. This gal's as sweet as pie. "The next morning, when I sat down at his bedside, he took my hand in his and slid this onto my ring finger." She points to the sparkler on her left hand and it's still a beauty. Just like Helen. "Helen Louise Parker, will you be my driver for the rest of our lives?"

Her voice catches in her throat, trembling now, but the faraway look in those bright brown eyes are a million miles away. With Jim. In a dream I let trickle from my hand to hers.

Finally, she looks up at me. "And that beautiful Englishman, the love of my soul—he said that he wanted to ride beside me for all the rest of his days. And that's just what he did."

Tears slip down my face and I cry with her. I see the images, but I haven't let myself feel them for a long time.

"Thank you, Leo," she says, patting my hand, tears funneling down her face. "For the next seventy years—even if it's only in a dream." She squeezes my hand, her voice softer now. "If I could go back and drive him around for another seventy years, I'd do it all over again."

She will. In her dreams. And I'll see to it. Damned allergies!

"Leo, let me tell you about my rose garden," she says, and I grip her hand.

So many dreams! They all bunch together into a tangle of emotions that push down my spine and through my chest. She tells me how the weeks bud into green leaves and stretch into long, willowy tendrils of months then years that climb across trellises, past the window, and onto the porch, maturing into full blooms. Years then decades. A lifetime of springs and winters. Until that one last sleep under the winter snow. But see, the blanket of snow's too cold and heavy and it stays too long. And when spring finally warms the ground and melts the snow, there's only blackened thorns and leaves. And the memory of those full, fragrant blooms.

Helen's story moves me like a Mack truck jackknifing on I-5.

"For now, these two young'uns keep me busy," says Helen with a deep sigh, hugging her great-grandkids to her chest. "Another part of my Jim that still goes on."

I look over at Helen's granddaughter, phone smashed against her ear. I can't help rolling my eyes. So oblivious. Missing some of the best moments in her life. She needs to put down that phone and live her life.

Helen nods at her granddaughter. "Don't be too hard on Tara, Leo. Being a single mother's hard enough even before the accident—"

"Accident?" I ask, frowning.

Helen smiles through teary eyes and pats her granddaughter on the hip. "Right now, Tara's takin' care of her mother, my daughter. There was a terrible car accident." Her voice falls to a sharp whisper. "Her dad didn't make it. That's his ring on her thumb."

I feel a massive spike of guilt drill through my breastbone and pin my heart against my shoulder blade, exploding in a rolling wave of guilt.

"She's talking to her former high school crush," says Helen. Again, Helen's face brightens, a smile on her face. "He was driving the ambulance the night of her parents' accident. He's an EMT studying to be a doctor."

My whole body is a pile of jelly now, overwhelmed by the emotions surrounding me. And history repeating itself.

Okay, who the hell's cutting onions while my allergies act up? That you, William?

I get to my feet and hug Helen. "Thank you," I say in a choked half-whisper.

"Thank you," she says.

I reach over to Tara and squeeze her shoulder. She glances over at me and nods.

Turning around, I take in the sea of faces throughout the room. Nurses. Patients. Residents. Family and friends. In each face, there's a story. About people they love. People they've lost. And in each pair of eyes, memories and emotions churn, ready to surface at the first kindness shown to them.

And behind those memories are dreams.

Dreams are my business. But for so long, I've made those dreams safe, sanding down corners and softening emotions so nothing hurt, nothing cut, and nobody bled. I hid the scary dreams. Muted the angry dreams. Protected everyone from the hurt and pain when they dreamed about people they lost. People who died.

Those dreams have to get through. They have to continue. Just as they are.

Once more, I look around the room, looking into every person's face, realizing that the one thing I no longer see is a stranger.

Well, okay—there's still Fred sprawled out on one of the couches, snoring his ass off. Stranger than anyone else I know. The room dims and William walks through the closed door, still in his robes, still carrying that scythe.

"You're a quick learner, Leo," he says, patting me on the back. "Thought you'd have to get through half the room before you understood."

I reach up and squeeze his hand. He returns my gesture and I feel the warmth of family against my palm. In my heart. Feels good.

"My protection was hurting people, I get that now," I reply, bowing my head.

William nods. "I look forward to seeing how their dreams change. Here and everywhere else."

He meets my gaze and holds it, one last moment of warmth until that hollow fragileness returns to his eyes. But just for an instant, I see the pain of that burden in his gray eyes. And then it's gone. Cousin William, always the professional, but I feel the chill of that responsibility dance across my heart. And I'm glad I just handle dreams.

William is back on the job again.

In the reflection of his scythe, I see a blond-haired man in an olive military uniform, holding a red rose in front of him. Waiting. I gasp. Jim!

"So soon for Helen?" I ask, wincing.

William shakes his head. "Not right away, but soon."

My muscles go slack, feeling relief. I have time to craft some wonderful dreams for Helen. And Tara. I'm not going to waste this chance to heal. And love.

A loud, rasping snore draws William's attention to Fred.

Fucking Fred, sleeping away on the couch. He jolts up from the couch, his own snores rattling him awake. With hooded lids, he stumbles around until he's standing beside William.

"Cousin," he says to William in a sleepy voice. "How are you?"

"Working. And you? Dreaming of your next assignment?"

"Hey, that's my job!" I shout.

Fred glances at me. "Cousin Leo," he says, nodding. His attention snaps back to William. "Say, about that—where exactly is Lavrentiya? Minnesota?"

I hold in a laugh. "It's on the beach, Fred," I say. "Balmy weather —you'll love it!"

It's the first time I've seen Cousin Death laugh out loud in years. Fucking Fred.

MAKING AMENDS

DAVID STIER

David Stier is a US Army Veteran from the 32nd Armored Regiment 3rd AD (tank driver), studied world and US History, and has toured the Ardennes in Belgium where the Battle of the Bulge took place. A graduate of UCSC in Creative Writing, and the Odyssey *workshops, David lives in Twin Falls, Idaho, where he writes fiction inspired from his studies, travels, and his army experience. His stories have appeared in* F Magazine, Elemental Anthology, Stars in the Darkness *and* Pulphouse *and also in four volumes of* Fiction River, *most recently in* Hard Choices.*

David based "Making Amends" on an actual event. The story wonderfully documents the often surface-rough yet pure and strong love that two lifelong male friends can share with one another.

———————

I was in a hurry to get to Dick's, so turning onto Mattison Lane was the shortest way to go. Then I realized that passing by Ken and Coco's house was also a part of that scenario. Ken had really pissed me off last night at the meeting. I'd left by flipping him off and telling him to go to hell.

As I neared their address I resisted the urge to speed up and also forced myself to look at the house. Coco's SUV was gone because she was on an all-girl's camping trip for the weekend but Ken's pickup was there. I really liked the way they had privatized the front yard by cultivating ferns and other Central Coast groundcover around mature live oak trees to create a unique personal space. They both loved gardening, as evidenced from the hours spent together in crafting their private little world.

After I passed the house I thought about the meeting last night. What was it exactly that had pissed me off? The more I thought about it the less I remembered about it, which convinced me it was a stupid reason to get PO'ed about in the first place.

Just love to take yourself too seriously, don't ya, pal. When are you going to grow the fuck up?

Once more I'd been an asshole. I thought about turning around with the aim of making amends. Ken had been my AA sponsor for most of the sixteen years I'd been clean and sober. In all honesty, he'd probably saved my life, or at least kept me out of the slammer the nuthouse or both. My face flushed in a flash of realization—not for the first time and definitely not the last—that Ken was the most important man in my life. He was maybe the best friend I'd ever had, for God's sake, so why would I allow a stupid resentment I couldn't even remember impact upon that?

I almost turned around, but Dick's call last night about a new stack of 1950s Korean War comics and the offer to have first crack at them sealed the deal. I'd swing by Ken's later this afternoon to make the amends.

The phone rang and the caller ID said it was Coco.

Smooth move, asswipe! You forgot to see Ken yesterday.

"Hi Coco," I said.

"Hi Don," Coco's voice, even over the phone, told me that something was definitely wrong. "I'm at Dominican Hospital. Ken suffered a stroke yesterday morning while I was on that camping trip. Then once we got him to the hospital he had a second stroke."

"Wha—"

Coco kept talking, as though she needed to get it all out at once. Every word she said felt like a dagger thrust to my heart. My gut turned over and a lump formed in my throat. I lowered my head in shame. What if I'd stopped by yesterday on the way to Dick's? Maybe getting him to the hospital sooner would have made a difference.

Fucking comic books were more important than a friend's life, right, pal? All you had to do was stop by and make amends for being a jerk, you fucking asshole.

"He's in ICU right now," she said, "after having open heart surgery last night." She sobbed and started to cry. "He probably had the first stroke early yesterday morning. He was alone for about

32

twelve hours. If I hadn't gotten home earlier than expected he'd probably be dead right now. Can you swing by Dominican sometime today?"

"I'll be there ASAP."

I'd been in Dominican to have my appendix out a few years back, but I'd never been to the ICU. This part of the hospital seemed cleaner. The smells of disinfectant that almost but not quite veiled the body odor, vomit, and other sign posts of human illness weren't present like they'd been when I'd had the appendectomy. The walls were painted a lighter shade of white, too. This wing smelled very clean, as though the chemicals were fighting and winning the battle to save lives.

Nothing like stating the obvious, pal. What a maroon.

I followed the signs and as I got closer, the lump in my gut grew. Finally, I reached the ICU entrance and pushed though the scarred, heavy, double swinging doors.

Coco stood in the waiting room talking to a doctor. As I moved closer, I caught his last comments.

"—was successful. I don't want to alarm you, Mrs. Conklin, but the post-operative bleeding hasn't yet ceased. Ken's chances are still good and coagulation may be restored fairly soon. For now, however, we have enough of Ken's blood type to avoid complications."

Jesus Christ! This guy's bedside manner could do with some polish, huh? I hope he's a better surgeon than a diplomat.

When Coco saw that I was about to tee off, she nodded to me and tried to smile. Seeing this, the doctor turned.

Knowing me as well as she did, Coco gave the warning look she'd perfected over the years. It was a look I knew very well so I shut my pie hole and tried to smile.

"This is Doctor Yasminsky," she said. "Ken's surgeon."

"Hi, doc. I'm Don Campbell, a close friend. I couldn't help over-hearing what you just said."

"Hello Mr. Campbell." He smiled what I thought of as the *doctor-neutral-being-polite-smile* then we shook hands and he turned back to Coco.

Ma always said I wore my thoughts on my sleeve.

Guess she knocked that one out of the park, right, pal?

"I'll keep you updated, Mrs. Conklin. You know how to reach me if you need to." And with a perfunctory smile in my direction, the doc left.

"Where'd he learn about bedside manner?" I asked. "The Acme Medical School of Etiquette?"

Coco smiled, which was my intent.

"We were lucky to get Dr. Yasminsky on such short notice, he's the top cardiovascular surgeon on the Central Coast, but it's been several hours now and the bleeding hasn't stopped." She gave me another one of the looks she'd developed over the years. This one I called *shut-up-stupid-and-listen-real-close*.

"We really need to look at the reality here, Don."

When I met Coco after Ken agreed to be my sponsor, it was a real oil and water reunion. We'd met six years earlier when I was going to college. She was a bus driver for the Santa Cruz Metro and I took the bus to college. She was easy to remember because she would stop the bus just about anywhere and grab hubcaps she saw lying on the side of the road. It was hilarious watching her skinny and quick form race across streets and sometimes through traffic to grab those chromium disks. The hubcap collection in their backyard was impressive. I'd made beaucoup points with her when I'd found an old stainless steel 1935 Desoto hubcap that she mounted next to the front door.

Also, she always had an open book on the dashboard, which she read whenever her bus was picking up or dropping off passengers. I thought of her as a real ex-hippie weirdo.

She told me I was easy to remember as well because I'd acted like a "pompous-ass weirdo" whenever I got on her bus. We laughed about it now but even after sixteen years we could butt heads. She called it a "jaw-jutting friendship," which I couldn't argue with.

Her mind jumped from subject to subject just like mine. We cracked up watching other people—Ken included—who were left totally in the dust when we hit our stride, switching topics—usually about Dickens or Dostoyevsky—at lightning speed and still understanding each other.

And we'd both been labeled weirdos as kids, so we understood what it felt like to spend a lot of the time looking in at life from the outside.

Like Ken, she always called me on my shit and most of the time she was right.

"Why did he have to have open heart surgery for a stroke?" I asked.

"There was a blood clot in his heart that caused both strokes," she said. "Dr. Yasminsky thinks it was there for years. It was necessary even though he was still in shock. They all say it's a wonder he's still alive and an even bigger deal that he survived the surgery."

And then she started to cry again. For a moment I just stood there, not knowing what to do. Coco was one of the most caring and toughest people I'd ever met. Today I'd heard and seen more tears from her than in our entire friendship. Finally I took her in my arms and tried to give what comfort I could.

"Can I see him?" I asked after she'd calmed down and dried her eyes.

The patients in ICU were behind remotely operated doors. I'd heard that only immediate family could get in.

"I'll break down the damn door if they say no," she said.

Jesus, he looked bad. The first time I'd seen him he was just *Ken the Painter*, the contractor I'd worked with on several houses over the years and the dude who'd helped me learn how to be a man. The first house I'd helped him paint was a 3,500-square-foot three-story monster. I thought I knew something about house painting, but man, Ken really taught me otherwise. He'd been doing it for decades after quitting his job as a high school art teacher. The job took two weeks, but when I first saw the place I thought it would take two months.

I considered myself Mr. Speed-o-matic but when Ken got going you could hardly follow the brush strokes. He left me totally in the dust. I watched in jaw-dropping unbelief as his magic brush whipped out doors in three minutes. He'd told me a story once about how he'd worked on a job for three days with a broken elbow, which reminded me of the time my pop worked for three days as a plumber with a broken wrist. Ken was into coke back then so I could only guess how fast he was before he'd gotten clean and sober.

Now he lay in one of the most high-tech hospital beds I'd ever seen. The smell of alcohol and of other things reminiscent of Pop's last night of life were present. Ken was on a ventilator and had tubes coming out of his chest to containers on the floor beneath the bed— probably collecting the blood Yasminsky mentioned. He had catheters in both hands leading to a blood bag and saline drip suspended over the bed. Behind him were monitors whose purpose I could only guess at, except for the oximeter like I'd had clipped to my finger after the appendectomy to monitor oxygen levels.

Ken's face was pulled down on the right side. His color wasn't bad but his breathing reminded me of a lesser version of Pop's painful wheezing on *his* final night. At the top of Ken's hospital gown I could see the first few inches of the dressing that covered the chest incision. I looked from Ken to all the monitors to the nurse and then to Coco—who looked as scared as I felt—then back to Ken. Never had I expected to see him reduced to such a state of helplessness. He'd always been a larger-than-life presence to me and while he could piss me off at the drop of one of his *Ken the Painter* baseball caps, I realized—sooner but usually later— that what he said was given in love and directed toward my welfare.

For the first real-life time, I understood that I loved this man for who he was and for what he had done for me. The only out-of-pocket costs for his mentoring and support had been his time—given freely and with boundless affection for me as a person.

Watching him fight for every breath, I looked back on our sixteen-year friendship, trying to remember the times I'd thanked him for anything. And sad to say, I kept drawing blanks.

That's you all right, pal. Mr. Gratitude in the flesh.

I started to tear up and hurriedly wiped at my eyes with the back of my hand.

"Is it okay if I take his hand?" I asked.

The nurse, a friend of Coco's—Coco seemed to know half the town of Santa Cruz—smiled.

"Yes, please do," she said. "It could help—maybe a lot."

I bent closer and gently took Ken's hand in both of mine, being careful not to squeeze it because of the catheter. I studied his face some more, wondering what to say, if anything.

"If you don't snap the fuck out of it, you old fart, I'll kick your sorry ass."

Behind me the nurse laughed. In front of me I thought I saw Ken take a deeper breath while his eyes moved behind closed lids. I briefly stroked his arm, then turned around.

The nurse, wearing a shit-eating grin, shook her head.

"Good job, Don," she said.

Coco, with tears in her eyes, gave me a grateful smile, then came over and hugged me tight.

"God bless you, Don. I think you reached him with that." She kissed me on the cheek.

"Patented Don Campbell."

For the next twelve hours it was touch-and-go. Once they even had to bring in the crash cart to restart his ticker. Doc Yasminsky said that it was up to Ken now to decide if he wanted to live. I told Coco after that observation that Ken was home free. She looked at me with I took to be hopeful doubt.

"You'll see," I said. "He's not done with life yet."

A couple hours later his condition stabilized. An hour after that he briefly opened his eyes and smiled before nodding off again.

They kept Ken in ICU then CCU for two weeks then transferred him to the rehab facility on Fredrick Street. The first time I came to visit him there Coco was sitting by his bed. Truth be told, she'd been at his side almost constantly since the surgery. Ken was sacked out and as soon as I came in she motioned me to step outside.

"How's he doing?" I asked.

Coco looked away for a moment then shrugged.

"The physical therapists say that his entire right side was affected by the stroke. Also, as I suspected, he has aphasia. But on the plus side, he understands everything people say and can already speak a few words."

Her expression was easy to read—looking with dread at a life of wheeling around an invalid. Who could blame her? I'd also bet my life that she'd stand by him no matter what.

"Have they said if he'll be able to walk and use his right arm again?"

Besides being a house painter, Ken was also talented artist. My ma—also an artist who knew quality when she saw it—had a painting of his with me standing in front of Stonehenge and another of Ken and Coco's living room. His work adorned most of the walls in their house and the walls of who knew how many other houses in Santa Cruz. They all had a marked Expressionist feel. Once you saw one you remembered it. He'd given me the Stonehenge painting gratis. If anything killed him it would be the inability to create more art.

"They haven't come out and said as much," she said, "but it's plastered all over their faces."

"Of course you know that's bullshit, right?" I said.

Coco looked back toward the closed door of Ken's room and remained silent.

Seeing her defeated look really pissed me off, but I managed to bury the anger.

"Look, Coco," I said. "My ma's an RN and I talked to her last night about stroke recovery. She told me that the first six months after the event is what determines if a stroke victim bounces back —or not."

She again looked from Ken's room back to me. "That's what they told me, but they also said not to get my hopes up."

Damn! Do they all go to the same goddamn school to learn about bedside manner?

"Well I think they're full of crap," I said. "I don't claim to know Ken as well as you, but I *do* know he's no quitter."

I took her by the shoulders and made her look me in the eye. "I'll bet you my first edition of *Bleak House* that he'll use his right arm again and walk, *and* I'll bet my first edition of *Little Dorrit* that he'll paint as good or as better than before—and I ain't talking about houses."

She tried to stare me down and lost.

"How long have you been here? All night, I bet."

She shrugged, smiled. "You know me so well."

I hugged her once, hard.

"Well, go home and get some rest. I'll sit with him for the rest of visiting hours, then I'll stop by and we can go out to dinner someplace."

Ken was asleep, facing the window. The blinds had been drawn back, giving him a twilight view of some oak trees and blue cloudy sky. There was another patient in the second bed but I couldn't see much because the curtains were partially closed.

Ken's face still had that right-side-droopy appearance, but it seemed to be a little better. As I pulled the wooden chair closer to his bed, the legs scraped across the linoleum floor, which woke him up. For a moment his eyes remained unfocused, then he saw me and smiled with the left side of his face.

Okay, pal, you sold Coco, now don't blow it with the protagonist, huh?

I gave him what friends called my *smart-ass-slash*.

"Lucky you, man. I sent Coco home to get some sleep. Now you get to look at my ugly mug."

He smiled again and I smiled what I hoped passed for a big fat shit-eating grin. It must have worked for his smile widened too. Even the right side of his mouth quirked upward.

I sat down and moved the chair a little closer to his bed. He still had a catheter in his right hand connected to a saline drip. Coco had said he still couldn't eat solid food because he had trouble swallowing. That was one of the first things the therapists were working on, she'd said. I noted the remains of his dinner—what looked like some kind of horrid, thick green slop.

"That the stuff you have to eat? Damn that must really suck," I said.

Ken nodded, shrugged. He opened and closed his mouth several times, making a series of grunts. Then: "Yath...taths...lk...cp," he finally got out.

The nurse who was helping the other patient in the room looked up.

"Well, Ken," she said with a mock-serious expression. "The sooner you learn swallow, the sooner you won't have to eat crap." She moved to my side and whispered into my ear. "That's the first understandable sentence he's said!" Then she moved back to the other patient.

I motioned with my head to the nurse. "Listen to the doctor—I mean nurse—if you want some real *man's* food."

We talked—or actually *I* talked for a while. Telling him about friends of ours and how they all wished him well. Like Coco, he seemed to know half the town, so when I mentioned mutual friends and if they'd come by, he nodded *yes* a lot. After what seemed a right amount of time, I switched gears.

I picked up his right arm. He followed my movements with his eyes. It was very warm and when I moved the fingers and released them, they moved back to their original half-closed position. I let the arm drop back onto his lap.

"They told me you'd never use this arm again and I told them that was fucking bullshit."

He shrugged, then stared out the window.

I stood so he had to look at me. "They also said you'd be stuck in a wheelchair for the rest of your life and I told them that was fucking bullshit too. You're not going to make a liar out of me, are you?"

He just shrugged again, kept looking out the window.

"Ma told me last night that the first six months after a stroke will decide whether you'll ever use that arm or walk again, so unless you want to be a fucking cripple for the rest of your goddamn life, you'll snap out of it and get with the fucking program."

He'd stopped smiling now. In fact, he looked really pissed off.

I moved back to the chair and he glared at me as I sat down.

"I need to make an amends, man," I said. "I was an asshole after that meeting." My heart began to pound and my gut did several flip-flops. Acid rose in my throat and I swallowed it back down. In spite of my determination, tears formed in my eyes. Ken's look of anger morphed into one of questioning concern. I felt the tears run down my cheeks, angrily wiped them away.

"I passed by your house the morning of your stroke. I was still pissed from the night before so I didn't stop. If I had, you wouldn't have been alone till Coco got home. Maybe if I'd been there to call 911 you wouldn't have had that second stroke."

I forced myself to keep eye contact. "I'm sorry, Ken. You're my best friend and I'm nothing but a useless self-centered shit."

I looked away, down at the floor. More tears ran down my face.

I felt his hand on my shoulder. Looked up, expecting to see anger —maybe even hatred. Instead, he was crying too.

"No...Dah...not...ur...faa..."

A nurse came by, took one look then quickly left.

I told Coco too over dinner that night. She said it wasn't my fault either, but to this day I feel it to be the most selfish mistake of my life and something I will probably never forgive myself for. Her love for me hasn't changed, but to me the failure is ever-present.

As I said before, Ken had tons o' friends so he was never alone. When I stopped by, someone else always seemed to be there, so I'd usually hang out for a while, then leave. Slowly, his speech began to improve.

A couple of days before he was to be discharged and sent home, Coco called.

"Don," she said. "Can you swing by Ken's room now? We need your help."

When I entered both he and Coco were the only ones there. Ken had a smile on his face. Most of the paralysis was gone.

"Ken has something to show you," Coco said with a smile while her eyes began to tear up.

Ken looked down at his right hand. His face turned red and his face muscles tightened up with strain. Slowly, he raised his right arm, then let it fall back into his lap.

"Thank you," he said.

And for the record, the two Dickens first editions are still mine. *That* had been a safe bet.

FROSTWITCH VS. THE RAVAGES OF TIME

DAYLE A. DERMATIS

Dayle A. Dermatis is the author or coauthor of many novels and more than a hundred short stories in multiple genres, including the urban fantasy novel Ghosted. *She has lost count of how many issues of* Fiction River *her stories have appeared in, but we haven't. Dayle's been in sixteen volumes, most recently in* Hard Choices, *with more on the way. She'll also edit a volume called* Doorways to Enchantment, *which will appear in mid-2019. She is a founding member of the* Uncollected Anthology *project, and her short fiction has been lauded in year's best anthologies in erotica, mystery, and horror.*

"When faced with the challenge of writing a story for an anthology titled Feel the Love, *my first goal is to come up with an idea nobody else is likely to," Dayle says. "Challenge accepted! I tossed away love for parents and children, romantic love, love between friends.... And then I probably watched too much superhero TV and movies—especially the ones in which the hero is fighting to save their home." And that was how* Frostwitch *was born.*

"I think there may be more stories from Frostwitch in the future," Dayle says.

And, I, for one, am glad. Dayle captures this spirited hero in a most brilliant way; coming to terms with age and the fact that she might no longer be able to continue saving the city that she loves. But the love in this story isn't just our hero's love for her city.

There are at least four kinds of love in this story. Can you find them? Do you see more?

I moved stealthily along the upper gallery of the Greenview City Natural History Museum, keeping to the shadows. It was the middle of the night, so the museum had a lot of shadows cast by emergency lighting or the low glow of display lights. I was rather glad the lemmings case was covered, because I didn't want to know what they smelled like. They looked a little moth-eaten.

The shadows were a boon, because my superhero outfit was a

very unstealthy silvery-gray. Kind of like the inside of a freezer storage bag. Only a little sparklier.

The museum dated back to the late 1880s and had the strength and solidity of Victorian architecture: the gallery railing of Gothic trefoils was made of thick walnut, polished smooth from a century of trailing hands and a serious dose of Lemon Pledge. I stifled a sneeze.

I could be over it and on the main floor in the space between heartbeats, if need be. Rappel down, line back in my tool belt a moment later, faster than you can say Frostwitch. Which is what they call me.

It was a stupid moniker, but if you didn't pick your own super-hero name fast enough, the public would do it for you, and then you were stuck with it. I'd missed my window of opportunity years ago.

There were worse possibilities, I suppose. Once Bad Penny had made a lewd comment comparing the shape of the icicles I could form and throw to the shape of a certain part of the male anatomy.

You couldn't incarcerate someone for having abysmal social skills, but I confess it had given me a smug satisfaction to see her locked away for all her other crimes.

And still. *Frostwitch* beat *Icicle Queen* any day. Even despite the fact that pretty much every supervillain called me "Frostb*tch" behind my back, and sometimes to my face.

I'd decked every last one of them, of course. Laid them out cold. Ha ha.

I kept to the side opposite the Diplodocus skeleton, because I didn't want to dislodge any bones on the way down. Plus, ow. She took up a good portion of the marble floor below, but the object at the other end of the main hall, the special exhibit, was what had my attention.

The Uluru Opal, on loan from Australia. Four oval inches of rainbow flame trapped in a rock. Gorgeous.

I was here because there was a rumor that Bad Penny wanted the opal and her henchpeople were planning a heist. The Creator came to earth on a rainbow, according to Aboriginal dreamtime, with a gift of peace, and where he stepped, opals shimmered into existence. The Uluru Opal in particular was supposedly imbued with powers, and of course a supervillain would want to pervert something with the powers of peace into something designed for chaos.

Why Bad Penny would want the opal when she was still incarcerated in Greenview City's maximum security facility was beyond me. Whether she stayed there was another matter. There's a reason she has the name she has.

Wait. This is a superhero tale, so you probably want an origin story. Here's the Wikipedia-esque version.

Bianca Frost grew up as the privileged eldest child of Greenview City billionaire philanthropists Helen and Grant Frost. An adrenaline junkie from early life, at twenty-two she was caught in an avalanche while climbing Mt. Everest. Official medical reports are unsurprisingly sketchy, but it was believed she was briefly dead, and when she came back to life, she had superpowers.*

Unfortunately, while she was recovering at a remote Buddhist monastery in Nepal, Greenview City turned into a hotbed of crime, and Frost's parents were killed in an explosion designed to take down the city's power grid. She is somewhat estranged from her younger brother, Dr. Brian Frost, who was injured in the attack and remains in a wheelchair to this day, and who blames her for not being home to oppose supervillain ElectroKing.

Now, she fights crime. It's her calling to keep Greenview City safe.

*(Also, my hair had turned pure white, which was a funky fashion statement then. Now, some thirty years later, it almost looked like it belonged on me. I keep it in a short bob, because who needs hair in their eyes when they're fighting, or a ponytail for their opponent to grab? Function before fashion. Ditto with the ridiculous sky-high ankle-breaking heels. Seriously.)

Go figure why supervillains love Greenview City as much as they love Gotham City, Metropolis, Star City, etc. I suspect they just like a challenge. Can you be a supervillain without having a superhero to keep you on your toes? It's like the chicken-egg question.

The Uluru Opal sat on a steel-and-cement pedestal surrounded by walnut panels to keep with the feel of the museum. It was covered by unbreakable, uncuttable tempered glass, and of course everything was wired with so many alarms, a ladybug could set them off.

But Bad Penny and villains like her had their ways.

Their ways probably would include the network of tunnels beneath Greenview City, because of course there was a network of tunnels beneath Greenview City. I'd finished my sweep of the gallery, so now it was time to police the main floor.

The museum's regular security guards were on site, of course. They didn't know I was there. The material of my suit meant I wouldn't show up on security cameras, and I knew their schedule. I was able to slip down the wide marble staircase, its railing a match to the one around the gallery, unnoticed. Back into the shadows near a meteorite that had hit farmland outside of Greenview City and no doubt spawned some superhero or villain back in its day. Because of that, I was glad it was behind reinforced radiation-blocking polymer that was as see-through as glass. It was the size of a Corgi and could very well still be emanating something that could mess with my abilities.

I eyed all the entrances and exits, cast a keen glance at the iron-banded reinforced glass skylights high, high above me, and kept alert for any vibration that would indicate someone was drilling up through the floor.

If they drilled up through the marble, a pale cream interspersed with gold-veined evergreen to form borders and compass roses, I'd be seriously pissed.

The opal was part of incumbent Mayor Novotny's campaign, sharing goodwill with a similarly monikered city in Australia. I'd provided backup security at his fundraiser a few nights ago, and now, as I stalked silently around the perimeter of the open hall, his speech came back to me. It'd been a good one, full of his passion about the city he loved and how he planned to make it even better, for his children and his beloved wife and all the citizens.

I shared his dream for Greenview City. Otherwise, what would be the point of my being here? This was my city, and I would protect it from anything that threatened it or the people who lived here.

Unexpectedly, emotion rumbled inside me like the avalanche that had triggered my superpowers, threatening to gain speed and tumble down and overwhelm me. As I blinked back the unexpected prickle of tears, I heard the voice of Gwen Leoni in my in-ear monitor.

"Everything okay, boss? Your vitals just did some kind of hinky swoop I've never seen before."

I swallowed against the annoying clog in my throat. "I'm fine," I murmured. "Anything on the monitors?"

Back at our home base—the Art Deco train station abandoned in the eighties when the city grew sideways and unimaginative people clamored for a modern (*cough*-boring-*cough*) station more convenient to the city center—my right-hand woman monitored security feeds, police scanners, and my blood sugar levels, among other things. For all I knew, Gwen had X-ray scanners to see through people's clothes. I couldn't keep up with it all.

My job was to keep myself in fighting shape, and that takes a lot of time. At least four hours of training every day, running (which I'd always loved anyway), weights, sparring in a variety of methods, weapons practice, and yes, I even had a metal salmon ladder climbing thingie because Gwen had had too many drinks with Felicity Smoak, Green Arrow's techie, one night.

I have better triceps than the Green Arrow, though. I think about that every time I use the salmon ladder, because it I hate.

Between training and actually keeping the city safe, I don't have time to worry about the details, although lately I thought Gwen had been getting a little shoddy with the details. She said I've been unusually picky lately.

"Picking up some activity in one of the storage rooms," Gwen said. "Movement. Two—no, three people. Not security; they're all accounted for."

I swore and ran for the nearest basement access door. Its alarm was activated, but Gwen was half a step ahead of me, and a moment later the alarm light blinked off and the coded lock clicked open.

She'd lock up behind me so nobody else could piggyback on the access.

"I thought you were monitoring the tunnels!" I said as I took the cement stairs down two at a time. I leapt around and over from one flight of stairs to the next, bypassing the landing, one hand on the metal railing to orient myself, my body responding to what needed to be done. Muscles flexing, joints twisting, adrenaline lending its assistance. I didn't have to think, just act and react.

"I *was*," Gwen said. "They didn't come in that way, unless they have some super-new, super-strong, *Star Trek*-worthy cloaking tech, and a way to get through the security doors without setting off alarms. I'm the only one who's developed that. And no, we haven't been hacked," she added before I could ask. She knew me too well.

I cared less about how they'd gotten in than I did about stopping them before they got to the Uluru Opal.

Gwen directed me to the correct storage room. I weaved between open crates with the packing material sticking out, around sturdy metal tables bearing artifacts being cleaned or prepped for display, burst through the door.

I took in the situation within a few heartbeats (and my heartbeat was a little faster than it ought to be, oddly, given the amount of training and meditation I did—I didn't need Gwen to tell me that, and she knew better than distract me during a confrontation).

They'd come in via crates themselves—I saw breathing apparatus and what I guessed was waste receptacles but I refused to think about that—and also smuggled in equipment that they'd begun assembling. Electronics.

Explosives.

They *were* planning to bust through, destroying that gorgeous hundred-plus-year-old marble floor.

The woman and one of the men turned toward me, leaving the second man to continue working on placing the explosives.

Adrenaline morphed into anger that surged into rage.

I temporarily disabled the woman by sweeping her legs out from under her while shooting one of my patented icicles at the man with the equipment.

My super-freezing power didn't outright harm people. The icicle found its mark in the man's arm, but didn't puncture him. Instead, in an eyeblink it spread over his entire body, immobilizing him in a layer of ice. He wouldn't freeze; he could still breathe.

The second man came at me, and I ducked his punch, and growled low in my throat and clocked him hard enough in the chin to lay him out.

The woman tried to get up, so I nailed her with an icicle, too.

I wasn't even breathing heavy when I stopped, but the rage still boiled inside me, and I had to restrain myself from kicking the man nearest to me while chanting "Stupid, stupid, stupid!" Instead, I muttered, "She didn't pay you nearly enough for this."

"What?" Gwen asked.

"Nothing. Goons are down." I covered the detonator with ice, just to be safe. "Call the bomb squad."

"On their way. B, your vitals shot all over the map again, and I'm worried. Get back here so I can check you out."

"I'm *fine*," I insisted through gritted teeth. "Stop mothering me, and find out how these guys convinced the museum to haul in crates filled with them and all their gear."

I'd have to file a report later. Being a superhero didn't absolve one of paperwork, and paperwork was the one thing I hadn't been able to foist off on Gwen.

I fought the urge to growl, then turned and strode out of the storage room. I felt a slight twinge in my hip as I did, but I walked it out, walking out my anger at the same time.

(I didn't walk all the way back to the train station. I have a car. It's not a Frostmobile per se, but it gets me where I need to go. Every mayor since I became Frostwitch has authorized government plates for me, too.)

I wanted out of my supersuit and into a hot shower, but I knew better than to do that before Gwen checked me, and the suit with all its monitors, out.

Gwen Leoni is a few inches taller than me, but more willowy, so she seems even taller. She has long black hair in a thick braid halfway down her back and a Roman nose that suits her angular face. We've been friends since the first time we jumped out of a plane together to celebrate our eighteenth birthdays, but Gwen's thrills come more from her work here. Inventing things, being at the heart of things.

She's more likely to run a marathon than a tough mudder, but she's a decent sparring partner when I need one.

She's also my gadget inventor, security monitor, and First Aid provider. (By this point, she probably knows more about basic emergency medicine than my brother, the doctor.) Now, she peered at a scanner, ran a thermometer over my forehead, strapped a blood pressure cuff around my arm.

I suppose I should describe our superhero fortress, second only to the origin story in importance.

Like I said: abandoned Art Deco train station. Three stories high with dark mosaic inserts in the pale wooden ceiling, from which brass filigree and frosted glass Art Deco lamps twice as tall as me hang down. The windows are full-length, and we replaced the original glass with a non-breakable kind that also blocks visibility from outside while still pouring in light during the day. That way we can use the enormous terminal space without prying eyes. We stored the original waiting room benches downstairs, because I couldn't bear to throw them away.

The floor was a parquet marble, but we threw down some carpets both to protect it and to cut down on the echoey nature of the space.

Gwen's computer system, with its multiple monitors, is actually in the ticket office. Half the main area has been taken over by my workout equipment, and one corner near the bathrooms is screened off so I can make quick changes when I need to throw on my superhero outfit. We renovated the bathrooms in a period style to include showers, a Jacuzzi tub, steam room, and massage area.

Downstairs there's storage for extra weapons and equipment. Upstairs, over the ticket offices and baggage claim, is our living space. We weren't up there much, between my superheroing, my training, my philanthropy work (carrying on my family's legacy), and Gwen's support of all of that. I couldn't survive without her.

We were in the bathroom, with its sea-green wall tiles and sinks, and hexagonal white-and-black tiled floor. The massage table doubled as an exam table. The room smelled of lavender and cedarwood—aromatherapy, according to Gwen.

Forget the hot shower. My hip still hurt a little, and my muscles felt tight even though the fight had been short. A steaming bath with Epsom salts sounded divine.

Through the open door, I could hear the Roomba making its way around the floor of the main hall. Superhero lairs attract dirt and messes like any other place, but we couldn't exactly hire a cleaning service.

"Your vitals look fine now," Gwen said, setting the stethoscope aside and unwrapping the blood pressure cuff with a satisfying rip of Velcro.

"Maybe your equipment is faulty," I suggested, not helpfully.

Gwen made the squinchy face she always made when I suggested something under her purview wasn't up to snuff.

I amended my desire to get out of my outfit and into a hot Epsom salt bath, to getting out of my outfit and into a hot bath and then having a nice chilled glass of wine. The latter was mostly for Gwen.

"Could it have been the meteorite?" I suggested, more helpfully.

Gwen had a technical explanation why the meteorite wasn't the culprit, including the fact that I'd been two floors below it at the time.

"I'll take a blood sample, run some tests," she said. "If it's something more serious, we should ask Brian..."

Brian Frost, my brother. He was the only other person who knew my secret identity. He'd never forgiven me, but he was invested in my continued work to keep the city safe. Still, any encounters with him could be classified as Code: Awkward, so I avoided them.

"I'm fine," I said for the thousandth time. "Just a little stress." I didn't mention my hip. I suffered bruises and muscle aches all the time.

The fact that they seemed to be more frequent and healed a bit slower was all in my mind, I was sure.

Had to be.

The alternative was unthinkable, so I didn't think about it.

I didn't have time to think about it. Greenview City criminals didn't give me the chance.

Mayor Novotny's son was kidnapped, in a bid to shake up his reelection campaign. I knew this because it gave me the opportunity to prove the masterminds behind the kidnapping were Liana Lu, his opponent, and Javier deFranco, her husband.

When I returned their son, the mayor and his wife cried.

I almost cried, too.

What the hell was wrong with me?

I mean, I'm only human—of course I have feelings. But I'm also a superhero, and I have to ooze conviction, make everyone feel they're in good hands, that they're safe. Seeing the protector of your city bawling like a baby doesn't inspire confidence. Imagine Batman or Black Widow sobbing. Go on. I dare you. See?

The following night was a regular patrol session, with Gwen keeping an ear on the police scanner and monitoring other equipment I didn't entirely understand. Things like video feeds from drones over the city, infrared cameras, maybe earthquake-sensing equipment.

I ended up at a holdup at a random bodega. Small beans, but I was in the neighborhood, right place at the right time.

I'd gone inside to pick up a bottle of water, because I was feeling hot and sweaty. It wasn't an overly warm late-spring evening, and I was starting to wonder if my suit was malfunctioning somehow.

The freckled, redheaded kid behind the counter went all wide-eyed when I walked in. I was used to that. But instead of asking if it was really me, he said, "Are you okay? You're really red."

I glanced in the security mirror. My face did look flushed.

"I'm fine, thanks," I said, smiling, because superheroes should always be nice to people who aren't villains.

I didn't want to ask Gwen about my suit, because she'd get cranky. Maybe I had a fever. My fast-healing abilities usually knocked any illness on its ass, but archvillains were always trying to take me down, and someone could have invented a Frostwitch-specific supervirus.

I was getting water out of the cooler on the back wall—okay, maybe I was lingering a little with the door open—and about to ask Gwen about my vitals when the punk came in.

One guy in a hoodie with a gun. Pfft. I could handle this with one hand tied behind my back, fever or no fever.

The bodega was empty except for the clerk and me. I tiptoed up the snack aisle, formed an icicle, and threw.

Except it was the lamest, weeniest icicle I'd ever created since getting my powers, and instead of encasing the punk and immobilizing him, it hit him on the hip and covered only his left leg in ice.

He shouted in surprise and to my horror, the gun went off as he slipped and fell backwards. The clerk jerked and dropped behind the counter. I kicked the gun away from the punk, wrestled him over, and hogtied him before leaping behind the counter.

The clerk wasn't moving, and only years of training kept me from panicking. A moment later, I breathed a little easier: the bullet had just grazed his upper arm, and he'd apparently passed out from the shock. He was conscious by the time the cops arrived, and I owed the bodega for the bottle of vodka I'd splashed over the wound before improvising a bandage with Kleenex from one of those little travel packs, tied with Red Vines.

I gave my report to the cops, handed over the perp, and left.

My hands were shaking.

The kid had gotten injured on my watch. Had gotten injured because of me.

What was wrong with me?

We went through the same routine in the bathroom, where tonight the smell of lavender and cedarwood seemed especially strong, cloying almost to the point of being nauseating.

Gwen did some tests, took more data, drew more blood. She said my body temp had actually dropped two degrees during the time I was bright red and sweaty.

She said, patiently, that it wasn't my suit but that she would run more tests on it, too. She was gentle when she pointed out that it was a different suit than the one I'd been wearing the night at the museum, and she didn't need to add that the likelihood that two different suits failing at the same time was infinitesimally small.

Then she told me to take a shower and meet her upstairs.

I do keep a home in town, fairly nearby, for entertaining when I need to host a fundraiser or otherwise put on the appearance of having a normal life. (Brian got the family manor house, and he was welcome to it; I didn't need the space.) It's just convenient to have an apartment here, with a kitchen and comfortable living space to relax and bedrooms where we can catch much-needed catnaps.

I opted for comfortable, practical furniture; antiques where they fit and a few pieces of art to keep the place from looking austere.

I found Gwen on the big distressed leather sofa, a warm chestnut color. She was reviewing something on her tablet; the TV on the wall showed the local news channel, but the sound was off.

Two cut crystal glasses of whisky, probably Speyburn, sat on the cherrywood coffee table, one of the antiques in the room, its legs carved like swans.

The sofa cradled my body as I sank into it. Gwen handed me a whiskey. I took a sip. Honey and vanilla, with a spicy finish. She raised a dark eyebrow, tilted her head a fraction of a degree. Okay, then. I took a heftier swallow. She did the same, and we put our glasses down.

"How bad is it?" I asked.

She took my hand. "Sweetie. It's menopause."

I busted out laughing.

Then I stopped.

"You're joking."

Gwen slowly shook her head. "Hot flashes, mood swings, heightened sense of smell... You don't have an infection, you don't have a fever, you're showing no other signs of being ill."

My fault for not admitting everything. "I've had some unexplained pain, too—nothing serious, though—and sometimes I feel like my reflexes are a hair slower."

She squeezed my hand. "You're fifty-four years old, B. It happens. I'm fifty-six—remember when I hit menopause."

I closed my eyes from the horror of it. She'd hit full-on anal retentiveness. The station couldn't be clean enough or neat enough, her equipment couldn't run fast enough, and gods forbid that we get below a quarter carton of almond milk.

I pulled away from her and knocked back the rest of the whisky, a waste because I didn't savor it, but there you have it. "I need some air," I said.

Yes, it's a cliché that superheroes brood on rooftops, but rooftops are one of the few places we can be alone and mostly safe. You could see danger coming, and you could pace.

It was hard to brood effectively if you couldn't pace, too.

Plus, the rooftop gave me a view of Greenview City, each window another citizen lighting up the skyline.

This was my city. *My* city. I'd fight for it with my last breath, from the history museum to the modern train station, from the iconic old St. Stephen's cathedral to the glass monstrosity of the Ardmore Hotel. More importantly, for the people. For Greenview City to be a safe place to live, to love, to raise children or parakeets or whatever you want, to grow old.

And that was the problem. I'd never expected to grow old—I'd assumed I'd go down in a fight. Instead, my body was betraying me, not from injuries but from age, telling me I was mortal in the end, no matter what my superpowers were.

Telling me I couldn't protect the city I loved.

Telling me I couldn't protect the people, like that bodega clerk tonight.

"It's just me," I murmured. "There's no one else."

"B? Everything okay?"

I'd forgotten to take out my earpiece. I wore it more hours of the day than not, so I never noticed it. Gwen had had to remind me more than once when I was, um, indisposed.

"Sure," I said, knowing my voice was clipped, but also knowing, based on the churn of emotions in my chest, that if I said much more, I'd lose it, and Gwen didn't deserve that. "Fine."

I took out the earpiece and slipped it into the pocket of my jeans. The late-spring breeze ruffled my short hair as I looked out over the glittering lights of Greenview City.

Who would I let down next? Whose life would I endanger, rather than protect?

I did the only thing I knew how to do: I faced the obstacle head-on, and just tried harder.

I upped my workouts to compensate for any aging effects as well as to be better prepared if my powers failed me again. And I tested my powers whenever I had one of those awful "power surges," as annoying people tried to term them, determining how they were affected, what limitations I had. Then I worked on how to compensate for them.

I'd always appreciated my powers, and although it had never occurred to me they could leave me once they became a part of me, I'd tried to never take them for granted. I'd honed my body and mind into a fighting machine as a complement to my freezing abilities.

Now I had to hone my body and mind even more.

The body part, I understood how to do that. I switched up my workouts and added to them, challenging myself.

The mind part, that was more difficult. There's only so much meditation a girl has time for, and the mood swings weren't something I could control, just learn to ride through and manage.

Gwen was working on her end, and I didn't get in her way. We'd learned a long time ago how to make things work, and that included me not lurking over her shoulder asking for updates. For one thing, most of the time I wasn't even going to understand her answer.

For a while, it worked. I was in top physical form, and I'd found a few workarounds for my powers, creative alternatives I'd used once or twice and forgotten about.

Like freezing a villain's weapon, or the floor beneath them so they just fell down. There was a reason I'd been wearing special non-slip shoes, and there wasn't always a need to completely immobilize someone. It'd just been easy, so I'd fallen back on it.

You could say I was in the Bargaining stage of the Kübler-Ross model.

Or maybe I was still in Denial and, well, denying it.

I tried not to think about it.

I knew Gwen was working overtime on her overtime, researching my problem. She didn't talk about it, and I didn't ask.

Until one night after patrolling, I came back to the train station to find her sitting in one of the remaining benches in the lobby.

She wasn't alone.

My somewhat estranged brother, Brian, was with her.

"This looks suspiciously like an intervention," I said, easing down on the bench across from them. I'd twisted funny when fighting with Parrot, because an archvillain with wings (not to mention bright plumage—he was visible miles away) requires some unusual techniques, and my right knee was a little sore.

My brother, three years younger than me, had some white strands in his hair. I hadn't seen him in at least six months, whenever we'd last had a fundraiser for the Frost Family Foundation. He was trim— he was far from an adrenaline junkie like me, but he was smart enough to take care of himself—and if he let his hair go white, we'd look even more alike. We both had our mother's generous mouth, our father's expressive eyes.

I had no idea why he was here.

"It's not an intervention," Gwen said. "Don't get mad, B, but I looped Brian in on what's been going on with you, because I thought he could help."

I felt my face contort into an expression of massive confusion before I could stop myself, and Gwen quickly added, "He helped me when I went through menopause."

"He's your *doctor*?" I'd had no idea.

"Well, he is the best in the city...."

I took a deep breath, trying very hard not to feel ganged-up on. "Okay. Shoot."

"First of all, Bianca, I want to help you," Brian said. "Not just because you're Frostwitch, but because you're my sister. This...this has been a kick in the ass for me. We lost our parents so young...we have only each other left, and we have only so much time left. It was stupid of me to blame you for not being here when Mom and Dad died."

Crap, here came the waterworks. I blinked rapidly, cleared my throat. "I'm glad."

He nodded, looking a moist around the eyes himself, but then he composed himself. Went into doctor mode.

He proposed hormone replacement therapy, and supplements to boost my calcium and other, um, stuff (Brian was as adept at medical-babble as Gwen was at techno-babble). He'd reviewed the data Gwen had provided him, and he wanted to run a few more tests with equipment she didn't have access to. Obviously I could see him as Bianca, not Frostwitch. And he'd be on call in case I needed anything.

And then the three of us went to the best Italian place in town—which was willing to open back up for us in the middle of the night because we were the Frosts—because they had the moistest, richest chocolate cake in town. Don't worry, we tipped really, really well.

Hormone replacement changed me almost as much as the avalanche did. Within a week I was on a *much* more even keel, and my powers were back to full frigid glory.

Just as Bad Penny herself discovered when she busted out of prison and made her own attempt at the Uluru Opal and I stopped her before she crashed through the glass Victorian roof over the museum's main hall. (Really? *Really?*)

"I heard you were melting, Frostb*tch," she sneered, running a hand over her short, spikey, coppery hair.

"You heard wrong," I said, and precisely immobilized her while she still dangled in a harness from a helicopter. Then I climbed up the strapwork into the helicopter, knocked out her pilot with one blow, and flew to the prison, where I lowered her into the prison yard along with the pilot.

Cool. Now I had my own helicopter, too. Maybe I'd call it the Frostcopter. Or *Snowflake*.

Mayor Novotny won the election, of course.

I stood at the back of the podium during his swearing in and waited to see if all hell to broke loose.

He'd chosen the Ardmore Hotel for the event, and the Ardmore was a glass-and-chrome monstrosity. I glanced to my left, squinting, calculating from which of the surrounding buildings Dark Matter could hit the mayor with one of his quantum arrows, or, hell, a sniper could do the same, with the right ammunition to punch through one of the windows. The three-story glass walls and the blazing lights inside made the atrium a fishbowl in the evening darkness.

This place was the least defensible building in Greenview City. For crying out loud, the city's open air central plaza had more trees to block an attack.

But Dark Matter was behind bars (for now—like I said, they

never seemed to stay incarcerated for long,. See, e.g., Bad Penny.). Honestly, there wasn't anyone else I could think of who'd be opposed to Novotny's reelection, but you never knew when some new supervillain would try to make his or her mark.

I continually scanned the crowd, the sweeping tangle of clear staircases that crisscrossed the atrium, and all the entrances and exits. I was only half listening to Novotny's speech, because politics, blah blah blah.

Then he said, "I'd like to take this opportunity to honor someone who's not only responsible for ensuring my family's safety during my campaign, but for the safety of each and every person in our fair city: Frostwitch."

He turned to me, beckoned me forward on the stage.

I'm not one much for ceremonies, but to run away would be rude. I moved to his side.

"But you don't need to hear it from me," he went on. "So many of you have written to me about how much she's done for you and for Greenview City."

He then read parts of some of those letters.

It was overwhelming. I'd had no idea—had never really thought about—the fact that people took much notice. I figured they went on about their lives, and my job was to allow them to do that. So much of what I did was behind the scenes. Stop the criminals before they hurt someone, before they steal the Uluru Opal, before they take over the city's water supply and poison everybody.

When he finished, the entire place clapped politely.

Kidding. They erupted into cheers, which went on much longer than I would have ever expected.

Guess how I felt about the city was mutual.

And if I shed a few tears at the ceremony, I think that was to be forgiven.

Frostwitch would still be saving the city for years to come.

THE GODDESS KILLER

LAURYN CHRISTOPHER

Lauryn Christopher writes marketing and technical material for the computer industry. In her spare time, she writes mysteries, often from the criminal's point of view, as in her Hit Lady for Hire series. Among other places, her stories have appeared in multiple Fiction River *volumes, including* Editor's Choice, Feel the Fear *and* Justice. *For information, links to more of her work, and to sign up for her occasional newsletter, go to www.laurynchristopher.com.*

About "The Goddess Killer," Lauryn writes: "Conversations around our family dinner table are often loud, filled with a lot of laughter and more than their share of inappropriate remarks, such as the one in which our adult children speculated which of them was the parents' favorite and which would be sacrificed first in a zombie apocalypse. It was a short leap from there to writing the story of a man faced with choosing who he loves the best."

I admire this story because it provides an intriguing combination of the dilemma in Sophie's Choice *with the tension and action of* The Purge.

A summer thunderstorm raged, rain pelting the large picture window, the streetlight shining in flickering strips of light barely visible through the partially open wooden blinds. No lights were on in the house, but I could still see the three people seated in my living room, arranged in a row like game show contestants.

Lydia, my mother.

Angela, my wife of eighteen years.

And Hillary, my fourteen-year-old daughter.

The three women I loved most in the world, each duct-taped to a dining chair of her own, arms strapped to their sides and mouths covered with wide strips of tape.

And then their eyes widened as he came up behind me, laughing maniacally, a parody of the Joker mask he wore. He leaned close, the flat of his knife blade cold against my cheek, and murmured in my ear.

"It's time to choose, Tommy. Who do you love the most?"

***

The press called him "The Goddess Killer" after the mythological Triple Goddess—the Maiden, the Mother, and the Crone—who were the basis of his pattern. He always chose a man in his early forties who had a single child, a teenaged daughter (the Maiden); who had been married to the same woman for about twenty years (the Mother); and who had a good relationship with his own mother (the Crone), who also lived with the family.

He would barricade the family in their home and force the man to choose which of his women was to die.

Sad thing was, whichever one the man chose was the one the killer let live.

He'd struck six times over the last four years, and it had always been the same. He slit the throats of two of the women, while telling the third that he hoped she could live with the knowledge that her son, husband, or father—who he also left alive—didn't love her as much as the others.

Then he'd dial 911 from the house phone or one of the victims' cell phones, leaving the call active while he left the house. By the time the first responders sorted out the situation and arrived on the scene, the killer was long gone.

It was a sick, twisted game.

And the media ate it up.

***

"You'd tell him to kill me, of course," my mother said, as though this was a perfectly ordinary dinner conversation for the four of us to be having.

Perhaps it was. We'd all gone to dinner at an Italian restaurant not far from the real estate office where I work. And whether it was the result of dining under the watchful gaze of the mafiosos who stared at us from the collection of reproduced black-and-white photographs adorning our booth, or simply the result of Hillary reading us the latest media speculations, the topic of conversation had naturally turned to the murders.

Mother continued calmly, neatly cutting a bite of lasagna as she spoke. "Hillary has her whole life ahead of her, and she'll need her mother. I've already lived my life. It's only logical." She avoided eye contact with me as she put the bite into her mouth.

"Lydia!" my wife exclaimed.

"I'd do no such thing—" I protested.

"You've got it wrong, Gran," said Hillary, cutting me off. She ripped a piece of garlic bread into three pieces and arranged them on a small plate. "If Dad picks you," she said, pointing to one of the chunks of torn bread, "the creep kills me and Mom." She dribbled marinara sauce on the other two chunks of bread to illustrate her point. "Isn't that what you said he does, Dad? So, if he wants me to *live*, he has to tell the guy to *kill* me."

"No one's killing anyone," Angela said. She was a nurse, and was wearing the same calm expression required by her profession, but after eighteen years of marriage, I recognized the way she masked her emotions. The tension in her neck and shoulders causing her to sit with almost perfect posture. The sight tightening of her cheek muscles as she ground her teeth. This conversation was bugging the hell out of her, and I couldn't blame her.

Hillary shrugged, popping one of the marinara-covered bites of bread into her mouth. "Guy's effed-up, that's all," she said around the mouthful.

"Hillary," Angela warned.

Hillary just rolled her eyes at her mother and dove into dinner.

"Look," I said, setting down my silverware and looking around the table at the three of them. "I didn't ask you out so we could decide which of you should live and which of you should die. I love you all. I want you *all* to live. For a very long time..." I wanted to say more, but the words stuck in my throat, and I just left the thought hanging.

My mother and daughter both sat there, poking at their meals, and Angela reached over and took my hand. In the awkward silence, I was suddenly aware of the other conversations going on around us. We'd opted to eat inside rather than on the outdoor patio, where large fabric umbrellas deflected a share of the heat but did little to defend against the oppressive humidity of late July.

The booth where we were seated in air-conditioned comfort was separated by high, padded cushions from similar booths at either side, but provided a clear view of several tables in this section of the restaurant. Not that I could hear anything specific that anyone was saying—the level of chatter was such that it provided near-absolute privacy to each table.

Still, I lowered my voice before I spoke again. "Hillary's right," I said. "He is 'effed-up.' And if it came to it, I'd kill him before I let him kill any of you."

The glowing numbers on my bedside clock read 3:30.

I don't know what it was that woke me—a clap of thunder, a door closing, a footstep in the hall, probably just someone using the bathroom—but I lay there, listening, trying to push past the fog of sleep to identify the sound. It was a common enough activity, determine if a random sound was worth investigating, and, if not, catalog it as one of the many squeaks and creaks of an old house during a proverbial stormy night.

Thump.

"What's that?" Angela murmured, her voice fuzzy.

"Don't know. Stay here while I check it out," I whispered, sitting up and swinging my legs out of the bed. "Probably nothing."

"Hmmm..." Angela replied, already drifting back to sleep.

I padded quietly across the room, snagging a T-shirt from a chair on the way. Carefully turning the knob, I silently eased the door open.

The bedrooms are on the second floor of our house, opening

onto three sides of a wide landing at the top of the stairs that we'd turned into a small reading nook. To my right, Hillary's door stood open, her room dark except for what little light filtered in from the streetlight on the corner. The adjacent bathroom, windowless, was completely dark. To my left, my mother's room mirrored Hillary's, dark and empty.

Across the landing, a light shone up from the lower level.

I crept forward, still not entirely sure that it wasn't just my mother or Hillary that I'd heard moving around, until I reached the balcony railing overlooking the living room.

Three of the dining room chairs had been pulled into the middle of the living room, placed side-by-side so they faced the dining room. My mother was bound to the chair nearest me, her hands and arms at her sides, a wide strip of duct tape across her mouth. Her head lolled to one side and her eyes were closed. I could only hope she was unconscious, but still alive.

The second of the three chairs was empty.

And a large man was busy binding my daughter to the third chair, her rainbow-colored tank top and cat pajama bottoms a bright contrast to the rows of silver gray duct tape stretched tight across her torso. Hillary also appeared to be unconscious, as I couldn't imagine her allowing anyone to tape her to a chair without a protest.

It was that guy, the one from the news. The Goddess Killer, here, in my house.

My bluster at our dinner a few weeks before notwithstanding, I'm a real estate salesman, a desk jockey, not a muscle-bound, leap-over-the-railing action hero. I covered my mouth with both hands to keep from making a sound and revealing my presence, and took a step away from the rail, putting my back to the wall to keep from falling over. When I thought I could trust myself not to shout at the guy downstairs, I dropped one hand, but left the other one at my mouth, biting on the knuckle of my index finger while I tried to think of what to do next.

Breathe in. Breathe out. Don't hyperventilate. Don't freak out, or we all die.

I eased back toward the edge of the wall, peering over the balcony.

He was exactly as they described him on the news. Male, between six-feet and six-feet-two-inches tall. Brown leather work boots with heavy soles. Blue jeans. Close-fitting, long-sleeved shirt tucked into heavy yellow gloves, probably the latex kind from the grocery store. A rubber Joker mask—the colorful one from the old Saturday cartoons. He hummed as he worked.

I turned around to head back to my room for my phone and almost screamed like a little girl. Angela was behind me, her face as pale as the thin pink nightshirt she wore.

She'd seen.

I gestured her back, and when she didn't move, took her by the shoulders and guided her into our room, closing the door silently behind us.

"He's got Hillary," Angela said. Her voice was barely a whisper. "And your mother."

"I know," I whispered in reply.

Keeping one arm around my wife's trembling body, I scooped up my cell phone and dialed 911.

"911, what is your emergency?" said a woman's voice at the other end of the phone.

I told her.

It felt surreal, like a scene out of a television cop show, as I recited my name, address, and the details of the situation as calmly as if I was dictating a report. I described the intruder, what he was doing downstairs at that moment.

As I talked, I pulled Angela into our walk-in closet, and pointed upward to the small attic access panel in the ceiling. She nodded and started to climb up the built-in shelves like a ladder, paused, pushed the phone away from my face, and wrapped her arms around my neck.

I hugged her tight, and kissed her.

Tears streaming down her face, she resumed her climb, holding onto the shelf with one hand while pushing open the access panel with the other. The sound of the storm was louder up there, and a chill draft wafted down to us. Angela shivered, then pulled herself up into the attic, raising a cloud of dust.

"Toss me those," she whispered, pointing down at a pair of jogging pants and a top on one of the shelves. I did.

"You find the flashlight?" I asked. The 911 operator had asked me to stay on the line while she passed the information to the authorities.

Angela nodded, stifling a sneeze, and clicking the LED flashlight we keep up there to its lowest setting.

"Come on," she said.

I shook my head. "Close the panel," I told her. "Stay out of sight, quiet. It will frustrate his game, and should buy us enough time for help to arrive."

"Don't try to be a hero."

"I'm not going to let him hurt Mom or Hillary."

"Isn't that exactly what he'll do when he can't find me?"

"Not on my watch," I said. "Go."

"I love you, Tommy."

"I love you, too, Ange. Never forget it."

My house is a 1970s tri-level—one of those where the living room, dining, and kitchen are at ground level, the same as the garage, while the rest of the house is split into two floors, with the bedrooms a half-flight up from the main level, and other rooms a half-flight down. Sadly, this is not a style that is typically equipped with secret passages; a feature that would have made sneaking around and surprising the killer a much easier process.

However, the master bedroom does open onto a small, private deck, and we keep one of those roll-up emergency ladders in each of the upstairs rooms—a precaution we'd never had to put to the test, but which might now turn out to be a lifesaver.

Once Angela was safely hidden away in the attic, I pulled on a pair of jeans, grabbed my keys and a second LED flashlight from the nightstand and tucked them into a pocket of my jeans. I slipped my phone's headset into my ear so I could stay connected with the 911 operator, and slid my phone into another pocket. Then I retrieved the roll-up ladder from the armoire by the balcony doors, and went out onto the deck.

I had forgotten about the thunderstorm.

But there was no turning back now. The wind drove the rain at me like needles, and as I tossed the emergency ladder over the rail, I decided that the sound of the storm might at least cover any noise I make climbing down. Assuming I didn't get hit by lightning, or get blown into the side of the house, or slip on the wet metal treads of the ladder.

Shoes probably would have been helpful.

I'd nearly reached the bottom when the ladder suddenly jerked, throwing me to the ground. I lay there flat on my back in the wet grass for only a split second before rolling to my feet and darting away into the shadows of my backyard.

The killer had been standing there on the balcony, studying the ladder.

I don't know if he'd seen me or not; I hoped he'd assumed that Angela was with me.

"Are you still there?" I asked into my headset.

The reply was garbled, as though the storm was interfering with the signal. I didn't know how much the operator could hear, but I gave an updated report anyway.

"I'm outside, my wife is hiding; I think the intruder is looking for us. Are the police on their way? The FBI? Anyone?"

Again, all I received in reply was a collection of garbled syllables.

"I can't understand you," I said, knowing there was a strong possibility that she'd just said the very same thing to me. "I'll try again when I get back inside."

I huddled under an elm tree that was doing a pretty poor job of sheltering me from the wind and the rain, and watched lights switch on inside my house as the killer moved from room to room, looking for Angela and me.

I considered my options. There weren't many.

I don't own a handgun—a choice I was now regretting—nor much else that could be used as a weapon. As a result, my best plan was to sneak in through the garage, see if I could find anything at all useful, and from there get into the house. If I could make it to the utility room on the lower level, I could shut off the power to the house. I knew my way around better than the killer did. Hopefully, that would give me some sort of small advantage.

I ran across the yard to the far side of the house and fumbled with my keys until I found the one for the garage door. By the time I got inside, I was soaked through, my teeth were chattering, and my phone wasn't even giving me static anymore.

I could only hope that help was on the way.

Crossing through the kitchen and dining room without stopping to try to help my mother or Hillary was probably one of the hardest things I've ever had to do in my entire life. I could see them in their chairs, moving slightly, coming out from under whatever anesthesia had been used on them. But I knew that the best way to save their lives was to distract and delay the killer.

And then I heard screaming and a series of thumps from upstairs —followed by the screams abruptly cutting off.

Angela!

I practically jumped down the half-flight of stairs to the lower level and raced to the utility room. Tearing the breaker box panel open, I reached up and flipped the big switch marked "Main."

The house plunged into blackness, relieved only by what little light came in through the outside windows. I slipped out of the utility room—not a corner I wanted to be trapped in—and tried to figure out what to do next. In my hand, I held a broken-off broomstick, the best thing I'd been able to find in the garage. I had no skill in martial arts, but I'd played baseball in high school and knew how to heft a bat, and learned a little bit of stick-fighting with a college buddy who was into historic re-creations. So with three feet of solid wood in my hand, with a jagged end where I'd broken away the bristles, I at least felt like I had a passable weapon.

Okay, you SOB, you're on my turf now.

Maniacal laughter echoed through the house. "You're changing the game, Tommy," a crazed male voice shouted. "That's not fair. If you change the game, I'll have to make up new rules, and I'm not sure you'll like them very much."

I heard his heavy tread on the stairs, and an "ooof" as he dumped Angela onto the third chair. As I crept toward the stairs, I heard the familiar hiss of duct tape being pulled from its roll.

A wave of relief washed over me. Whatever he'd done to Angela, she wasn't dead yet, or he wouldn't feel the need to bind her to her chair.

I moved up the stairs quietly, one step at a time, broomstick ready if the killer should make a move on me. But the steady hiss and tear of the duct tape never wavered, and I made it to the top of the stairs without incident.

He'd shoved the coffee table back against the couch, and positioned the three chairs in the center of the living room, with a fourth chair—presumably the one for me—facing them, a few feet closer to the kitchen.

I could see him clearly from the top of the stairs, but thought it unlikely that I could sneak up on him from the side without him doing something to Angela. So I tiptoed across the dining room and into the kitchen, made my way around the island, and crept toward the kitchen door, expecting to have a good opportunity to come up on him from behind.

Except when I stepped to the kitchen doorway, the killer was gone, and only my mother, my wife, and my daughter—my personal incarnation of the Triple Goddess—were there, bound and gagged and clearly terrified.

And then the killer came up behind me, laughing maniacally, a parody of the Joker mask he wore. He leaned close, the flat of his knife blade cold against my cheek, and murmured in my ear.

"It's time to choose, Tommy. Who do you love the most?"

The only thing that makes sense is that he hadn't seen the broken broomstick in my hand. Because when he nudged me forward, I held the stick close to my side, and when I was clear of the door and clear of the table, I raised it and spun and clocked him a good one across the side of his head, knocking him back and onto the table.

The knife went skittering across the smooth wood into the darkness.

It wasn't like he actually needed it. He was an easy three or four inches taller than me, and the close-fitting shirt he wore bore witness to a workout schedule far more rigorous than my twice-weekly trips to the gym. If he'd thought to give me a swift kick in the face with one of his heavy work boots, it would have been all over for me right then.

But instead, he bounced back up off the table like a rubber ball and lunged at me.

I swung again, but this time he was ready for me and ducked the swing, barreling at me with his head down, driving me back against a bookcase with his shoulder, fists doing a one-two-one-two on my midsection.

I flailed at him with the stick, but with the bulk of his body pressing mine back, could get no leverage, and my swings were ineffectual at best.

The bookcase behind me, however, presented an opportunity. It was a large, heavy piece of furniture, about four feet wide and standing about a foot taller than me, and loaded down with hardback books on the lower shelves and a collection of photographs and other family memorabilia on the upper shelves. And as the killer pummeled me, my back was bouncing off the outer edge of the bookcase, causing it to rock against the wall.

I stopped trying to hit him with the broomstick and tossed it aside, then grabbed at his upper arms, twisting my body to the right and away from the bookcase as his left arm pulled me forward, putting the killer directly in the path of the bookcase as it toppled over.

I stumbled backward, barely managing to stay on my feet, gasping in pain from bruised, possibly broken ribs. Beneath the bookcase, the killer was already struggling to extricate himself, the Joker mask grinning up at me crazily as the man wearing it swore at me.

It was then, as I scooped up the broomstick and was a heartbeat away from driving the ragged end of the stick into the killer's throat, that the front door suddenly burst open.

Dark figures piled into the house, rough voices shouting "Police! Drop your weapon!"

I dropped the broomstick and raised my hands. "It's about time you guys got here," I said.

Needless to say, the next several minutes were a little crazy while things got sorted out. Eventually, the officers on the scene got the lights turned back on, and hauled the killer away.

In the meantime, a couple of EMTs had cut away the tape binding my family to their chairs and given them a cursory checkup. My mother and Hillary were still a little woozy from the chloroform the killer had used on them, and Angela had several bumps and scrapes from when he'd pulled her down from the attic, but other than that, they were all just fine. They'd also wrapped my ribs as a precautionary measure, and recommended I go to the hospital for an x-ray.

At the moment, though, I was sitting on the living room couch, my mother on one side of me, Angela and Hillary crowded together on the other side. Our arms were all wound up with each other's, as the four of us all tried to hug each other and reassure each other that everything was going to be all right.

"That was good work you did," the lead FBI investigator said, sitting down in an easy chair opposite us. He had his notebook out, and looked like he was about to ask us a bunch of questions.

"There was no way I was playing his sick game by his rules," I said, shrugging—and then wincing as my ribs twinged with pain. "Choose who I love the most and let the others die? Impossible. I love them *all* the most, in very different ways, and would have done anything to save them. That was my choice."

I looked at my family around me, at their shell-shocked and tear-stained faces, and squeezed Angela's hand. "That was the only choice."

LOVE LOCKS

DALE HARTLEY EMERY

Dale Hartley Emery writes fiction in a variety of genres that include fantasy, science fiction, and mystery. His Fiction River *short stories include "Inhabiting Sweetie," in* No Humans Allowed; *"Four-hundred Yards," in* Hard Choices; *"Cassidy's Ghost" in* Editor Saves; *and "As Fast as Wishes Travel" in* Wishes. *When he is not writing fiction, Dale writes software that helps the financial industry remember peoples' bank balances.*

"Love Locks" was inspired by trip a Dale and his wife took in the spring of 2014 to Venice. "Our first-floor hotel room had a small balcony on the Grand Canal," Dale says, "giving us a view of the passing gondolas, vaporettos, and tour boats, as well as the Accademia Bridge 100 yards away." He says that almost everything in the setting, including the ritual that inspires Christopher and Jessica's morning mission, is real, except for the giant poster of Emma Watson.

I was particularly intrigued, not just with the beautiful setting of what is often thought of as a romantic getaway, and the perfect setting for a popular and frowned-upon love lock ritual, but the way Jessica and Christopher's adventure reveals the dynamics of their relationship. I was especially appreciative of the unexpected place where this story ends up.

Chris felt Jessica's warm, soft hand slip into his as they stepped out of the alleyway between the sagging, settling buildings into the south end of Campo Santo Stefano.

They were still in shadows, but the glare from the fifty-foot-high white stone facade of a small church across the campo blinded him.

He raised his arm to block the glare.

"I should have worn a hat," Jessica said, her arm also shading her eyes.

"Want to go back?" Their hotel was less than a minute behind them. And the narrow walkways winding between the buildings were all in shadows.

"I'm good," she said.

Chris's eyes adjusted.

To the right of the church, four long rows of small round tables draped in yellow tablecloths extended out in full sunlight onto the dull gray brick that paved the campo. Three people sat in purple plastic chairs around one of the tables, and three more around another, all sipping from brown stoneware mugs.

The tables were fifty yards from the nearest of the cafés and restaurants at the north end of the campo, on the eastern side, in shade. Apparently, these people liked the sun.

To the north, in the middle of the wider part of the campo, an elderly couple sat on the stepped stone base of a statue. Above, on a tapered square base, a thoughtful, bearded, stone academic looked down at the campo, lost in thought, arms folded, one hand clutching a scroll, a pile of thick, stone books at his feet.

Other than that, the campo was empty.

It was nearly eleven a.m. It looked as if most of the other tourists had slept later than he and Jessica had. He doubted that their lazy mornings had been half as wonderful as his.

"We could go back to bed."

Neither Chris nor Jessica had felt any great rush to get out of bed this morning. They had lain in each other's arms, listening to the infrequent *vaporetti* and small motorboats cruise along the Grand Canal just outside their open window. Then they had made love, listened to the boats for a while longer, and finally showered, dressed, and ventured out of their charming hotel room.

To Chris, the canal smelled faintly of fish. All of Venice did, for that matter. That was his only complaint.

Jessica said it smelled like the ocean. She had no complaints at all.

And Chris was starting to almost like the smell. Almost.

"Might be fun," she said. But she nodded to her left, toward the path that led a hundred yards between the church and a narrow, zigzagging garden of leafy shrubs and conical trees toward their destination.

Ponte dell'Accademia. The Accademia Bridge.

She tugged his hand and he followed.

Beyond the church, the walkway opened up into a small plaza. On the eastern side, yet another trio sat around one of a small group of tables, sipping from brown stoneware mugs. In the sun.

"You love her, yes?"

A man sat in the shade of a tall, conical tree, his skin dark brown, his head shaved. He was skinny, and his jeans and blue-and-white striped oxford shirt hung loosely on him.

He waved his hand over a selection of padlocks, each standing on end, arranged in neat rows on a thin, white cloth in front of him. Some were thick and heavy, and others small and thin, with narrow hasps. Some were brass colored, others steel. A pair of keys was fastened to each hasp by a yellow twist tie.

At dinner the night before, a loud British woman at a nearby table had claimed that the handbag vendors in the streets were all from one African country, the sunglasses vendors from another, and the shoe vendors from a third. "All fakes," she had said.

Chris had no idea whether she was right about the sellers' origins. But he suspected she was right about their wares.

She hadn't mentioned padlock vendors.

Jessica said, "Well, that's a good omen."

Chris laughed. He knew what she meant. Bumping into a padlock vendor so soon into their big mission for the day.

They had seen two padlock vendors on the bridge the day before, each selling a selection of sizes and colors, each standing next to a bloom of padlocks attached by other lovers in tight clusters along the curved steel bars that held the handrail onto the bridge's old wooden railing.

Lucchetti dell'Amore. Love locks.

You and the love of your life write your names on a padlock. Attach the lock to the bridge. Throw the key into the water.

Chris had said, "Hey, let's do it," and reached for his wallet.

Jessica had touched his arm and stopped him.

"Might be fun. Tomorrow."

She had been right. Today was better.

Their first anniversary.

Chris had met Jessica exactly a year ago. June 9. On Venice Beach.

Maybe it was a good omen. But probably just good business. There were surely always padlock vendors here, so close to the bridge. And more at the Rialto Bridge and whatever the bridge at the far end of the canal was called.

"Which one?" Chris said, pointing at the padlocks.

"The sturdiest one," Jessica said.

The thicker locks with the thicker hasps had the highest prices. Good business.

Chris pointed at the thickest lock. Brass colored. A blue plastic band around the bottom of the lock had the word "Master" printed on it.

He remembered the loud British woman's words from the night before.

All fake.

Chris shuddered.

Using a fake lock in a symbolic ritual was probably a bad idea. Even if the ritual was all in fun.

Chris paid the man, who handed him the lock. It felt heavy and warm in his hand. Weighty.

It felt right.

It felt like the real thing.

He unwound the twist tie and tried the keys. Each one fit and unlocked the lock.

Jessica said to the vendor, "Do you have a marker?"

"Extra," the man said.

Chris reached for his wallet again.

Jessica touched his wrist and said, "I'll get this."

Chris nodded. As she opened her purse, he handed the twist tie to the vendor.

The vendor smiled and nodded his appreciation.

He held out a thin, red Sharpie to Jessica.

"For free," he said.

"See?" Jessica said. "An omen."

Chris and Jessica headed around the last zig of the garden.

The bridge came into view, fifteen feet wide, its weathered, gray-brown wooden steps arching up to the midpoint over the 150-foot expanse of the canal.

Jessica squeezed his hands and they started up the steps.

They had picked out the spot for their lock the day before. Halfway down the far side of the bridge, near the spot where they had seen the first vendor. One of the clusters of love locks was not as tightly packed as the others. So there was plenty of room for one more lock.

As they climbed the steps, two teenage boys descended, wearing shorts and T-shirts. One of the boys tapped the other on the arm with the back of his hand, pointed at the padlock in Chris's hand, and laughed.

The other boy laughed, too, glanced up at Chris, and said something in Italian.

"What?" Chris said.

The other boy said something as the two of them passed Chris and Jessica. Then the two of them laughed again.

"Come," Jessica said.

"Did they just insult us?"

"They're young. What do they know of love?"

"They're Italian," Chris said. "Isn't love in their blood?"

Below in the canal, a small, flat tour boat heading eastward toward Saint Mark's Square swerved to avoid a larger *vaporetto,* a water taxi filled with people heading westward. The tour boats all looked alike. Squat and shiny, made of polished tan wood, the middle of the boat a recessed, roofed room with windows all around, big enough to seat a dozen tourists. Chris didn't know whether the sameness came from tradition, like the ubiquitous gondolas, or some kind of regulation.

Four people stood at the back of the boat, their arms resting on the roof of the seating area. One raised his cell phone in both hands, aimed its camera at the *vaporetto,* and fingered the screen.

The tour boat driver waved the back of his hand at the *vaporetto* and shouted something. Probably rude.

"Love is in everyone's blood," Jessica said. "Most of the time."

They passed one of the clusters of love locks, jammed so tightly together that they stuck out in all directions, defying gravity, and reached the long flat stretch of wooden planks at the top of the bridge.

As they reached the top of the steps heading down the other side, Chris stopped short.

Two women in bright white shirts, navy blue pants, and white hats with navy brims chatted with each other halfway down the steps. They had navy blue epaulets on their shoulders.

Police officers.

Behind the officers, at the handrail, were two men in pale green T-shirts and jeans, one on his knees, and the other hunched over, his elbows out.

Between the two men, leaning against a wooden post that held up the old wooden handrail, was a plastic, lime-green bucket.

Chris heard a snap, then a rattle of metal on metal.

The man who had been hunched over stood and rubbed his back with one hand. In his other hand was a long pair of bright red bolt cutters.

They were cutting the love locks off the handrails.

"Oh," Jessica said.

"Maybe—" Chris stopped himself from pointing out that the vendor's position might have been an omen after all. Just not a good omen.

"Maybe what?"

"That's why the lock guy was so far from the bridge."

"And why those kids laughed at our lock."

The worker with the bolt cutters snapped another lock, sending it rattling into the bucket with the others.

Jessica said, "Now what?"

At the foot of the bridge was a small piazza. Three small souvenir booths lined the edge of the canal, each shaded by a green, white, and red canvas awning. Chris and Jessica had bought postcards at one of them the night before.

And beyond the souvenir booths was a *vaporetto* stand.

"Try the Rialto Bridge?" Chris said. "We could catch a taxi."

Beyond the end of the bridge, across the piazza, the fifty-foot-high walls of the Galleria dell'Accademia were entirely covered with three identical posters of Emma Watson stretching from the brick pavement below to the line of the terracotta roof above. In each poster, Emma jammed her hands deeply into the pockets of the pale gray trench coat cinched tightly around her thin waist by a thick, pale gray belt. Her long brown hair blew in the breeze, her face pale, her eyes glaring out from the deep shadows cast by harsh lighting from above.

She seemed to be scolding whoever was looking at her.

Jessica was looking at Emma, too.

"I think our little mission of love is doomed," she said.

"We could come back later."

"They'll just cut off the lock next week, or next month," she said. "Kinda spoils the whole idea, don't you think, knowing that?"

"So what you're saying is that it's all—"

"Oh, God, no."

"What?" Chris said.

She sighed in mock disgust.

"Go ahead. Say it. I know you can't help yourself."

"So it's all academic, then."

Jessica walked to the handrail, leaned over, poked a finger into her mouth, and made a retching sound.

Chris said, "That's the response I'm hoping for."

When she returned, she was looking past Chris.

"How about the Guggenheim?"

He turned. The Peggy Guggenheim Museum squatted a few hundred yards away, halfway to the end of the canal. It was short and wide, white and stark. It looked nothing like the ostentatious, ornate facades of the other buildings that lined both sides of the canal from one end to the other. He had read that it was not nearly as modern as it looked, having been built in the 1700s.

But it stuck out, especially with the majestic domes of the Santa Maria basilica rising up behind it.

On the other hand, there was a Picasso inside. He had never seen a Picasso. And the museum was a five-minute walk from the bridge.

"It's not quite the same as declaring our undying love by writing our name on a lock and clamping it to a bridge," he said. "But it might be fun."

As they passed the workers, Chris dropped the padlock into the bucket with a clank.

The wooden stairs ended at a wooden landing that was raised ten feet off the ground. From the landing, wooden stairways led down to the left and right. The one to the right led to the small piazza with the souvenir booths and the *vaporetto* stalls on one side and the Galleria dell'Accademia on the other. They would take the stairway to the left, then wind through the narrow streets and alleys to the Guggenheim building.

A man stood on the landing at the foot of the bridge stairs, arms folded, one foot forward, watching people descend. A half-rolled scroll dangled from one hand. He wore a heavy, brown woolen robe that must have been uncomfortable in the late morning heat. If there had been a pile of thick books at his feet, he would have looked just like the statue in Campo Santo Stefano. He even had a bushy, stiff beard, almost the same gray color as the statue's stone.

Chris took Jessica's hand and stepped to the left to pass by the man.

Ahead, across the piazza, three fifty-foot tall Emma Watsons glared at him from three tightly cinched trench coats.

"You love her, yes?" the man said. His voice was soft and high-pitched. He had an Italian accent, adding little vowel sounds on the ends of words.

Another vendor. The line seemed to be a standard attention grabber, at least for couples.

Chris couldn't see what the old man was selling.

He nodded curtly at the man and stepped forward.

"Love is in their blood, too," the man said.

Chris turned.

The man's arms were still folded, but one finger pointed toward the police officers and the workers on the bridge.

He looked at Jessica.

"Most of the time, as you say."

Chris looked back toward the crest of the bridge. They had been on the other side of the bridge when Jessica made her comment about love in the blood. From here, that spot was out of sight and almost certainly out of earshot. It must be a hundred feet or more.

Had the man been behind them the whole time? Chris didn't think so, but he wasn't sure.

"You shout," the man said. He touched his chest with his fingers. "In here."

Chris tugged on Jessica's hand.

She squeezed and pulled back, not moving. She looked at the man, a half smile on her face, her eyes crinkling, her head cocked. The look she got when she was trying to figure out one of Chris's pranks, or one of his jokes.

"You give up so easily," the man said, "your little mission of love."

"What's your game?" Jessica said.

"*Sempre amore*," the man said.

It sounded like some Latin words Chris had learned here and there, and he guessed at a translation. Forever love.

Jessica frowned. "*Lucchetti dell'Amore?* Really? You're selling padlocks?"

Chris pointed a thumb over his shoulder. "No thanks. We already donated ours to their collection."

"*Lucchetti dell'Amore!*" the man shouted, raising a hand, the tip of his thumb touching the tips of his fingers. He turned and spat pointedly on the ground, then said something else in the same disgusted tone in Italian.

Chris caught the words *turista* and *denaro*. Something about tourist and his money? Probably close enough. In any case, the man clearly did not approve of the popular love locks ritual.

Or maybe his outrage was all part of his schtick.

Chris said, "So what *are* you selling?"

"*Sempre amore,*" the man repeated. He smiled. "Always love."

Jessica laughed. "It might be fun."

"No," the man said. "Very serious."

Jessica stifled her laugh and put on her "okay, now I'm being serious" face.

"How does it work?" she said.

Chris said, "What do we have to buy?"

"You love her, yes?"

Ah, back to that line of patter.

"Yes."

"Very much, yes?"

A common sales tactic. Get the prospect to lean forward, to commit to something. To overcommit. It was surprisingly difficult to back down later, when the seller used your own conscience against you and twisted the overcommitment to make the sale.

Difficult unless you knew the tactic. Then you could watch for the invitation to overcommit, and the twist.

"Yes, very much."

He looked at Jessica. She smiled.

"Also you love him, yes?"

"Very much," she said. She slipped an arm around his waist to demonstrate.

"*Molto bene,*" the man said. "I make *permenante. Sempre amore.*"

Jessica cocked her head again.

Chris had to admit, he was curious about what the man would do next.

Curious what Jessica would do next.

On their third date, he and Jessica had gone to a Renaissance fair in Santa Barbara. Jessica spotted a fortune teller. "It might be fun," she said, a playful grin on her face.

Chris could not resist Jessica's playful grin.

Inside the dark tent, thick with nose-tickling incense and dim candlelight, the fortune teller launched into her cold reading mumbo jumbo.

Chris noticed Jessica reacting with little ooohs and ahhhs to the fortune teller's pronouncements and vague visions. And the fortune teller's visions slowly became more vivid and precise.

Jessica was playing the fortune teller.

Chris joined in.

Between the two of them, they guided the fortune teller to foretell the great fortune Jessica's fictitious sister would inherit (causing strife in the family) and the sudden (if mercifully painless) death of Chris's fictitious uncle.

On the drive back to Los Angeles, they had laughed and laughed.

That night they made love for the first time. The fortune teller somehow didn't foresee that.

That had been a good day.

Now Jessica had that same playful grin on her face.

"All right," Chris said. "What will it cost?"

"One hundred and fifty."

That was a little more than one hundred fifty dollars. More than five times what the fortune teller had charged.

"That's a lot of money."

"Is not so much, yes?" the man said. "For always love?"

"Chris, let's do it." Jessica smiled at him. "My treat."

The man held out his hand. "Gilberto."

Chris and Jessica introduced themselves.

Chris said, "What next?"

"Next we sit," Gilberto said. "And feel the love."

Chris and Jessica followed Gilberto across the piazza, paved like the Campo Santo Stefano in dull gray bricks in a herringbone pattern.

He expected the man to lead them to some small, dark room filled with wizardly paraphernalia, where he would chant arcane syllables and draw arcane symbols in the air with his finger.

Instead, he stopped on the far side of the piazza between the *vaporetto* stand and the Galleria at a small cluster of tables covered in vinyl, red-and-white checkerboard tablecloths.

Every restaurant on every piazza in Venice had a cluster of tables like this in front. And many piazzas had clusters like this one, far from any restaurant or café.

Venice was a very tourist friendly place.

Gilberto motioned for them to sit.

They sat.

Gilberto folded his hands in his lap and looked back and forth from Jessica to Chris.

"You must take this very seriously."

Chris didn't dare look at Jessica. She had a great poker face, but he didn't want to provoke her into laughing.

In the corner of his eye, he saw her nod.

Gilberto said, "First the money. To show you are serious."

To show they were serious. Chris had to admit, that was a nice touch.

Jessica fished the bills out of the purse and laid them on the table.

"Now you must prepare yourselves very carefully."

Gilberto made no move to pick up the money. Instead, he spread his hands over the table.

"This is comfortable for you?"

"I don't know," Jessica said. "What do we have to do?"

"Prepare your heart. Is not a little bit too public here, maybe? To feel most deeply your love for one another?"

"I'm good," Chris said.

Privacy was not an issue. They were the only people seated at the tables.

And he had no trouble feeling love for Jessica anywhere.

"When you feel the deepest love in your hearts, I touch you very gently. Like so." He touched the back of one hand with the fingertips of the other. "Is okay I touch you?"

Jessica nodded and smiled.

"You want to look in the eyes, maybe? Touch hands?"

Jessica leaned forward, put her hands on the table, and looked at Chris.

Chris reached out and intertwined his fingers with hers.

Jessica chuckled.

"When I touch, you feel the love always."

"Okay," Jessica said.

"No more, no less."

"What?" Chris said.

Jessica's fingers tensed, and she frowned. She slid her hands back from Chris's.

Gilberto said, "You will feel this love always for each other. This love, *precisamente.*"

"No more?" Jessica said. "Really?"

"*Sempre amore.*"

"But...don't people grow to love each other more over time?"

Her frown deepened.

She seemed to be taking this very seriously all of a sudden.

The old man had done something the fortune teller had been unable to do.

He had gotten to her.

"*Even* more, I mean."

Gilberto shrugged. "*Si. No.* Who can say this thing?"

"Whoo," Jessica said. She laughed nervously. "That's a lot of pressure all of a sudden."

Gilberto touched the bills on the table with his fingertips.

"Perhaps I cannot accept your money today."

Oh, that was a nice touch. Offer to back out. Let the prospect make the move to continue the sale.

But Jessica had already handed over the money.

Unless this was the setup for something more expensive.

Chris said, "Maybe we should go."

Jessica laughed and drew a breath.

"No, this is good. Let's keep going."

She entwined her fingers in his again.

Chris had never seen her this way. Thrown for a loop.

Gilberto said, "You must make certain."

Jessica nodded and looked at Chris.

Then she laughed. A melodious, happy laugh.

"Feel the love," she said.

"Fill your hearts," Gilberto said.

Chris gazed into Jessica's eyes, and she into his.

She looked beautiful. She always looked beautiful.

He stroked her thumb with his. Her fingers felt soft and warm and good.

He loved her.

He let his love flood into his heart. He could feel his love through her fingers. Through her eyes.

It filled his body.

His being.

He never saw Gilberto reach for them, but he felt the man's fingertips, warm and cracked and dry, touch the back of his hand.

He took a slow breath. The air smelled like the ocean.

Gilberto's fingers slid away.

Chris and Jessica looked at each other for a moment longer. Her eyes were shining.

He could stay this way forever.

She blinked, squeezing tears down her cheeks. She pulled one hand from Chris's and wiped her cheeks with her fingers.

"Thank you," she said, turning toward Gilberto.

Her eyes went wide.

Gilberto's chair was empty.

"Whoa," Jessica said.

The old man must have gotten up while Chris and Jessica were staring into each other's eyes.

Damn, the guy was good.

He looked at the table.

The money was gone.

Chris laughed.

Yeah, the guy was really good.

Jessica pointed over Chris's shoulder.

He turned.

Gilberto was halfway across the piazza, plodding toward the bridge, his heavy, brown robe fluttered in the breeze like Emma Watson's hair.

Chris turned back to Jessica.

She was wiping more tears.

And he could feel the tears welling in his own eyes.

The old man had done nothing more than invite them to feel their love.

Feel it deeply.

The love they already felt for each other.

Gilberto had sold them their own love.

And it had been worth every penny.

LOVE BOTS

DÆMON CROWE

Dæmon Crowe is one of four pseudonyms that write Crowe stories. Two of the four author names (Dory and Dæmon) have appeared in nine Fiction River *collections, including* Feel the Fear, Pulse Pounders: Adrenaline, Last Stand, Tavern Tales *and* Justice. *Crowe stories have appeared in* Alfred Hitchcock's Mystery Magazine, *in* DAW Books, *and in* Level Best Books' Best New England Crime Stories *anthologies.*

"My obvious inspiration for this story," Dæmon says, "is the then and now political situation, where I find it impossible to fathom how certain politicians can hold even a small percentage of the population in thrall. They must be using some magic or technology, hence the birth of the love bots, a perversion of everything love stands for in service to an egotistical buffoon. Can't say much more. Those blinded by their own love bots will hate this story. Those who have escaped may find even more bitter laughter and a modicum of solace."

This dystopian tale is one that conjures up the essence of Orwell's 1984. *The story also, of course, speaks quite brilliantly about elements of leadership that are the cause of much debate and divisiveness in recent Western culture.*

B illy Flowers woke to the chime of his iMplant announcing the impending arrival of the New Year's love note from His Most Imperial Majesty The Grand Poobah himself.

Billy squeezed his eyes shut, pulled his mildewed feather pillow over his head and pressed it against his ears, further muffling the sounds of early morning traffic already clogging the predawn Brooklyn streets five stories below. His identical twin, Geordie, threw back the covers on his side of their double bed. A whisper of cold air tickled the small of Billy's back where his flannel pajamas— last year's hand-me-downs from older brother Trent and two sizes too small—left a bare patch no longer shielded by the thin fleece blanket.

Geordie's stockinged feet hit the unpainted concrete floor of their public housing tenement with a thump. The bedsprings creaked and the mattress rocked as Geordie shifted his weight to his legs and slid open the door to the windowless cubicle they called a bedroom. The aroma of fresh brewed chicory mingled with the clatter of plastic plates and stainless cutlery hitting the top of the Formica dinette table and the slap of Mom's mules against worn linoleum.

Billy opened his eyes.

On the rough cinder block wall appeared the projected shadow of their little sister, Gracie Ann—a miniature version of Mom, without the etched-in worry lines—standing in the kitchen doorway with her hands on her hips and, no doubt, a scowl on her face.

"Hurry up, you two. The Poobah knows when we're late. You'll get us in trouble."

Geordie shook Billy.

He groaned and turned farther toward the cinder blocks, trying to carry the blanket with him.

Geordie tugged the blanket away.

"You heard her. Get up before I turn you in myself."

Billy's iMplant pinged the two-minute warning.

He rolled onto his back and stared at the brown water stains connecting the dots on the acoustic ceiling tiles. If he squinted, the largest one became a silhouette of the Poobah himself, complete with bulbous nose, bouffant hair, double chins, and pockmarked cheeks. Surely the Russo Sino American Empire could produce a more attractive leader.

The thick synthetic weave of Billy's one-piece, winter Boy Ranger uniform landed across his face. Still warm from the dryer, it smelled of lye-based detergent and chemically fresh-scented fabric softener.

"Get dressed," Mom said in her most do-it-now-or-else tone.

Billy zipped himself into the blue-and-gray camo-printed jump-suit over his too-small flannel pajamas. He thrust his feet into a pair of Trent's castoff combat boots—the blood-stained ones the Marines sent back with his belongings—and secured the Velcro straps.

The sultry female voice of his iMplant started counting down.

Ten.

Billy secured the Boy Ranger belt buckle around his too-thin waist.

Nine.

He shuffled into the kitchen.

Eight.

He grabbed a four-ounce tumbler of reconstituted orange juice.

Seven.

Chugged it down without stopping.

Six.

Slid two slices of crisp New Year's bacon off the faded plastic plate at his place at the table.

Five.

Stuffed them both into his mouth.

Four.

Chewed.

Three.

Leapt over the back of the couch that divided the not-so-great room from the kitchenette.

Two.

Squeezed between Gracie Ann and Geordie on the lumpy sofa cushions.

One.

Swallowed.

The concrete wall in front of the couch shimmered. It smoothed into a static, 3-D close-up of the Grand Poobah's smiling orange visage.

Billy stole a glance at the enraptured faces of Gracie Ann and Geordie. Even Mom—sitting ramrod straight in the recliner once reserved for Dad, before he got the call and marched off to save the world—displayed the goofy grin his entire family wore in the presence of the merest hint of His Most Imperial Majesty. It was the same besotted look he saw on everyone at the mere mention of the Grand Poobah or any member of the Imperial Family. If the Poobah told the entire populace to jump off the Empire State Building, they'd line up a thousand deep to do it.

Everyone but Billy.

For the life of him, he couldn't see the attraction of a fat, fifty-year-old man who did nothing but demand sacrifices from everyone but himself. Why didn't anyone else see it?

The Poobah's face morphed into the Poobah sitting on his golden throne in his golden penthouse in his golden tower in Central Manhattan. He wore his New Year's red-, white- and blue-striped cutaway suit and star-spangled top hat.

Mom's eyes went glassy. She sighed.

Gracie Ann squealed as though the Poobah were the lead in the hottest boy band.

Geordie stiffened and leaned forward, ears pricked to catch every word.

Billy imitated his twin. Long ago he'd learned not to slouch or openly mock the coming clownish performance.

"My fellow citizens," the Poobah's trenchant voice rang from the speakers hidden inside the hanging ceiling. It echoed in Billy's iMplant. The Poobah waved his delicate hands and pointed through the screen like a recruiting poster. "Today we celebrate our ally's New Year and a new beginning for our great countries. This morning our gallant troops will march the length of Fifth Avenue, where I will review them before they march on to the Battery and board the ships I have provided to join our Russian friends in our fight against the forces of evil arrayed against us."

Mom clasped her hands to her breast and sighed.

Gracie Ann squirmed and trilled.

Geordie jumped to his feet. He clicked his heels and gave a stiff-armed salute.

Billy's heart sank. More troops. How many of these wouldn't return? Why didn't anyone else care?

He studied the stains on his boots.

"Join us along the parade route to send off our brave men and women." The Poobah's face broke into a cap-toothed rictus as the national anthem piped through the speakers and iMplant.

Billy wanted to throw a bloody boot at the Poobah. His face set in a neutral mask that he hoped passed for the best traditions of the professional Boy Ranger, he stood and joined Geordie in a half-hearted salute.

They joined the throngs walking across the Brooklyn Bridge and into Manhattan, Mom and Gracie Ann in their faux fur maxi coats, Geordie and Billy in their ankle-length Boy Ranger greatcoats over their one-piece uniforms. They all wore faux fur hats down over their ears with red stars sewn to their fronts. Gracie Ann skipped ahead with a gaggle of tweenager girls from her middle school. Geordie marched in lock step with a troop of Boy Rangers singing martial songs and passing a joint. Billy hung back with Mom.

The February wind whistled in the bridge cables and bit at the exposed skin on their faces. Billy shoved his hands deep into the pockets of his great coat and wished he had three more layers and two more pairs of gloves. For all the unbearable warmth of summer, New York winters were cold and snowy and miserable for all but those who lived inside the climate-controlled luxury towers clustered in Central Manhattan.

They followed the crowd north through the Village and Washington Square to the bright lights of Broadway. In the crimson glow of predawn they arrived at portable metal barricades across the sidewalk at the corner of Fifth Avenue and 51st Street, where uniformed guards checked for IDs and grandstand tickets. Only the chosen few would get any closer to His Most Imperial Majesty.

Gracie Ann and her friends pushed their way to the front of the crowd hanging on the parade route barriers along the curb. Geordie hung with the troop of Boy Rangers under the awning of a delicatessen. Billy directed Mom to a steam grate beside the open doors of a basement elevator sunk into the sidewalk.

At the crack of dawn, as the sun rose in slivers in the canyons of skyscrapers leading to the East River, a military band began playing a Souza march in Billy's iMplant. Mom's toes started tapping to the beat. Soon the music echoed up the street as the drum major of a Naval band lead ranks of sailors in battle dress uniforms and pea coats down Fifth Avenue. The sailor's noses were red and running in the cold, but they kept their cow-eyed gaze forward and their step lively.

"Why?" The question escaped Billy's lips before he clamped back his thoughts. *Why do they do it? Don't they know where they're headed? Don't they care?*

"Why what?" A girl around his age, maybe fifteen or sixteen—dressed all in black from her watch cap to her ski parka and stretch leggings and the shiny leather boots on her very small feet—stood on the raised platform of the sidewalk elevator. Her deep green eyes shone with the lively intelligence Billy worked so hard to conceal from all but his private mirror. Her mouth curled up in a smile that twinkled into her eyes and pierced Billy's heart.

"Um." His tongue wouldn't work. His brain froze.

The girl jerked her chin toward the Marines now marching past them to the squeals of Gracie Ann's gaggle. "You mean them?"

Billy nodded.

The girl nodded back. "You cold?"

Silly question. Yet, somehow, a warm glow had entered his chest.

"Come on down." The girl waved him toward the elevator as she pushed a button.

With only a cursory glance at Mom warming herself on the steam grate, her eyes glowing with the stupid ecstasy of love for the Poobah and his endless lines of troops, Billy stepped onto the elevator and it began its slow descent into the maw of Manhattan's underworld.

The elevator jerked to a stop in a basement storeroom lined with stacks of cardboard boxes labeled with the wares of the delicatessen over their heads: deli dill pickles in gallon glass jars; gallon plastic tubs of mayonnaise, ketchup, and mustard; number 10 cans of sauerkraut; crates of cabbage; trays of bread, rye, pumpernickel, and whole wheat; bags of bagels by the gross. It smelled of vinegar and damp concrete. The overhead doors clanked shut, leaving them in the light of a series of single bulbs hung by their wires from a concrete ceiling.

The girl stepped off the elevator and sat on a large box of paper napkins. She pointed to a box labeled Toilet Paper Jumbo Rolls.

"Have a seat."

As though in a dream, Billy sat.

"You're different," the girl said.

Billy's heart skipped a beat. He swallowed.

"The name's Louise, by the way."

Billy nodded. His tongue felt three sizes too big for his mouth.

Louise leaned forward. Her startling green eyes stared directly into Billy's.

"How'd you do it?"

He cleared his throat.

"Do what." His voice cracked and broke.

"Get rid of the nanos?"

"The what?"

Louise took Billy's chin between her hands and turned his face one way and then the other, always keeping her gaze on his eyes. She let go and sat back.

"Tell me true. Do you love the Poobah?"

The question should have sent a dagger into Billy's heart. Nobody admitted to not loving the Poobah. Nobody who wanted to live another day.

He shrugged.

"You don't, do you. I can see it in your eyes." She pointed up. "The rest of them out there, there's nobody home when it comes to the Poobah. He says jump," she snapped her fingers, "they ask how high. Unconditional selflessness—the definition of love. Perverted love. But you," she pointed at Billy, "you're not like them." She tapped her temple. "You've got somebody home. So I'll ask again. How did you get rid of the nanos?"

"I never had any nanos." At least he didn't think he had any, whatever they were.

She shook her head. "Not possible. Not unless you're slumming in that Boy Ranger outfit and you really belong up the avenue in your protected penthouse. You slumming? What's your name, anyway?"

"Billy. Billy Flowers from Brooklyn. Not slumming. No nanos I know of. What's a nano?"

She took him by the wrist, dragged him up a set of wooden stairs to the back of the deli. He didn't resist. He couldn't have resisted if he'd wanted to. She had him under a spell.

"Wait here."

It was all he could do not to follow her behind the deli counter, where a man dressed in white with a blood- and mustard-stained apron stood chatting with a customer while he sliced ham onto his open palm. Louise leaned up, cupped her hands around his ear and whispered into it. The man turned the same open, intelligent green eyes toward Billy.

He felt blood rush into his cheeks. He gave a palm out shaky wave and tried to smile.

The man finished wrapping a ham on rye sandwich in butcher paper and handed it to a woman behind the cash register. He wiped his hands on his apron and entered the back room.

His large hands took Billy's chin and wiggled it, looking into his eyes the way Louise had.

"I told you, Dad. No nanos. He doesn't even know what they are."

Billy rubbed his chin as Louise's father let go. "What are they?"

"Nanobots," Louise's father said. "They inject them with your baby vaccinations."

"Unless you're rich and famous and part of the Poobah's elite," Louise said with bitterness. "Or like our family" she pointed to herself and her father, "who can't get the vaccines for medical reasons. Then, if you're lucky or smart, you don't get the love bots."

"Love bots?" Nanos. Nanobots. Love bots. What the hell were they talking about?

"Tiny robots that work on your brain and endocrine system to make you love the Poobah with the kind of unconditional selfless-ness a mother feels for her child or a lovesick teenager feels for his first crush. They use that perverted love to fill their armies and fight their wars," Louise's father said.

"So if you're not slumming, Billy Flowers, how come you're not in love with the Poobah? How come no bots?" Louise asked again.

"I don't know," Billy said, but he had an idea. "I have a twin brother. He's more in love with the Poobah than anyone else I know. Even more than my father or older brother, before they got killed in Iran. I got the measles once."

Louise slapped her forehead. "They must have vaccinated him twice and missed you."

It made sense. The wonderful girl with the green eyes that made his stomach all queasy and his cheeks go red had to be right. No wonder he didn't fit in.

"What if they find out? Will they inject me?" The last thing he wanted was to fall in love with that fat old man, not now that he'd found Louise.

"How old are you?" Louise's father asked.

"Sixteen next month."

Louise jumped forward, wrapping her arms around him in a bear hug. "Too late. It only works before the onset of puberty."

She planted a kiss on his lips.

It was the sweetest thing he had ever tasted.

He wrapped his arms around her.

He was never, ever going to let go.

LOVING ABBY

ANGELA PENROSE

Angela Penrose watched the original Star Trek *in its first run, played scenes from the television show on the playground when in first grade, and has been a science fiction fan ever since. She writes SF, fantasy, and some crime fiction as Angela Penrose, and romance under another name. Her first professional SF publication was a story called "Staying Afloat," which appeared in John Helfers'* Fiction River: How to Save the World. *It was later reprinted in John Joseph Adams's* Loosed Upon the World, *and was required reading in Duke University's 2017 Global Ecological Humanities class.*

She lives in Seattle with her husband, where the two regularly enjoy nature documentaries. One of those documentaries inspired this story.

I enjoyed how this story explored those elements of parental love, but I am also intrigued by the way Angela allows us to reflect on the way humans interfere with other species all in the name of protection and conservation.

This tales reminds me of a memorable line in Michael Crichton's Jurassic Park, *conveyed brilliantly in the movie adaptation by actor Jeff Goldblum when Ian says: "Your scientists were so preoccupied with whether or not they could, they didn't stop to think if they should."*

I love my little girl.

Of course I do. I'm her mother. I carried her in my belly for... well, I'm not sure how long. Nobody knows anymore, really, although we all have guesses.

We landed here on Colorata just over eight years ago, ninety months of ship-time and 312 years of slowtime back on Earth. We were the seventeenth colony expedition to leave the Sol system, heading for a planet that'd been found, studied, investigated, and seeded with some key Terran plants and animals and microbes, by robot probes.

The ships landed in a green, Earth-grass valley with a wide, fertile floor and a quiet river winding through it. The river flowed about thirty kilometers into a round, sandy bay with good fishing. The probe data promised temperate weather, there were no really dangerous predators nearby, and there was nothing on the planet smarter than, say, a lion.

That last is important. There were no intelligent beings on Colorata when we came.

The first years were hard, but generally went well. We started exploring, building, farming, mining, learning about our new home and doing our best to make lives for ourselves.

And we started having children. Because of course this was all pointless without future generations to hand it off to.

It all went pretty much as we'd expected—which is amazing enough—until the Boomers came.

We didn't know they were Boomers then, or even that there was a "they."

I was outside at the time, kneeling in the dark, damp soil, weeding onions, when suddenly I felt tingly. It reminded me of one afternoon back home when I'd been walking down the street in the rain and suddenly a lightning bolt struck a tree across the street.

I was already looking up when I saw a ripple trail appear in the clouds, all in a split second, and then a sonic boom hammered on my ears.

I'm a botanist, not a meteorologist, so my first thought was that it was some weird weather thing we hadn't run into before. On a strange planet, you never know what you're going to run into—we'd all had that pounded into our brains before we were allowed to commit to the expedition.

I was in a community field, not my own garden patch at home, so there were other botanists working around me. We all looked at each other, grimacing and rubbing our ears. Clara said, "Sonic boom! Meteor, maybe?"

Su-Nan Chen, still kneeling between onion rows, said, "That fast? I've seen videos of meteors and they're much slower."

"Then what?" I asked.

Nobody knew.

Our governing council decided to send some drones to look around in the direction the cloud-streak had gone. If it was a meteor, it would've been carrying enough energy to leave an obvious crater when it hit. If it was something else, maybe they could find it, figure out what'd happened.

The drones searched for a couple weeks but didn't find anything. Most of us shrugged and went on about our work, of which there was plenty. We put the sonic boom out of our minds, mostly. It's what you do when you don't know much, and don't think something will affect your life any.

It was almost a year later when Brett Donnelly hurt little Alvin.

Brett was a geologist and had a climbing accident on one of his exploratory hikes. He lost his leg and fell into depression. I can't blame him—I can't imagine what it'd be like. Back on Earth, he could've gotten one of the nice robotic prosthetics and gone right back to climbing mountains, but we didn't have that capability. So he had an old fashioned J-hook style leg, which let him walk and run all right, but was iffy for rock climbing. He spent most of his time supervising mining robots, and was pretty bitter.

His son, Alvin, was only two when Brett got into a shouting, cussing argument with his wife, Libby. Libby says Alvin, who'd been crying in a corner while they argued, toddled up to Brett when he called Libby something particularly foul, and said, "Bad Daddy!"

Brett leaned down and backhanded him so hard he bounced off a wall. He broke two ribs and his collarbone and his jaw, and his brain swelled with concussion.

Dolores, one of our surgeons, got Alvin put back together and stabilized, and Brett was hauled into detention. Seeing little Alvin's still body shocked Brett into a sobbing wreck, but I'll say most of us didn't care. I was ready to vote to lock him up for a good long time, and Libby had Brett's things tossed out of their house by the next evening.

Brett insisted he loved his son, that he hadn't realized what he was doing or how much strength he'd used. He said he understood that Libby didn't want to live with him anymore, but he begged for visitation rights. Libby said over her dead body. The advocate said maybe, after counseling, possibly. Libby raged. The colony divided up, most of us on Libby's side.

The next morning it was all moot. Alvin vanished out of the infirmary.

There was a lot of shouting and accusations, and Libby was escorted everywhere for weeks, but it turned out it wasn't any of us.

Two months later, Grace Chen, the oldest Coloratan-born child at age five, fell out of a tree and broke her arm. She spent the night in the infirmary, and the next morning she was gone.

Greggy Filipeppi, age two months, disappeared after his mother, Fabiola, rolled over on him in her sleep. She woke up before he smothered, but she liked a firm bed and he had some cracked bones. Four days after her baby vanished, Fabiola was found back in the woods, both wrists slit.

It was obvious by then what was happening, but we didn't know who was doing it or how. We put cameras everywhere, but they never showed anything. At most there was the occasional flicker.

Parents grew frantic and paranoid about their children, and everyone talked—in strained, tight voices—about serial killers and undiscovered predators and horrible infections that got into injuries and consumed entire bodies, although none of the adults who'd been hurt vanished so that was just ridiculous.

After we lost Greggy, no one had any children for about ten months. People were trying, but no one was catching. Chemists analyzed everything they could pin down—soil, air, water, plants, animals.

They searched for microbes and toxins and weird chemicals, and found quite a few, but none that shut down fertility.

We might've thought it was a huge coincidence, Nature falling into step for a strangely long period with a strangely large group of people, but we knew better. They were doing it, somehow. Whoever had taken our children, they weren't letting us have any more.

Hysteria built up, and it took a lot of persuasion and shouting and gentle support and harsh punishment to get some folks to keep doing their jobs every day. Herman Johnson was on short rations for six weeks before he gave in and went back to tending the sheep.

The sheep didn't even need much tending. We had fenced Terran-grass pastures up the valley. All Herman had to do was watch the sheep, help any that got tangled up in fencing or the wiry native bushes that sprouted up here and there, and move them to the next pasture in rotation when one got grazed down.

We'd worried at first that the sheep might not "take" in this new environment—sheep are good eating, and their wool is a valuable fiber crop. Sheep aren't very smart, though, and need watching. Especially at lambing time; if a ewe dies in the birthing, or occasionally refuses to care for her lamb, the shepherd needs to step in and take care of it himself. Sometimes he can persuade a ewe whose lamb was born dead to "adopt" the orphan lamb, but if not, it's bottle feeding for a while, until the lamb can take care of itself—as well as a domestic sheep ever does—and rejoin the flock.

But that's all in the spring, during birthing season. Tending the sheep in the summer is one of the easier tasks, is my point. Herman spent most of his work time sitting in a patch of shade with his knitting, keeping half an eye on the sheep while his dogs did most of the watching. He had an airgun by his side to chase off the occasional carnivorous bird or lizard that thought a browsing wool-ball might look yummy. There weren't many native carnivores big enough to go after a sheep, though, and projectiles scared them away pretty easily, so there weren't many people who sympathized with Herman when he insisted it wasn't worth working anymore. He finally rejoined the real world.

Most people just ignored Herman and the few others like him, and focused on more immediate issues. And in the middle of an argument about whether we should try to move the colony to the beta site, a good six thousand kilometers away, the children reappeared.

Or at least, that's what we thought at first.

Grace Chen appeared early one morning. She just walked into the settlement, up the spray-pave road that led down to the bay, lugging Greggy in her arms and herding Alvin between the river-stone pillars that marked the edge of town, like a prim little sheep-dog. Alvin toddled ahead of her, and yelled, "Mommy!" when someone called Libby out. She snatched him up into her arms, crying all over him and laughing at the same time.

Su-Nan came to scoop up Grace, and someone got Ettore from the iron mine to take Greggy. He held his little son, silent and dry-eyed, but something in his shoulders relaxed. I was there and I saw.

I'd worried about him, losing his wife and his baby, practically at the same time. Watching him get his baby back was really wonderful, and we wondered whether it was all over.

I know, but I think it was a natural reaction. We were helpless to change our situation, so when it seemed to fix itself, we all grabbed onto that. It was nice for a while.

Two weeks later, Dolores announced that she was pregnant. We all cheered and felt relieved. Whatever had been happening, it was over with.

Eleven more women got pregnant over the next month, as if everyone decided to strike while the iron was hot. After some consideration, I chose a sperm sample from the huge collection we brought from Earth, went to the infirmary, and came home pregnant.

I was barely showing, still tending crops, testing soil, doing genetic analyses on our latest hybrids, when I first heard the gossip about the kids.

It was summer, hot and humid, and Clara and I were working in the lab. My bench was in the blank corner, with just walls on both sides. No one else had wanted it when we set up, but once summer had set in, the heat coming through the windows got the folks working there sweating and complaining.

Clara wandered over to my cool corner, a flask of juice in her hand, and said, "Have you noticed anything...off, about Grace?"

Clara was better friends with Su-Nan than I was, but I saw her with little Grace every now and then. I thought back a few days, when we'd both decided to eat supper in the cafeteria on the same night, and eat together.

Grace had followed her mother to the small, round table we'd claimed that evening, pouting over her bowl of stir-fry.

"She decided to have cake for dinner," Su-Nan explained with a wry smile.

"Well, there are times when we'd all like cake for dinner," I said, grinning back.

"I want cake!" Grace glared at us both, dropped her bowl onto the floor, where it bounced, spattering vegetables and sauce all over the tough carpet, then dashed back toward the food line.

Su-Nan muttered something under her breath, set her own bowl on the table, and dashed after Grace. She caught her at the dessert display, picked her up, and carried her shrieking, flailing kid back to the table. She set her down on a chair, squatted in front of her and just watched her until Grace quieted down to sniffling.

Grace ended up eating her stir-fry. She actually liked stir-fry, but little kids aren't always rational. I was uncomfortable for a few minutes, but I thought Su-Nan handled the tantrum with patience, and that's just how five-year-olds were sometimes.

"No," I said to Clara. "I haven't seen anything weird. What's up?"

She lowered her voice and said, "My friend Danny works in child care, and he said Grace has been acting weird since she got back."

She paused, and I nodded. I thought it made sense that the experience might've had an effect. Grace was the only one of the children who was able to talk well enough to have explained what happened, but she hadn't. When asked, she'd said, "I don't know," and if pressed, she cried. Nothing on the children themselves or their clothing gave a hint of where they'd been.

"Not that kind of weird," said Clara. "Nightmares or some withdrawal or normal acting out would be, well, normal. Danny says she's been acting out more than usual, but there's a pattern to it."

"Maybe she's cranky when she's tired?" I suggested.

"Sometimes," said Clara. "But Danny kept notes, as he's supposed to, and he showed them to me."

I gave her a look, and she said, "I know, he shouldn't, but it's so weird, he's not sure it's real. He wanted some other eyes on it before he brought it up to Maria, much less Su-Nan. And he was right—there's a pattern!"

She paused, and I said, "Well? What kind of pattern?"

"While she's in care, she acts out twice with each caregiver—no more and no less. So Danny knows she'll act out with him twice a day, although not when. And after the second time, he knows she'll be an angel until Su-Nan comes to get her. And she always is."

I leaned back a little and stared at her. "All right, that *is* weird. Is he sure?"

"He's sure about himself. He's not always sure about how she is with others—he has to pay attention to whichever kids he's working with himself—but from what he can see, she's the same with everyone. And there's more."

I scowled at her. She was enjoying drawing this out way too much. "So?"

"He doesn't usually work with babies anymore, but he's got toddlers sometimes, and he noticed Alvin does the same thing."

"That's...I don't know what it is." I tried to think. This was more than weird. It was scary, and the only explanations I could come up with made me shiver and lay a palm on my barely rounded belly.

"Do you think he should take it to Maria?"

"I think he should take it to the Council. Or Maria should."

"But what if—?"

"Really?" I sucked in a deep breath. "We all know what's happening. Children who were hurt vanished, then suddenly we couldn't have kids anymore. Then the kids came back and we can get pregnant again, but the returned kids are testing us. Testing the people who take care of them." Grace's tantrum the other night suddenly looked different. Yes, it was the sort of thing little kids did, but I wondered how many times per day Su-Nan had to be patient with her—had to prove she was a good parent to Grace.

"There's someone out there. I'll say it if no one else will. I have a baby coming and ignoring what's happening is stupid!"

Could I be a perfect mother? Would I be allowed to keep my child?

"It has to be something, someone out there, yes," said Clara, her voice carefully controlled. "But how could the kids be 'testing' us? They're too little to even think of that. Yes, kids test their parents, but they're never that organized about it."

"I don't know. Maybe they're being controlled? I don't know. Let's go talk to Danny."

We—all right, I—persuaded Danny to talk to Maria, and Maria to take him to the Council. Word got around that there was a problem with the returned kids, and almost everyone showed up for the next meeting.

The kids had all been examined when they returned, of course. They got thorough physicals, blood tests, that sort of thing. Now they got full scans. The colony only had one scanner and it was an energy sucker, and whenever it broke down, we wouldn't be able to fix it, probably for decades at least. Getting used to relying on it would be all kinds of trouble. We'd agreed to save it for emergencies, but we all agreed a threat to our kids was an emergency.

What the scans showed was something even I hadn't imagined. They weren't human.

Gloria Hunter, the chief pathologist, called them androids. They were artificial constructs designed to mimic human children perfectly. Someone on Earth might have been able to build something similar, but the kids had been back for weeks, and baby Greggy had been growing at a normal rate.

Building something that looked just like a child was one thing. Making something that would *grow* like a child? That was apparently even more impossible than making something that *acted* like a child.

Ettore refused to believe Greggy wasn't real, and stalked out of the subsequent meeting, clutching his baby son to his chest. Alexander, a mechanical engineer and Council member, pointed out (to Ettore's retreating back) that the thing that looked like Greggy was technically colony property, but Pat, a carpenter who sat next to Alexander, jabbed him with an elbow and told him to shut up.

"He's not going to lose it," Pat pointed out. "It'll be around if we need it for anything."

Su-Nan and Libby took some persuading. They insisted on witnessing scans of their children, and the Council voted to allow second scans, energy costs or no. Libby was a tech and understood exactly how the scanner worked. She watched the ring passing over Alvin's body, and the picture building up as it went. Her mouth got tight and tears ran down her cheeks when she turned away and walked out, leaving the thing that looked like Alvin behind. He cried, "Mommy!" and she walked faster until the door closed behind her.

Su-Nan watched the scan of Grace, then followed Libby.

We sent the drones out again, sweeping in all directions, section by section. We sent them farther than we ever had. We hadn't needed to do much exploring beyond our valley, after all; we had a full set of maps from the probes, different views and filters taken with different electromagnetic bands, so we knew what things looked like and where resources were when we outgrew our current territory.

Now we were looking for something the probes wouldn't have seen, because it wasn't there when they were scanning the planet.

None of the drones found anything.

At least now we were talking about them, about the aliens or whatever they were who took our kids. Who were probably watching us all the time, who had some way of preventing us from watching them, or even catching a fuzzy glimpse at the edge of an image.

After some debate, the Council decided to let the three android children stay in the colony. What else could we do? Destroy them? Chase them away, out into the forest?

They were exactly like children, like babies. Exactly. No one, including the people who argued that it'd be just like turning off a washing unit, wanted to be the one to "turn off" the child-things.

So we let them stay. They lived at the care center, where Danny and his co-workers staffed three shifts, seven days a week, ready to take care of the colony's children whenever their parents couldn't. These weren't actual children, but they were close enough, and the care center had been built to serve a population growing up from ten thousand.

It was a small expense in food and labor, but the Council reasoned that watching them would give us valuable information. How they grew, how they behaved as they got older, might give us some clues as to what their creators wanted.

Still, it was a shock, and the therapists were busy for a while—I saw Janice myself, and she gave me some relaxation exercises that helped with the nightmares—but then everything slid back toward normal, at least on the surface.

Except that Su-Nan and Libby, who both wanted to get pregnant again, couldn't.

Su-Nan tried three times (according to Clara) the old-fashioned way, what's called the "turkey baster method" for reasons I can't figure out, then requested an in vitro fertilization and implantation. The fertilization went well, but the embryo wouldn't implant. They tried again with the same results.

I didn't know Libby well, nor did any of her friends suddenly decide to share gossip with me, but as the months went by, she looked more and more depressed.

I was six months along when Dolores, the first woman to get pregnant, had her little boy. We celebrated in the community hall, and Herman gave her a bright yellow baby blanket he'd knitted for her. It had a cable pattern that made chains of hearts all up the length of it.

Four days later, Dolores took baby Miguel to the infirmary and demanded a scan.

Apparently he'd been fussing exactly twice each day.

Summer rolled into Fall, and a quiet depression settled over the colony, reflecting the gray clouds that filled the sky from mountain to mountain. It rained every few days, spitting little drizzles that were just wet enough to get you cold and uncomfortable, but not enough to actually water the crops. We still had to run the irrigation systems for that.

My belly grew, but I had a hard time finding the happy anticipation a pregnant woman was supposed to feel. I spent most of my off hours searching through the knowledge base.

We'd brought with us books, articles, videos, photos—as much information as we could fit onto the storage media allocated to our ships. We had a good percentage of what the world had generated in the last few centuries.

What I wanted to know was why?

Why take our children? Why give back these artificial substitutes?

We'd pretty much settled on aliens. Some people thought there'd been intelligent aliens hiding on Colorata before we came, but most people thought they'd arrived with the sonic boom and the streaking pattern through the clouds. That they were newcomers here, just like us. We called them Boomers, even the people who insisted they might be native.

A particularly paranoid group of us thought the children were being eaten. It's a horrific thought, but unlikely. If the aliens were able and willing to eat us, why take only children?

And why *all* the children? Because we eventually confirmed that every child in the colony, including the older children who'd been born on Earth, was an android. And we started scanning newborns immediately—all androids. The substitution was happening before birth. Paranoia swung high once more, and I found myself staring down at my belly at odd times of day, wondering whether what was growing in me was a baby or a machine.

But still, why take *all* the children? If the aliens are treating us like herd animals, then taking all of our children is very foolish husbandry. And surely a species who just wanted to eat us all and move on would, well, eat us all and move on.

No, it had to be something else. And I was sure that if I could figure out what they were thinking, what their purpose was, that the next step could be communicating with them somehow, persuading them to stop.

I knew it wasn't likely, but it was the only hope I had.

Some weeks later, another child returned to us.

I was working in the tomato field, testing soil samples every few meters. I caught sight of something moving out of the corner of my eye and glanced up quickly, then looked back and stared in a classic double-take. I suppose it would've looked funny, if anyone had been watching.

A young girl, almost my height, stood there swaying. Her clothes were odd—they fit her, but they didn't look like any of the styles I recalled from the colony stores. Her hair was cut short with a part down the center, very plain but neat. She stared at me, blinked a few times, then squinted.

"Tonina?" I said. "Are you all right?"

We'd gotten into the habit of treating all the children as though they were real. A few avoided them completely, some glared at them like they wanted to attack the monsters who'd replaced our kids, but most of us had fallen into a new normal. It was a wary civility, rather than the affection children should get, but the child-machines had all their needs provided for—they whimpered or cried or screamed if they didn't—and it *felt* normal. It was habit, so that's where we ended up.

Tonina was about eleven, the daughter of a plumber and a chicken farmer. I saw her around the settlement periodically, a serious child who strode about her business as though she were a decade older than her true age.

This child looked lost and confused, and half asleep.

"Tonina?" I dropped my test kit to remind myself of where I was in the field, then took a step toward her. "Do you need something?"

She blinked a few times, then seemed to see me, despite her eyes having been pointed in my direction all along.

She coughed and said, "Caroline?"

"That's right. Are you okay?"

"I..." She looked around, swallowed hard, then moved toward me, stepping carefully over and around the plants. There was no one within sight, so although she didn't know me very well, she came into my arms, leaned into me hard, and whispered, "I...I got my period. So they let me go."

I froze, then gasped out a hiccupping sob and hugged her to me. It didn't matter that she wasn't mine. She was *ours,* and she was back.

"We missed you so much, honey. All of you. Come on, the doctors will want to look at you, and we'll call your parents."

Tonina nodded quickly and let me lead her away. She kept her arm around me and leaned in, like she wanted to stay as close to me as she could without climbing into my skin.

I was fine with that. While we walked, my thoughts zoomed down one path and then another. They'd let her go. If it was actually the real Tonina—please, let it be the real Tonina!—that meant there was hope. Real hope, not just an airy fog of hope that melted into air when you tried to touch it.

No one noticed us walking into the settlement and down the main road. It was just me and Tonina, and we'd both been there yesterday, so far as anyone knew. I had an urge to call out, to shout to someone to go get the Bianchis, that their daughter was back, but I didn't, for the same reason I didn't pull out my pad and call them myself. I didn't know for sure, and didn't want to get their hopes up.

It would be bad enough if my own hopes crashed into rubble that day; it would be so much worse if it was her parents'. I walked with her down the street, as fast as she could go, which wasn't very fast, but eventually we got to the infirmary. I explained to the doctor on duty where I'd found her and what she'd said.

A scan showed it really was Tonina.

Her sexual maturity apparently meant that she didn't qualify as a "child" anymore in the aliens' minds, so they returned her to the herd.

That was four years ago. Seven more older children have come back to us. None of them remember how they'd been taken or what they'd done—or what'd been done to them—while they were away.

Tonina came back, so far as we can tell, more or less as she left except for the detail of physical maturity. As children returned who'd been gone for longer and longer, though, their parents noticed that they'd learned some things while they were gone. Each child—and they *were* still children, regardless of what their captors thought, all between ten and fourteen so far—had somehow picked up bits and scraps of what their parents did in their work.

They were odd little skills, imperfect and incomplete.

Riley could frame up a building as well as his mother, but had to be shown which nails to use. And he had no idea how to hang wallboard, or how to spray flooring.

Sara could butcher a chicken as well as her own mother, but was unclear about which parts to leave on the cutting board and which to put into the compost bucket. She learned quickly enough, but I heard she was horribly embarrassed about the initial glitch.

Had the aliens been watching us? Had they scanned our minds? No one knew how they collected the skills from us, much less how they'd passed them on to the children.

Although it was clear they knew exactly who'd parented which child.

At least we knew we could get our children back, that the aliens would eventually return them to the herd.

Or the flock, rather.

Because I think I know what they're doing.

Mitigational zoology isn't my field, but I know how to do research, and I found something that struck a note with me.

Before reconstructive DNA processes were developed, people went out and watched endangered animals, and tried to help them along.

Some endangered birds occasionally broke their own eggs. Just carelessness, really. In a large population, it wouldn't matter. In a small population, it was a disaster. So biologists would sneak to the bird's nest or hole while it was gone, and replace its eggs with fakes —basically egg-shaped rocks. They'd take the egg to their lab and hatch it, rear the chick until they were sure it'd survive, then return it when the parent bird was gone. Mom or dad would leave the fake egg on a feeding trip, and come back to find a newborn-ish chick.

It was for the birds' own good—to protect their young.

So here we are, just a few thousand of us on the whole planet.

I think the Boomers came, found us, and believed we were endangered. They're trying to help. I have to believe that, or I'll hate them *and* their androids, and I can't do that.

Because the Boomers seem to have stricter rules than the old bird-saving biologists on Earth. The Boomers want us to be good parents to our children. They want them to get the best care.

We already failed at that, in the aliens' eyes. They've taken all our children, and will take any more we have. Out of the womb, just as the bird biologists took eggs from the nest.

I can't believe that I'll never see my little girl until she's twelve or fourteen. I want her back sooner.

We know the Boomers are watching us—maybe watching through the android children's eyes—so I'm going to prove to them that I'm the very best mother. I take the best care of Abby, feeding her exactly what she needs, bathing her and brushing her teeth for her. I hug her all the time, and tell her I love her. She's the happiest, best-loved little android in the settlement.

I really do love her. She looks just like Abby will look, after all. She's a perfect replica. I love her more than any woman has ever loved a child; my whole life is focused on making sure she's happy every moment of every day.

If I cry sometimes at night, Abby never knows.

I just hope I can get the real Abby back soon.

FOILED

BRIGID COLLINS

Brigid Collins is a fantasy and science fiction writer living in Michigan. Her short stories have appeared in Fiction River, The Uncollected Anthology, *and* Chronicle Worlds: Feyland. *Books 1 through 3 of her fantasy series,* Songbird River Chronicles, *and her dark fairy tale novella,* Thorn and Thimble, *are available in print and electronic versions.*

"I find it odd that I've written so many sports stories," Brigid sales about this story, "since I don't consider myself to be much of a sporty person. But I do love to fence, and what's more, my husband and I had our very own meet-cute through our college fencing club, something along the lines of 'love at first stab.' I guess you could say this story came to me naturally when I asked myself how I Felt the Love."

While I'm not a sporty person myself, this tale easily fenced its way into my heart and I enjoyed the way that the two are brought together via the tournament, as the tension and adrenaline runs high.

I'm in the middle of my third bout of the tournament, currently up four touches to two, when I catch sight of the disrespectful ass two strips over. She's just wrapped up her own bout, a victory of five to one according to my quick glance at their scoreboard, and she's disconnecting herself from the electric scoring system without so much as a handshake or removal of her mask to acknowledge the opponent she's knocked out of the tournament.

Pressure against the juncture of my shoulder and collarbone yanks my attention back to my own bout. I tilt my wrist to parry out of reflex, but it's too late. The electric system beeps, and our judge nods to confirm the point to my opponent. Four-three.

I shake myself as we reset. *Come on, Marcus.* Like every other fencer in this echo-y middle school gym rented out for the weekend, I'd like to win. Taking home the trophy, even for a casual tournament that won't give out official fencer ranks, would be a satisfying end to the day, and it would mean I got to fence the maximum number of bouts. A double win, really. But if someone better than me knocks me out it's no big deal. I'll only be upset if I lose because I wasn't giving it my all. The sport deserves respect, but it's also meant to be enjoyed.

A bead of sweat dangles from my eyebrow, and my right arm sings from its curved position behind my head with the urge to wipe the bead away. But with my heavy mask on, touching my face is impossible.

I focus instead on the point of my opponent's foil and how it dances in figure eights around my own steady weapon.

This guy is constant movement, rocking back and forth in his *en garde* stance, jerking with loud, heavy stomps to telegraph a hard lunge, then pulling back when I don't fall for the feint. The movements make the electric cord running from the back of his *lame* slap against the peach-colored strip. These tactics proved unpredictable enough to get him through his first two bouts, but I've let him get three touches on me now. I can see his pattern.

My calves burn with delicious readiness as I hold myself still, waiting for my opening. He's weaving and ducking, using all sorts of unnecessary flourishes to keep me distracted while he figures out where to make his next jab.

When the opening comes, it's wide as the Grand Canyon, but I can make it wider. I lunge forward and extend my left arm towards his shoulder. My motion is constrained, especially compared to his erratic flailing, but no less energetic. My muscles flow and tense to hold my body in the exact position I need to put my foil's point precisely where I want it.

His parry is as wild as I predict, and equally ineffectual. I'm not aiming for his shoulder, after all. By the time his blade has swept far beyond his un-endangered shoulder, I've disengaged my initial attack with a tight twirl and placed my point against a spot an inch below it on his chest. I use just enough pressure to depress the electrified tip of my foil against his silver *lame*.

The scoring system beeps, and the judge nods. On target, five-three, victory to me.

My heart thrums in my chest as I remove my mask and grip his gloved hand with my bare one. I replay the bout in my head, lingering on the events like a kid back from his first date. I bite my lip over the memory of his first point, a well-earned stab to my usual weak spot on my belly. My lips curl up in tandem with the giddiness swirling in my stomach when I think of my clean disengage, of the way I didn't fall victim to his scare tactics to counter with my own, more efficient feint.

I finally wipe that drop of sweat from my eyebrow.

It was a good bout.

And then, like my older brother swooping in to ruin the good-date vibes with his own special brand of girlfriend-insulting dickishness, the ass from two strips over makes her reappearance at the strip beside me.

She's still wearing her mask, a high-quality, competition-approved helmet that she's gone and ruined by painting a non-sanctioned skull-and-crossbones pattern across the mesh front, and she hasn't said a word to either her new opponent or the judge who will confirm their bout. She just hooks herself up to the system and drops into her *en garde.*

No salute. No nod.

Her opponent hesitates, then shrugs and drops into her own *en garde.*

My jaw hurts.

It's like watching some douche slip something into his date's drink, and I can't see any way of saving her from the horrible thing she's about to experience.

Someone taps my shoulder. "We need the strip, man."

"Sorry." I reach behind me to unplug the electric cord from my *lame* and hand it to him like you're supposed to, then tuck my mask under my right arm. I wish him luck, and he lifts the tip of his foil in a half-salute.

As I walk away, the judge at the other strip awards a touch to the ass.

Now that I'm not in the middle of my own bout, I register the cacophony of the gym. Swords clash, saberists holler as they hurl themselves at one another, fencing shoes whisper against the grounded fabric of the strips or squeak on the varnished wood of the basketball court floor. Scoring systems sing their monotones at every touch.

Sweat laces the air along with the greasy hotdog and popcorn scent of the concession stand by the bleachers. My mouth waters as I make my way over there to look at the brackets posted by the menu. You burn a lot of calories fencing, and I've gone three bouts now without a snack.

But the energy spinning through my nervous system drives me past the fencers clustered by the menu and parks me by the posted brackets. They've been updated with the results of the most recent group of bouts.

The ass is fencing foil, and in a casual tournament like this one, men's and women's aren't separated, so it's possible I'll have the opportunity to teach her some respect. I let my foil dangle by the plug in the guard and run my gloved finger down the list of strips.

Strip five, round three, McAlister vs. The Pirate.

I make a sound between a cough and a laugh. The list actually reads "The Pirate." The ass hasn't even registered under her own name.

But she's not in my bracket. The only way we'll get to face each other is if both of us make it through to the final bout.

I let my head fall forward until I'm staring at my scuffed fencing shoes and I feel the stretch in the back of my neck. Getting competitive has always been out of the question for me. If I care too much about winning, I can't enjoy the actual play of the bouts.

Sports are supposed to be fun.

It's not worth it. Someone else will knock her out. Maybe she's getting knocked out now.

I twist to look over my shoulder. Halfway across the gym, the scoreboard at strip five displays four-one. The ass parries a blow from McAlister and lands her riposte high on the shoulder.

Five-one victory to the ass.

I close my throat against a roar when she unhooks without a handshake.

And just like that, it's worth it. If I have to sacrifice my enjoyment of a whole tournament for the chance to defend the honor of the sport, I'll do it gladly. I love fencing enough for that.

Three more bouts stand between me and the final slot. Already, the burn of ferocity builds deep in my stomach, and I stomp past the concession stand and back to my fencing bag in the bleachers so I can let this unfamiliar feeling grow. My water bottle gurgles as I squeeze a stream into my mouth. When I finish, I toss the bottle back into my bag, and it clatters against my spare weapons.

My next bout is on strip seven, all the way at the far end of the gym. The ass's is on three. She's making her way there now, her Jolly Roger face mask still in place.

The Belgian grip of my foil lets out a squeak of protest before I kick my bag closed and head off to strip seven.

My next opponent is a petite woman with her hair pulled up in a ponytail that swishes with her every step. Her *lame* is too big for her, and she's having trouble hooking herself to the scoring system. The guard of the foil that dangles from her wrist is covered in scratches. The grip, a Visconti, is too small.

She's a hobbyist, or else she'd have invested in equipment that fitted her properly. Normally, I'd let myself assume an easy win, and if I turn out to be wrong, oh well, at least I had fun.

Not today. I have to bring my best game if I'm going to make it to the final bout.

The judge glances at his clipboard and nods at me. "Marcus Scheidler?"

I nod and hook myself up. With both of us wired, we test our blades, don our masks, and salute.

I dip into *en garde* for a moment before I'm launching forward into a blitzing lunge, and the scoring system sings without my opponent ever moving to parry.

"Wow, geez," she laughs through her mask. "Okay then."

I give her a nod as we reset, fully expecting her to try the same trick on me. She does, but it's half-hearted and easily parried. I have the advantage of reach on her, and I barely have to extend to complete my riposte.

Her openings gape at me, and it's like they suck the point of my foil right to them. I get two more touches on her without even having to fake her out. Makes me wonder how she made it this far, but I realize that's unkind of me. She's probably suffering from a classic case of don't-know-how-to-fence-a-lefty.

She almost gives me a good fight for the last touch, knocking two of my attacks away but never managing to complete her ripostes. It's only a matter of time before I get the touch, and the judge calls the bout at five-zero to me.

"You're really good," she pants as we shake hands. Her smile stretches wide. She really is cute, and I wait for the words to press against my lips, to ask her which club she usually fences at or if she'd like to get together some time.

But the questions don't come, and I find my head turning to catch the action over on strip three as I unhook.

The ass is still in the thick of her bout, two-two. I drop a word of thanks to my judge before hustling over there, feeling like a moth drawn to a bug zapper.

I've rooted for people before, cheered on my friends and fellow club members. I know how the hope for everyone to have a good day at the tournament pumps through me.

Watching the ass is different from that. I want her to win this bout more than anyone I've ever observed. She has to win just as much as I do.

And standing on the sidelines, I have to admit just how good she is. By the time I get there, she's earned another touch, and is pressing her advantage for a fourth. Her style is all about the disengage, sometimes feinting two or three times before finally going for the hit.

She's fencing a lefty now, too, and trouncing him. He's breathing hard, the sawing of his lungs rasping through his mask, his chest heaving. His feet shuffle against the strip, his footwork falling apart under her onslaught. Her breaths come even and silent as she gets around his foil for her fifth touch.

I find I'm breathing hard, too. I can taste my own sweat rising in hot waves from the neck of my fencing jacket. Her aptitude and perfect form set something in my chest coiling in tight on itself. I slump against the cinder block wall, the back of my *lame* scraping against the thick paint.

The judge calls it. Of course she keeps her mask on. Of course she ignores the offered handshake. The thing coiled in my chest gives a sour twist.

Then the ass looks at me. At least, her mask points in my direction. The Jolly Roger splashed across the mesh makes it impossible to see the details of the face behind it, so maybe her gaze is drifting somewhere over my shoulder. But it freezes every muscle in my body like I've just got blocks of ice clinging to my bones. I shiver in the dampness of my fencing gear.

"Marcus Scheidler, approach strip six for round five."

I jump, jam my mask on hard enough to burn against the stubble on my cheek, and rush for the strip. I swear I hear someone laugh back at strip three.

The next bout blurs by in a detailed dance, even though that makes no sense. It's like I'm noticing new things about an old friend, things that I'd seen hints of but never fully unearthed. We're having an argument, me and my sport, about how this bout should go.

I thrust forward with a need to score the touch and advance, but my sport needles me in the form of my opponent's riposte, arguing for a slower pace we can both enjoy. *Why rush the point*, she sighs along with my opponent's shoes on the strip as he dances away from my feint. *We're having fun, aren't we?*

I try to work an apology into my parry. *I can't do fun right now, babe. This is for you, for us.*

I win the point and the bout, but the argument continues into the next round. I've fenced this opponent before, often enough to know his style and for him to know mine. We flirt with each other, seeing who can push the other further back on the strip before either of us makes a real attack.

It's like you're not even paying attention to me, my sport whines in his guarded stance.

And I'm the bad boyfriend who's looking at other girls, because the ass is fencing on the strip right next to me, and while I'm totally paying attention to how my opponent is moving, my real focus is on the way she's flexing around the jabbing point of her opponent's foil. I'm straining my ears to pick up the hiss of the blade sliding along the front of her *lame* in the closest miss of the tournament. I'm holding my breath to see what she'll do to get the last point she needs to clinch her path to the last bout.

Almost absently, I parry-riposte my opponent's attack, get my fourth point, keeping everything else gunning for the win of the whole damn thing.

I want it so bad. I'm starting to realize I've always wanted it so bad, I just never let myself have a reason to go for it.

The scoring system beeps, and I find myself stretched out in a deep lunge, my foil pressed against my opponent's heart. It's one of those cartoonish poses I laugh at other fencers for using, for taking the sport too seriously. I don't feel so much like laughing this time.

My opponent takes off his mask and shoots me this look like he sees something in me I don't. Like he's been waiting to see it for a while. "That was a crazy good bout, Marcus."

He holds his hand out. Sweat trickles down my sides and my spine as we shake. I've never beaten him before.

It feels freaking amazing and nowhere near enough all at the same time.

I don't even bother unhooking as I ratchet my focus back to the ass.

The score reads 4-4. My jaw hurts again. She's never let her opponents get more than two touches on her before this. She's giving it her all, I can see by the way her back leg trembles as she parries and drives forward for a lunging riposte.

She misses.

Her opponent tries to stab her as she recovers, but the ass scur-ries backwards. She manages to keep her footwork fairly clean, but she has to bat the guy's rapid-fire attacks aside one after the other with every step she takes back.

He drives her far towards the end of the strip. She's two steps away from out-of-bounds, which will net him the point he needs to win.

My foil dangles from my wrist, the point dragging against the fabric of my strip, and I clench both fists and tear my lower lip to shreds. I will her to gain some ground, to show her opponent the skills I know she commands.

She and I are going to fence. The wrap-up of this bout is just a formality.

I can't see her face behind her painted mask, but it's like the fires of Hell burn in the place where her eyes would be. Slowly, with feints and disengages, the ass takes back an inch, then another. She stomps her leading foot in a fake lunge like the guy I'd been fencing when I first noticed her, and it sends her opponent back another step.

Her double lunge is beautiful, and I read her victory in the stretch and pull of her muscles.

But her opponent touches her at the same moment she touches him, and when the electric scoreboard sings, both sides are lit.

The gym falls silent, just the fading beep and the gasping breaths of the two fencers echoing in the rafters. Everyone waits to hear the confirmation of the judge.

"Pirate's attack is parried, Johnson's riposte is successful. Final score five-four."

It's like someone's jammed an icicle into my spinal column right where my neck meets my shoulders, and she's unhooked herself and stormed to the hall outside the gym before I can fumble at the plug on the back of my own *lame*. A couple tries finally get me free to chase after her.

She's standing there in the hallway, her mask still on, her shoul-ders heaving up and down and her breath hitching like she's trying not to cry. Her fencing bag lies open on the floor beside the glass display case full of the middle school's trophies.

Apparently she also fences saber.

"What the hell are you doing here?"

She's not looking at me, so I'm surprised to hear her address me. "Uh."

Her mask tilts towards me, and she sighs. "You still have another bout."

"I..."

What am I doing here? She's been knocked out, that should be the end. I should be able to go back to enjoying fencing the way I always have, happy to have good bouts but easy with keeping things casual.

But I can't go back to that, not after the thing this ass, this belligerent pirate, has woken in my chest.

"You...you should have shaken his hand," I say. "You should have shaken everyone's hands. You should have saluted before your bouts, and taken your mask off after."

"Why?"

"Because that's what you do, how you show respect for the sport."

"Do you know how many people I've fenced who've saluted me only to spend the whole bout contesting every touch I get? How many people shake my hand after a bout just so they can spit an insult in my face because they can't handle that they lost? At least when I stopped letting people see my face, they got pissed off enough to stop letting me win."

She steps up to me, close enough the painted mesh of her mask nearly brushes my nose. In the shadows, I make out the outline of her heart-shaped face. Light from the fluorescent bulbs in the ceiling panels glints off the tears on her cheeks, follows the contours of the patch that covers her right eye. "You show respect for the sport by winning the tournament, Marcus Scheidler. And one day, I'll make it past third place."

Then she backs off, leans to zip her bag shut, and hefts it over her shoulder. She walks out the double doors into the sun-baked parking lot. As she steps off the sidewalk, she finally pries her mask off.

Part of me, a really big part if I'm honest, says screw the last bout. Don't let her get away.

But I know she's right. If I truly love fencing, if I want to show my respect for the sport and for everyone who's ever wanted the win, I'll go in there and fight the last bout, and I won't settle for just having a good time.

I'll commit, and I'll win. For her.

At the next tournament, when I see The Pirate listed in the brackets, my heart pounds. This time, I know I'll fence her.

Then I'll ask her out to coffee. She might even say yes.

A LOVE TO REMEMBER

TONYA D. PRICE

Tonya D. Price has published short stories in many genres online as well as in Pocket Book anthologies. She has also sold a number of stories to Fiction River, *including for the* Hidden in Crime *and* Hard Choices *volumes. She holds an MBA from Cornell University in Marketing and Finance and is the author of the nonfiction series,* Business Books For Writers. *Tonya has written a paranormal romance novel that she hopes to release in 2019. She will reveal the exact date on her website, tonyadprice.com.*

When asked about the inspiration for this story, Tonya reveals that it is based on her parents. "When I think of a love story," she says, "I always think of theirs."

When I first read this story I was immediately intrigued by the way that Tonya divided up each of the scenes of the story with different styles of love derived partially from Latin and Greek and more modern author adaptations such as John Alan Lee, who brought them together in his 1973 book Colours of Love: An Exploration of the Ways of Loving.

But Eileen and Ray's story had me at the moment the two said hi in Fey's Soda Shop with Bing Crosby's "I'll Be Seeing You" playing in the background. And with each reading since, I became captivated at how those many elements of love came into play through their lives.

Tonya's prose is, of course, stunning, and brings their story to life wonderfully; but this is a fine example of truth providing a more compelling tale than fiction.

Storge: Love of the Child

Susan would never forget the phone call from her mother.

The blizzard had dropped fourteen inches of snow on Boston during the night. A new batch of flakes had started to fall on the storm's second pass through southern Massachusetts, bringing life to a standstill. Through the slider that led to the second story deck off the bedroom, Susan could see gusts of wind blow snow into drifts so tall they had buried her backyard shed.

On the television, the governor pleaded for people to stay off the roads so the snowplows could do their job. Only a fool would try to venture outside.

Being snowbound didn't bother Susan or her husband. Joe sat in his office memorizing the names of the students in his MBA International Trade course, and Susan worked on a budget report for the university's newest financial system. A peaceful day. Until the telephone rang, shattering the quiet.

Joe answered. He was a gentle man with a pleasant voice. His tone changed to one of concern. "Eileen? What's wrong?"

Susan sat waiting, watching, growing worried as the seconds ticked into minutes. The pain she saw in his blue eyes told her the news was bad.

He covered the phone's mouthpiece with one hand. "It's your mother. She's very upset."

Susan couldn't understand a word her mother said through her tears. Did her father have a heart attack? What was going on?

Her dad came on the phone.

"Your mother can't talk right now. We are at the Mayo Clinic in Phoenix. I just got the word from the doctors. It seems I have cancer."

Susan didn't ask any questions. All she said was, "Oh Dad, I'll be there as soon as I can."

"You don't have to come out here, Susan. The doctors are just running some tests. You won't be able to do anything."

Joe had bought the plane ticket by the time Susan had hung up the phone.

Eros: Love of the Body

Two weeks after buying a bus ticket from Franklin Furnace to Dayton, Ohio, sixteen-year-old Eileen Seidel sat on a counter stool at Fey's Soda Shop sipping her grape-flavored soda pop. Bing Crosby crooned, "I'll Be Seeing You" on the jukebox. The only other patrons were two old men in a corner arguing over whether Hitler had committed suicide or was shot by his men. After making sure neither of the two old men were paying attention to her, Eileen nudged the arm of her new friend, Fanny. "I just signed myself up at the YWCA for a speech class."

Fanny pulled her sweater closer around her shoulders and nursed her Coca-Cola. "Why, you don't need no speech classes. You speak just fine."

Eileen shook her head. "There's an opening at Bell Telephone Company. I can make $1.25 an hour. A woman at the grocery told me. She says all I'd have to do is learn to speak better."

"Why?"

"'Cause rich people with phones don't think we hill people sound educated. You have to learn to talk educated if'n you want to get a job up here. One that pays decent, leastways."

"Oh, Eileen." Fanny giggled. She buried her face into Eileen's arm. "Take a gander at that boy that just walked in the door."

Eileen didn't need any poke by Fanny. She saw him all right. The boy in question was gorgeous. Tall, athletic. He had thick blond hair, the bluest eyes, and a face that belonged on a movie screen. And he was a soldier. "He looks like William Holden."

"Oh, Eileen, William Holden wishes he looked that good. He's a blond Ronald Reagan, and he's in uniform." Fanny giggled so loud the boy and everybody in the soda shop turned to see what was so funny. Fanny didn't take no notice but just kept on talking her fool head off. "I haven't seen any boy our age in four years. And he's in uniform so he ain't got no deformities and he ain't sick in the head."

The boy walked over to where the two girls sat talking.

Eileen realized she had been staring. Embarrassed beyond belief she kept her head down, concentrating on finishing her pop.

"Hi, there." The boy sat down on the stool beside Eileen.

Eileen could not look up. She wanted to die. What if he said something to her? He'd hear how she talked. Hear how she butchered the English language. Those were words the man at the post office had said during her interview when she told him she was from "Franklin Furnace in Sowdie County."

Once she opened her mouth, this boy wouldn't want to have anything to do with her. She couldn't bear to hear him make fun of her.

"I'll have one of them Coca-Cola's." His voice was a deep baritone. And he talked with the same twang as Eileen.

She felt a tap on her arm. When she looked up, she saw his extended hand.

"I'm Ray."

His smile was perfect. She shook his hand, but couldn't bring herself to look at him for more than a second. He was just too good looking. Too good for her, for sure. She managed to choke out, "Eileen."

"What was that? I didn't quite catch your name. Say, did anyone ever tell you that you look just like Katharine Hepburn?"

Fanny leaned forward to reach her hand in front of Eileen. "I'm Fanny. Guys tell her that all the time. And she does, doesn't she? Once a reporter, he actually stopped her on the street in Dayton and asked her if she was Katharine Hepburn, and on account Eileen is so shy when she didn't answer, the reporter thought she was Katharine Hepburn and when I told him she wasn't, he didn't believe me and took her picture anyways. Ain't that right, Eileen?"

Eileen nodded. She could feel her cheeks burning. All she wanted was to get out without embarrassing herself.

"You girls aren't from these parts, are you?"

Fanny got up and walked behind Eileen to sit next to the Ray. "Nope. Eileen comes from Franklin Furnace, and I'm from Chillicothe and where you be from?"

"Up north. East Liverpool, but my people are all from West Virginia." Ray looked at Eileen as he answered Fanny's questions.

Fanny clapped her hands. "I knew it. Sure enough. I knew you must be from West Virginie."

A couple of teenage girls came into the shop. They went right to the jukebox and dropped in their nickels. Eileen recognized the introduction to Bing Crosby's "If I Loved You."

Eileen had to get out of the soda shop before Ray asked her any questions. "I...I have to go." That, she thought to herself, sounded educated enough.

"No." Ray rose from his stool. "I mean, please don't. We hardly have gotten to know each other. You haven't said two words to me."

"Well, I..."

"I need your address."

Eileen didn't know what to say. She turned to Fanny for help.

Fanny sighed. "Maybe she'll say more to you in a letter. I tell you, trying to get this girl to talk, now that's near impossible. Here, give me that paper and pencil, and I'll write her down for you. Say, when do you get out of the Army? The war just ended. Must be soon. What you doing in Fairborn? Long ways from East Liverpool, ain't you?"

Ray just smiled at Eileen, who felt more uncomfortable than before.

"My mom wouldn't let me enlist until I finished high school. I turned eighteen three weeks ago and got my draft notice the next day. I just finished boot camp. They're shipping us out tomorrow with the occupation troops. I won't be back for two years. Would you write me? Eileen? Will you? If you write me, I'll write you."

Ray seemed nice. He didn't sound like he was giving her a come-on line like most of the men she met. And he had the same twang in his talk she did, though his grammar was better than hers. "Yes. I'll write. But I don't have any paper to take down your address."

"Oh, that's okay. I don't know my address yet. I'll write you, and when you get my letter, you can write me back. You will write, won't you?"

For the first time, Eileen smiled. "Yes, I'll write you."

"And will you send me your picture?"

She hesitated, but she gathered her courage and said, "If you send me one."

"I can give you one now." Raymond pulled out a photo of himself.

"Here you go. I take lots of pictures. I love taking pictures. I wish I'd brought my camera with me, but it's back in the barracks."

Fanny looked at her watch. "Lord, Eileen. I totally lost track of the time. We have to get going, or we'll miss our bus."

Crosby had finished his song.

"Goodbye, Ray." Eileen slid off her stool. "Say. What is your last name? So I'll know the letter is from you."

"What, you get so many letters from GIs?"

Embarrassed, Eileen turned and started to walk out, but Ray jumped off his stool. He reached out and caught her arm. He stood there looking at her. Not saying a word. For a moment she thought he might try to kiss her right then and there. He kind of had that look in his eyes. Not that she'd ever been kissed. "Jones. Private Raymond Jones. Gosh, Eileen, you are beautiful. Don't let nobody tell you otherwise."

Later, Eileen had no idea what she had said back to him or if she even said anything.

Every day she went to the mailbox looking for a letter and picture. After a month, a letter arrived.

Philia: Love of the Mind

June 28, 1945

Dear Eileen,

I'm sorry it has taken me a couple of weeks to write you. They sure keep us busy here. I'm not allowed to say where here is, but I can tell you that the German people have been friendly to us. They like us better than the Russians. Can't say I blame them. As a Radio Engineer, I get to travel around. I'm going to get to see a lot of Germany. Did you know it is about the same size as Ohio? We don't stay in barracks, but with families. So I get to meet real Germans. They aren't so bad. I think they are a lot like us. I've learned a few words of German. "Madchen, bring mir ein bier." That means, "Waitress, bring me a beer!"

Sometimes it can be a bit awkward living with the families, though. There are not many men in the villages. Many German soldiers were killed in the war, and others are being held prisoner. Mostly the villages are filled with women and children.

The people here have little food. I didn't grow up with much, so I have taken to sharing my rations with them. The mother of the family I'm staying with has a ten-year-old girl and a six-year-old boy. The father died in the bombing of Dresden.

The little boy follows me around everywhere. I took my cigarette rations and traded them for chocolate. You should have seen him go after that chocolate. He couldn't remember having eaten any before, although his mother says he did have a candy bar one Christmas when he was two.

Not smoking is a big advantage. Sarge keeps telling me I'm supposed to smoke that tobacco, but it is better than gold here in Germany. You wouldn't believe what you can buy with a pack of cigarettes.

I grew up not eating every day so skipping a day and giving them my rations isn't much of a sacrifice. I worry about what will happen to these people. I gave them half my paycheck today. The other half I sent to my mother. It won't be the first time in my life I've had no money for a while. At least in the Army, whether you have money in your pocket or not, they still feed you. Some of the guys complain about Army food, but I say, any food tastes good, long as it is food.

Well, I have to go now. We're packing up to go to another town tonight.

Please write me back. I wish we had had more time with one another before I had to leave, but maybe if we write, we can get to know each other better. Like, what do you aspire to do with your life? I want to be an engineer. Sarge says he doesn't see any reason I can't be anything I want to be even if I did come from nothing.

About the letters. Don't be surprised if it takes a while to get a response. The post office system here was pretty much destroyed along with train lines and everything else.

Please write me back. Your friend,

Ray

P.S. I think about you every day.

August 2, 1945

Dear Ray,

Your letter arrived today. I wasn't sure you would write. I thought maybe you had forgotten about me or met some pretty German girl. I guess you could tell from my last name that my family is German. There are a lot of German families back in Portsmouth, but you wouldn't know it to hear them talk. They are even changing their names. Mueller is Miller now. Ritter is Rider. Well, there isn't much you can do with Seidel so I'm stuck with it. Not that I want to change my name.

I guess I might as well tell you my parents are divorced. I don't know much about my father's side of the family. My mother doesn't have much good to say about him. I've met him a couple of times, and I think he is a very kind man.

He was in the Army in World War I when he was sixteen and in this war. He's forty-two. He got home and came to see me last week. He grew up speaking German and has a thick accent, so people say mean things to him all the time. In restaurants and on the street. He had a hard time finding a hotel to stay in because people thought he was a released German prisoner. Gee, people can be stupid sometimes. What German prisoner would be walking around Fairborn?

Anyway, you are doing a good thing being nice to the family where you are staying. It speaks to your character.

I've enclosed the photo you asked for. It is my high school graduation picture. It's just wallet size, but that was all I could afford.

I would like it if you wrote me again. I'll write you back.

Your friend,

Eileen

. . .

November 29, 1945

Dear Raymond,

I haven't gotten a letter from you since I sent you my photo. I hope you are okay. If it were wartime, I would worry maybe you had been injured. Are you still interested in writing me?

I do hope you received my letter and photo.

Please write and let me know if you got my letter. If you don't want to write to me anymore, that would be okay, but I'd rather you tell me.

Yours truly, Eileen

Eileen waited for the lunch shift on the switchboard. She looked to the right and left. The last of the second shift girls had settled in and were taking calls. Never in her life had Eileen broken a rule.

Fanny removed her headphone set. "Go on, now. Call him."

Making personal calls could get Eileen fired.

Supervisor Wilson passed by on her way to dinner in the cafeteria room. Her dinner break would last exactly thirty minutes.

Eileen and Fanny had volunteered to cover for their third shift replacements as part of the plan.

"Fanny, it has been two years. He only wrote me once. He's not interested in me. He must have a girlfriend by now."

"You don't know that." Fanny raised her voice over the other phone operators' conversations with callers. "Go on. Give him a call and find out. I'm sick of listening to you mooning over him."

Eileen needed her job. "If I got fired, I'll never make this kind of money again."

"A five-minute call won't get you fired." Fanny put her headphones back on, flipped the switch under a lit bulb and inserted the cord jack into the circuit. "Good afternoon. How may I address your call?"

Eileen took a deep breath. She could hear her own heart beating as she gave a final look around the switchboard room. The coast was clear. She inserted her cord jack in her board.

All she needed to do was ask for him and leave a message. Then Ray could call her back if he wanted.

The phone at his home in East Liverpool rang three, four, five times. Eileen reached for the jack to disconnect the call.

"Hello?"

A woman's voice.

"Hello. I'm at trying to reach Ray Jones."

"Hold on." The woman yelled, out, "Ray, there's a girl on the phone for you."

No. He was there? She couldn't talk to him. That wasn't part of the plan. Eileen started to end the call, but she didn't act fast enough.

"Hi, this is Ray."

Eileen looked over at Fanny. She pointed at her the microphone end of her headset and mouthed the words, "He's on the phone. What do I do?"

Fanny just waved her off. "Say hello, you silly goose."

Eileen said, "Hello. This is Eileen Seidel, I...I..."

"Eileen! Boy, I never thought I would hear from you. I can't believe I'm talking to you."

At that moment all the frustration of the past two years came back. Those trips to the mailbox looking for a letter. The tears because he hadn't written. Her inability to quit thinking about him. "Well, I guess not after you never wrote me."

"I wrote you. You never wrote me back."

She hadn't thought him a liar. "Of course I wrote you back. Several times. All I got was your first letter."

"No." Ray fell silent. "Honest. I never got a letter from you. I kept asking the postmaster every week until the guys all started teasing me, saying you didn't exist. Every week I thought maybe that week I would hear from you. Finally, I figured you had found another guy."

"But..." She blurted out the truth. "I checked the mailbox every day too. I'd run home hoping to find word from you, and there were never any letters."

"Do you still live in the same boarding house?"

"Yes."

"Okay, then."

"Wait, are you going to write?"

The line went dead.

Walking home after their double shift, Eileen repeated her conversation with Ray for the tenth time to Fanny. She owed her friend that much since Fanny had worked the sixteen-hour double shift alongside her. Snow covered a thick coat of ice, making the sidewalks slippery. Eileen took care not to fall. She couldn't afford to pay a hospital bill for a broken leg.

The warm glow of the streetlamps reflected off the falling snowflakes, giving downtown Fairborn a magical look, or maybe everything felt like a fairy tale after talking to Ray.

Fanny asked Eileen to repeat every word of the phone call with Ray once more. Then she gave Eileen opinion on every sentence. Tired, Eileen finally raised her hands as they turned down Central Street to make their way the short distance to the boarding house. "Enough, Fanny. I don't imagine I'll ever see Ray again."

"Sure you will, Beautiful."

There on the steps to the boarding house sat Ray in his Army outfit, covered in snow. When he smiled, he looked even better than their first meeting. How could that be possible?

He was still the most handsome man Eileen had ever seen. She couldn't call him a boy any longer. As he stood, brushing flakes off his hair, she realized she had to be careful. She could lose her heart to this man who had just driven five hours in a blizzard from East Liverpool to Fairborn to see a girl he had only met once.

Ludus: Playful Love

Eileen didn't think it possible to crowd one more person on the narrow Indian Lake beach. One-hundred-and-one-degree temperatures had sent the little kids, the teenagers, and the old people to the lake. Like everyone else, Eileen and Ray sought refuge from the August heat wave in the cool water. Eileen just prayed her grandmother didn't find out where she had gone.

Eileen's mother abandoned her when she was nine months old. She would have been put in an orphanage, but despite having eight other children to raise, her grandmother took in Eileen. Like most hill people Grandma didn't cotton much to city ways. If she saw Eileen in her bikini, the old woman would mostly likely take a birch stick to Eileen's backside to save her soul from the devil.

Seeing the look of admiration in Ray's eyes when she removed her cotton robe, Eileen forgot all the hellfire and brimstone Grandma had taught.

Ray offered his hand. Eileen laughed and ran away toward the lake. If there was one thing Eileen loved to do it was swim and the only person who loved the water as much as she did was Ray.

She dived into the lake. Three breast strokes and she felt something grab her ankle. Fish didn't scare her, but she knew snakes often came in the water to cool off on hot days.

As soon as her head broke through the surface, she let out a scream, only to turn and find Ray laughing.

"Hey, it's okay. It's just me."

She swam further out, away from the kids playing in the shallow water. Ray followed her and caught her in his arms. Then, treading water, he reached up and pushed a strand of hair from her face.

"I love you, Eileen."

She laughed. They had dated for two years. He had said those words before. She was getting used to hearing them. Embarrassed, then thinking he might think she was making fun of him, she put a hand on his cheek. "I love you too, Ray."

Every person on the beach might have been watching when Ray

kissed her, but Eileen didn't care. Someone loved her. She didn't quite believe it could be true.

When he pulled away, he said, "I have something I have to tell you."

At first, she thought Ray might be about to tease her again, but then she could tell he was serious. "What?"

Ray began to swim further into the lake, his strong arms holding her securely in the crocked of his left arm as he did a sidestroke with his right. "I applied to college on the GI Bill and got in. I'm going to get an electrical engineering degree. Isn't that great?"

Eileen and Ray had often talked about wanting to go to college. "That is super."

She was proud of him, but what would this mean? "Where are you going? Ohio State?" Ohio State was only an hour and half bus trip from Dayton.

"No, New Tech State. In Fort Wayne, Indiana. It's a new school. They just started an engineering program funded by the government."

"Oh." Eileen tried to keep calm. Indiana bordered Ohio. Maybe they wouldn't be that far apart. "How long will you be gone?"

"Four years. I can't believe it. A kid from East Liverpool making it into college. You should see how proud my mother is."

"What's your dad say?"

Ray looked off at the horizon. "He left the family when I was twelve. I have no idea how to find him. Not that I want to."

Eileen tried to be happy for Ray getting into college, but all she could think was what would she do without him. "I'm glad for you, Ray. I'll sure miss you."

Ray put a hand under Eileen's jaw while they floated on their backs. He rolled over and with a gentle pull brought her face close to his. "Not if you marry me and come with me." He let go of her in the middle of the lake, reached down into his shorts' pocket with one hand, which he raised in the air. "Damn it, no!"

Without another word, he dived into the water.

Eileen treaded water, wondering what had happened. Where had he gone? She put her head underwater and could see Ray far below her. He still seemed to be swimming down to the lake floor. Not able to hold her breath any longer, she went back to treading water. *I might be a widow before I'm even married*, she thought.

A minute later Ray finally came back to her, holding one hand up. "I got it."

"You got what?"

"The ring. Here, give me your finger quick!"

She hadn't quite put everything together yet. She just stared at the diamond. "But what if you drop it again?"

Ray took her hand, kissed it, and slipped on the ring. "Then I would just swim to the bottom of the lake and get it again."

The ring had a white gold band—her favorite. The diamond was a chip but she didn't know anyone who could afford a diamond of any size. In her mind, the ring was perfect. But, you had to do these things right. "You didn't ask."

Ray's smile disappeared. "What?"

"You never asked if I would marry you."

"I didn't?" He swam back a bit from her. "I guess I was so worried about the ring." He took her left hand in his. "Are you going to marry me?"

Eileen had given marriage some thought in an abstract kind of way. "Your parents and mine were divorced. You know what that feels like to grow up with everyone looking down on you, like you did something wrong. Like you are less than everyone else. I need your promise, if we have kids we will never get divorced. No matter how unhappy we might be, we will never get divorced. That is my condition."

"I promise. And I promise you we will never be unhappy no matter how long we are married, Eileen Seidel."

Much as she loved him, she warned him, "Don't marry me unless you mean to keep that promise."

Agabe: Love of the Soul

The married student apartment at New Tech State consisted of one small room with peeling green paint, a kitchenette along one wall with a hot plate and no stove, a bathroom so small Eileen could reach out and touch any of the four walls from the toilet and a shower she couldn't turn around in. They slept on a day bed. Both their feet hung off the end of the twin mattress.

In the winter, they couldn't get the heat above sixty degrees. In the summer a fan moved ninety-degree heat around the room. Still, they were together.

Eileen found a job in the grocery mornings and making wreaths during the second shift at night. Ray went to school. He also worked the night shift at a local gas station.

She had never had such a horrible job as making wreaths. Her fingers bled from needle pricks. Her hands hurt when she washed the dinner plates, and if she got salt on her fingers while cooking, she would cry out from the pain. But they needed her paycheck.

November 18, 1949, three months after their marriage, Eileen fixed a romantic dinner, saving her cigarette money for six months to splurge on a steak and a birthday cake for Ray.

She stayed up until midnight, sitting on the day bed waiting for him, refusing to let herself fall asleep. When she heard Ray's key in the door, she lit the candles.

He opened the door, and she ran up to him and threw her arms around his neck. "Happy Birthday!"

All day she planned the scene in her mind. He would laugh and be happy, but he didn't laugh.

He broke into tears.

He turned around so she wouldn't see his face and buried his head in his hands.

"Ray, what's wrong?" She couldn't imagine what would upset him so much. "Did you get fired?"

His shoulders shook. He didn't answer.

"Did you get kicked out of school?"

He just shook his head. Finally, still unwilling to look at her he said, "I never had a birthday party. Nobody ever made me a cake."

"Never?"

He shook his head again. "Never."

She slapped him on the back. "Well, you have one now, and I can't afford any more candles, so you had better blow them out quick before I set the apartment on fire."

They sat in wooden chairs on either side of a crate they used for a dining table, eating on two plates they had bought at the Salvation Army Center. They split the steak. Afterward Ray ate a second piece of cake.

When he had finished eating, Eileen invited him to move to the daybed, the only comfortable place to sit. "I also have a birthday present for you."

"No, Eileen, you have already given me more birthday than I have ever had."

She put a finger on his lips, knowing he was thinking of the cost. "Here is my present to you. I picked up a second job. You can study and you don't have to work at the gas station."

"What? No, you don't need to do that."

For a moment, Eileen had worried he might not let her work. A lot of men didn't want their wives working. "Listen, it is a good paying job. It's a job at the telephone company. I'll be a telephone operator again. I know I'll like the work and you can drop the gas station job. You'll have more time to study and you won't fall asleep in your classes. When you finish college, you'll get a high paying job and then we can have kids and I won't be working. But you won't stay in school the way you are pushing yourself right now. I want to do this. I can quit the wreath job. And it will only be for three more years."

Ray didn't say anything for several minutes. Finally, he took her hand. "I want you to promise me something."

"What?"

"That when I graduate and get a job, you will go to college."

"Me?"

"Yes. You need to go to college to be a teacher. Once we have those college degrees, Eileen, no one can ever take them away from us. It doesn't matter how poor you started; you can become anything you want. That's what college gets you."

"I promise." No one had ever loved her like Ray did. She didn't deserve him. She doubted she was smart enough to get through college, but she would try for him.

'You know what we are, Eileen? Soul mates. Only together are we whole. We were meant for each other."

"Did you learn about that in school?"

"I learned about that when I met you and realized what I had been missing my whole life."

Philautia: Love of the Self

The school bus rumbled down Magnolia Lane in a puff of gray smoke. Eileen reached up to dry her tears, but more tears just fell.

Ray wrapped his arm around her. "That's okay, honey. It is only kindergarten."

Eileen stared down the wide suburban street. A squirrel, sitting up in one of two maple saplings in the front yard of their new ranch, chastised them for invading his territory. Eileen had never dreamed of owning a home. Any home. Certainly not one with two bathrooms. She felt ridiculous standing on the sidewalk crying. "I know."

Ray pulled her closer to him. "He will be home in four hours."

"I know." She made another attempt to dry her tears.

Ray handed her a Kleenex. "Come on inside. I need to talk to you."

She let him guide her through the side door and into the kitchen. Eileen sat at their table, a real maple table they had bought when Ray got his promotion to work on the Mercury space capsule's computer system.

He went over and put on a pot of water on their electric Kitchen Aid stove. "Eileen, it is time."

She had finally quit crying. "Time for what?"

"Time for you to go to college."

What a ridiculous idea. "I can't go to college. I have two kids."

"Yes, you can. You can take one course a semester. It will take you a number of years, but I figured it out. You will graduate when Alan finishes elementary school. Then you can get that job teaching you always talked about."

"I can't." She had given up hope of going to college. "It was just a little girl's dream, Ray."

"It was your dream. That makes it my dream. It's time, Eileen. Time to fulfill that dream. Once you get that degree, Eileen..."

"I know. No one can take it away from you."

Ray reached out to hold her hand. "You will think differently about yourself. You will know, without any doubt, that you are just as good as anybody else. You need to do this. You do so much for everyone in this family. It is time to do this for yourself."

"I don't know."

"Do you believe I love you?"

"Yes."

"Do you believe you are worth loving?"

She didn't have an answer. She didn't believe she was smart enough to get through college, but she didn't want to disappoint Ray. "Okay, I'll try."

Pragma: Longstanding Love

Voice Mail, May 10, 1994, 3:00 pm.

"Hi, Susan, this is your mom. Dad and I made it out to Anchorage, safe and sound. The RV held up well.

Alaska is beautiful. The mountains are unbelievable. The weather is warm and we've met the nicest people. I hope you and Joe make it out here sometime.

I'll call again next week. Love, Mom."

Voice Mail, August 1, 1994, 4:32 pm.

"Hi, this is your Dad. I got your letter. It was great to hear your girls are doing so well in school. Remember, tell them to work hard so they can go to college. Once you get that degree, no one can take it away from you.

I just wanted to let you know that your mom and I found out each town up here in Alaska has a senior center and meals are just four dollars. Our money is going further than we planned because of all the senior discounts. We've decided to stay another three months. We are going to take a helicopter trip up to Denali. I'll call you when we get back. I love you, Dad."

Voice Mail, September 3, 1994, 5:17 pm.

"Happy Birthday, Susan. This is Dad. Your mom and I are going to test the limits of our marriage and stay here in Fairbanks through the winter! It is a crazy plan for two sixty-eight-year-olds, but we want to experience living in the dark for three months. Your mother says it will be an educational experience. We will read. Write lots of letters. Play canasta. It should be very romantic. Write us! Love, Dad. We will call again tomorrow."

Storge: Love of the Child

The clock on the wall in Eileen's room read midnight when Susan's brother, Alan, arrived from DC to say goodbye to their mom. Most of the other residents of the Alzheimer's wing had settled down to sleep. A few roamed the hallway of the locked unit, free to wander in circles during the night.

A lone nightlight above the medical bed provided a dim glow over the heart rate monitor. Alan kissed the top of their mother's head. The nurse brushed her hand across Eileen's forehead. She held Eileen's wrist and squinted at the clock's second hand as she took their mother's pulse. "It won't be long."

Susan felt her mother's grip tightened in her hand. What kind of nurse announces a patient is about to die while the poor person is right there?

When the nurse left Eileen said in a quiet voice, "I'm afraid." Everything about her had become frail.

Susan wasn't surprised, but she also didn't know what to say. She knew what her mother meant. She thought sometimes when you voice your fears, they become less scary. "Of what?"

Her mother didn't answer.

Susan didn't need a reply. She had read once when you die your entire life plays in your head, but her mother couldn't remember her life. Susan decided to give her mother back her memories as best as she could. "Mom, you were born in Portsmouth, Ohio."

Her eyes were closed. They haven't opened for the past half hour. "I don't remember." She sounded upset.

"That's okay. I'm going to remember for you."

Her mother gave Susan's hand a squeeze.

"You went to school at Bath Township High School."

"Was I good a student?"

Always the teacher. "Yes. You were at the top of your class. You went to college. You completed the requirements for a Doctorate in Early Childhood Education, but refused to turn in your dissertation when you found out if you got your PhD you couldn't teach in the classroom anymore."

"That's good."

"When you were sixteen you took a bus all by yourself to Fairborn, Ohio, to find work during the war."

"I don't remember that."

Susan pushed on. "You met Ray then."

"Who is Ray?"

Things weren't going well, but Susan was determined to help her mother through this. "When you were a telephone operator, you broke the rules, and you called Ray to see if he was back from the war. You had met him at Fey's Soda Shop just before he shipped out to Europe. Your friend Fanny was with you. You called his house, and his sister answered. You didn't think he would be home, but he was, and he came to the phone. Your letters never got to him. After you had called he drove five hours to see you."

Her mother didn't say anything, but Susan kept talking.

"You married Ray."

Alan started to wipe at his eyes, but Susan pressed on.

"Ray died of cancer."

"Did he?"

"When he died the last thing he told you was that he loved you and would be waiting for you. It has been a long time, Mom, and I know it is scary, but you don't have to be afraid. Ray loves you. He loved you since that moment he first saw you in Fey's Soda Shop. And he's been waiting for you to join him."

Susan leaned forward to hear her mother.

"I remember."

Those were the last words Eileen spoke, but those were the only words Susan and Alan needed to hear.

THE REFURBISHED COMPANION

KELLY WASHINGTON

Many of Kelly Washington's short works have appeared in Fiction River *anthologies, including* Editor's Choice, Legacies, *and* Recycled Pulp. *Her short story, "The American Flag of Sergeant Hale Schofield," which originally appeared in* Hidden in Crime, *was selected* for The Year's Best Crime and Mystery Stories 2016.

When Kelly isn't writing, she works in the defense contracting industry in Washington, DC. A third-generation soldier, she is not afraid to push boundaries either in real life or in her fiction. Regardless of the genre— fantasy ` , science fiction, or romance—her writing style packs a powerful punch by featuring strong and independent, yet flawed, characters

"I'm fascinated by societal pressures to 'couple' up and thought I'd explore a new angle on it," Kelly says, when talking about the inspiration behind this tale. I'm sure you will agree that the angle and the perspective she brings to this tale, which explores an intriguing type of companionship that ends up being not at all what you likely suspect when you first start reading it, perhaps draws your mind to concepts that Philip K. Dick often wrote about.

The knock on Mirna Io-Kim's apartment door was hurried, as if the visitor wanted to get the appointment out of the way, which didn't surprise her. She was nervous, too.

The image from her security camera popped up on her television, interrupting the news. A tall man with a large box at his feet stood outside her apartment door.

Mirna frowned. Human? It wasn't what she was expecting, but she supposed companions came in all shapes and sizes. Who was she to be picky?

Though, she wondered at the box. No one said anything about a box.

Standing, she flicked off the television, and straightened her oversized blue sweater and the semi-matching blue-and-gray plaid skirt that did little to flatter her slim figure.

She adjusted her neck scarf before tucking her black hair behind her ears.

Once, at university, someone told her she had nice ears, and whether true or not, it was one of the best compliments Mirna had ever received, so she made a point of displaying them. Sometimes she wore accessories, like earrings, but not tonight.

She reconsidered. Earrings might be a nice touch. But she didn't have time and she didn't think her visitor would notice anyway.

Her carpeted living room was spotless. Mirna didn't like clutter, which dovetailed nicely given the fact her income didn't support more than owning the basic necessities.

A mounted television occupied the far wall, which faced a tan couch and love seat set. A recliner was positioned near the window and a rectangular coffee table sat between the couch and the television.

Her apartment was tiny but neat, and it had everything she needed, to include lightning-speed Internet, backup power, and a kitchen galley for when she had guests.

Since it was common for Mirna to bring work home, her bedroom, which came with a desk and Murphy bed, doubled as a workspace.

In her spare time, she enjoyed creating origami flowers. A bevy of them were pinned in shadow boxes, which hung from her walls, while the rest were on display in a large bowl that sat atop the coffee table. Free formed, they piled up and over, a confetti of blooms in various colors and sizes, many with metallic detailing, their points still crisp due to lacquer.

Would he like her artwork? Could she ask without sounding conceited? It might be best to let him decide the topics.

She was humbled the company sent her a human companion. She must be more valuable an employee than she thought, but that didn't erase her nervousness. Mirna wasn't much to look at, but she was highly educated and had a lot to offer.

When she opened the door, a clipboard was thrust in her face.

"Good evening, ma'am." The man bowed. "Please sign at the bottom."

His accent reminded her of her mentor, a gentleman law professor who lived in Itedi, near Mount Kamzuri. She didn't like him, but she loved the landscape.

In the fall, the mountainside blazed orange and red, and the view from the porch was priceless. After her lessons were complete, Mirna would sit by the hearth and write poems about the mountain and the spirit goddess who watched over Itedi's agriculture.

Her mentor thought poetry was a waste of time, but he humored her like he might a cherished pet.

Mirna did everything she could to forget about her mentor, but she still owned the poems. They were in a notebook in a shoebox in her closet.

So hearing his accent was a happy surprise. She'd have no problem talking about the region and Mount Kamzuri's beautiful scenery or Itedi's farming community.

Pleased with the turn of events, Mirna smiled and bowed as well.

Rising, she craned her neck to see his face. Young, tall, and thin, with a marathoner's form, her assigned companion had a head full of fine black hair. His brown eyes were warm and kind.

Mirna didn't consider him handsome, but she found the cut of his masculine jaw attractive.

She didn't mind so much that he was dressed like a deliveryman. Maybe he worked two jobs.

No matter one's citizenship status, New Koyomaha was an expensive city to live in.

His smile wasn't quite a smile. It was more of a smirk, which she found interesting.

Perhaps in time, and after a few visits, she'd come to understand and appreciate his sense of humor. Just like he'd come to like her shy nature.

But at the moment she was mortified he decided to do this part in the common hallway. Any of her neighbors could be watching.

"Sir, please, let us conduct business inside my apartment," Mirna whispered.

Her face was hot. Blinking, her eyes stung.

She didn't know how these things were done, but she'd never heard of a companion deliberately embarrassing a client. But, then again, most companions were humanoid, or virtual.

Companions were a company perk for single employees, and covered under a specific medical insurance plan.

It wasn't why she took the job with Krawl & Brist, a criminal defense firm in the heart of New Koyomaha. She didn't even know about the perk until the head of human resources gave her a brochure after she failed to enter the national matrimony lottery the month before.

By then, she'd been with Krawl & Brist for nine years, and hadn't gone out on a date in two. In her mind it wasn't something her employer should worry about, but her boss thought otherwise.

The implied threat felt real: coupled employees were *better* employees.

She didn't think they'd fire her, but she didn't want to take the chance. The citizens of New Koyomaha, as well as the nation, were competitive when it came to careers and romance.

Game shows were thinly dressed-up lotteries where contestants either competed for a dream job or finding a mate.

In order to keep her employer off her back about the recent matrimony lottery, and to keep them from asking too many questions, Mirna agreed to use the companion benefit, which brought her back to the man standing at her door.

He looked confused.

"Ma'am, I will be honored to assist you with the box, but first I must receive your signature for accepting the delivery."

It took her a moment to comprehend he was truly a deliveryman, and *not* her company-assigned companion.

The realization hit her hard enough that her mind froze and she needed the support of the doorframe.

Thick strands of hair fell into her face and she did nothing to correct it.

How could she be so wrong? A mere law clerk would never receive a *human* companion.

Mirna's nod was swift. She was grateful that the shame was hers alone, and she did her best to conceal her mask of humiliation.

"Of course," she said, using her inkan—her personal seal—to stamp the orange slip of paper.

She looked down. The box, which was wooden and nailed shut, was the size of a dishwasher.

After using a hand truck to bring it inside and a pry bar to open the top, the deliveryman bowed and left.

Mirna secured the door, reassembled her thoughts, and eyed the box. Fingers trembling, she lifted the top. Gasping, she stepped back when she saw the contents.

The lid fell to the floor with a loud clatter. Her downstairs neighbor would complain, but that was the least of her concerns.

Inside the box was a disassembled male humanoid with the word REFURBISHED stamped on his chest.

Rushing to the work terminal in her bedroom-office, Mirna's first thought was to fire off an unhappy note to the head of human resources, but that wouldn't be consistent with her usual demeanor, which was calm and measured.

Was the refurbished companion a form of subverted punishment for not being motivated at finding a husband?

A refurbished companion *she* had to put together.

Her boss must be laughing at her behind her back.

Mirna's shame doubled. She thought about the typical off-duty emails she received over the years.

Give the assignment to Mirna. She's got nothing else to do.

I've got plans this weekend, do you mind doing me a favor, Mirna?

Mirna, you won't be using your plus-one guest invitation for the holiday party, will you? Can I have it?

Last month alone, she received a dozen encouraging emails when the national matrimony lottery was announced.

Mirna knew she wouldn't qualify for the lottery, but she wasn't immune to loneliness. It was the one constant ache she was unsuccessful in managing.

She had no one to talk to. Not substantially, at least.

Her mentor died nine years ago, and casual conversations at the local market didn't count, nor did the multitude of emails she received from Krawl & Brist's lawyers.

It was her job to clerk for them. She worked hard and performed her duties with perfection.

It shouldn't matter whether or not she was married, but because she wasn't and New Koyomaha was a society that placed a higher value on coupled citizens, her employer found a crafty way to teach her a lesson.

She was heartbroken that her value within society would not rise until she found love and married.

Mirna returned to the crate in her living room.

Regardless of her personal feelings on the topic, the refurbished companion was here and he was hers. *He* was blameless in the situation.

It'd be unjust and cruel to keep him in the box. Doing so would go against the United Nations' Automatonic Protection Act, not that she needed legislation to behave humanely.

Mirna thought about her next actions while questions formed in her mind.

What was his name? What were his hobbies? She had one bedroom, so where would he sleep? Was he programmed with a skillset that would enable him to have a paying job outside of being a companion?

She thought of other things like, what if she didn't like him?

Or worse, what if he didn't like her?

Feeling overloaded, she bumped into the coffee table, which caused the bowl of origami flowers to fall to the floor.

It became increasingly difficult to form coherent thoughts as she knelt to restore the bowl and the flowers to their rightful place on the table.

"Small steps," she said, because she knew she was getting ahead of herself. Through her scarf, she rubbed the back of her neck, easing the tension she felt there.

First, she'd assemble him and then think about clothing because the idea of someone lying naked in her living room rattled her sense of respectability. In the morning she'd head to the flea market.

Everything else could wait.

Mirna was confident she could manage that.

Feeling better, she returned to the box. There she found a set of tools, but no manual. It was a setback but not an insurmountable one. Everything was online, anyway. Mirna opened her laptop and loaded the companion website after clicking the *Agree* button on the nation's IDA Banner—Internet Decency Act—and got to work.

Removing the head, limbs, and torso, Mirna noted that his parts were nicely contoured and made of heavy rubber. His skin, however, was soft, like fine suede. He was one of the newer models that felt human.

She lifted his eyelids and liked that his brown irises were natural-looking and warm with flecks of gold.

He will have a handsome gaze.

The pieces of him didn't match and it was apparent that other humanoid parts were mistakenly put in the crate, but Mirna didn't mind. It gave her options on how to build him.

Depending on if she wanted him short or tall, or thin or muscular, she could choose different limbs.

His head and torso were olive in color, and he came with accessories, such as hair, chest hair, and beard styles, and whoever owned him before her had his back tattooed. An elaborate dragon draped his backside, top to bottom, the watercolor-style ink still bright and lifelike.

If he was owned recently, why had he been refurbished? Did he do something wrong? As she thought about this, she was disappointed in her word choice of *owned*.

Perhaps the tattoo was *his* decision. Once a humanoid was online, they were free-thinking beings with authentic thoughts and feelings. Humanoids were a protected class of citizen. Not everyone agreed, but Mirna did, and she fully intended to treat her companion with respect and compassion.

She did not own him any more than he owned her.

His past was no concern of hers.

Yesterday didn't matter.

Today was their fresh start.

She placed his disassembled pieces on the floor and formed his anatomy while positioning limb options next to each other.

Once laid out, his form took on a comical shape because he had four arm and three leg options. It would have been four leg options, but one set was incomplete, so she left the longest leg in the crate.

As it was, she wasn't sure which to choose. Mirna lay down beside him to get an idea of how tall she should make him. The medium set of limbs would place him in the five-foot-six range, which was three inches taller than Mirna.

She thought that would be a healthy difference and one that would complement her height as well. If paired together, no one would give them a second glance. They'd be a young thirty-something couple.

She smiled at that and the unused limbs went back into the crate.

At the bottom she found a box she missed during the first inspection.

Opening it, she almost fainted, and the box tumbled to the floor.

Three penises fell out: small, medium, and large.

Mirna scrambled away as if each one might rear up and bite her.

She closed her eyes as she scooped the penises back into the box, snapping the lid tight.

She couldn't—wouldn't—entertain the possibility of *that* happening with her companion and if it did, they'd have a conversation about it first.

She knew others used their companions in that manner, but Mirna's dreams were strictly platonic.

Her desires were simple.

A lifelong best friend.

Someone to listen to who also listened to her.

She wanted friendly hugs and going for walks while holding hands.

Her ideal relationship was nonsexual: gentle, loving, academic, companionable.

She didn't want or need passion, and lust never entered her thoughts. Her mind didn't work that way and it was the reason Mirna was single.

Not many men would accept a nonsexual relationship. At least not the men she had met over the years.

In her heart, the love she craved was the basic human touch—the ability to reach out and not feel alone.

Because day after day, Mirna's loneliness was smothering.

But that was about to change.

An energetic spark of hope flickered inside her chest as she picked up the tools and physically assembled her companion. It wouldn't be long before he was conscious.

As she read the instructions' final pages, it stressed that in order for the humanoid's firmware to register all limbs and attachments, to include hair accessories, he shouldn't be powered on until fully assembled.

She selected short brown hair for his head, and thick brown eyebrows, which would complement his eyes, but left his strong jaw and chest hair free.

His appearance pleased her. Not handsome but not unattractive, either. If she were being objective about it, his average-level of attractiveness matched her own.

Mirna was about to connect the mini-USB port on the back of his neck to her laptop when she stopped.

"Attachments" also meant a penis, and he might be offended if she left him incomplete. She'd have to choose after all. Mirna's pulse picked up as she selected the medium-sized penis, and her hands shook as she installed it to the lower part of his torso.

That was it. She was done.

She didn't want him to wake up feeling cold, so she retrieved a blanket from the closet and covered his naked form.

Then, taking a deep breath, she plugged him into her laptop.

And waited.

When nothing right away happened, she distracted herself by removing the crate, straightening the living room, and watching the late-night news program, all the while trying to guess what his name might be.

She felt drained, but she couldn't possibly sleep.

In the background, the news anchors reported on the success of the national matrimony lottery. Two million applied and thirty thousand had been selected for arranged marriage screenings. Of those, one hundred would compete at the chance of having a televised wedding.

Mirna stopped listening when she saw movement from the other side of the coffee table. Then in one swift movement, the companion sat up and the cable pulled away from his neck with a sharp snap.

She said nothing as she knew he'd need a few minutes to become oriented.

The blanket fell away when he rose to test his legs. He moved about her apartment and she admired his natural movements. As long as the word REFURBISHED was covered, no one would confuse him for a humanoid.

They'd suspect her long before they suspected him.

When he returned to the living room she was already standing as she greeted him.

"Hello. I'm Mirna. This is your home and you are safe."

Her lack of nervousness surprised her. Perhaps it was because she felt they were on equal footing.

Warm eyes fell on her and he said hello in ten languages before he came to hers.

"My name is Theodoros. Are we meeting for the first time?"

She smiled. "Yes."

He closed his eyes for a moment and Mirna knew he was accessing his new programming. Then he said, "I believe I am your companion."

Ignoring his nakedness, Mirna walked around the coffee table and closed the distance between them.

"We are each other's companion." She removed her scarf and put his hand at the back of her neck. "Feel."

When his index finger skimmed her mini-USB port, she felt a touch of electrical familiarity, and her eyelids fluttered.

His did the same.

She'd been pretending to be human for so long that she forgot what that touch felt like, and that's all she wanted. To be connected to someone else.

Someone like her.

"We are alike, then," he said, his voice soft and pleasing. "Except I am naked."

Mirna laughed, which was something she hadn't done in ages. She handed him the blanket and he covered up.

"I'll fix that when the market opens in a few hours," she said. "Until then, we could talk and get to know one another."

"I'd like that."

So they did.

The sun rose before either noticed. Mirna was lost in conversation and couldn't remember a time she was happier.

The spark of companionship had formed, and her loneliness felt like a thing from the past, which was all she ever wanted.

THE SECRET OF CATNIP

STEFON MEARS

Stefon Mears is the author of more than twenty books, including the Spells for Hire urban fantasy series, the contemporary SF Telepath Trilogy, the Rise of Magic space fantasy series, and most popular, the Cavan Oltblood epic fantasy series. His short stories have sold to magazines such as Fireside *and* Strange Horizons. *His work has also appeared in five* Fiction River *volumes, most recently in* Pulse Pounders: Countdown.

"Cats have always been a part of my life," Stefon says about the writing of this tale. "They're goofy, wonderful, loving creatures, and I've had to say goodbye to too many of them. This story is a tribute to the cats I've lost."

I am sure that, like me, this tale will make you reflect on the love for any pet that you, like Little Warmth, have loved and lost, or perhaps are still fortunate enough to have in your life. I am certain that, after you read this story, you might be drawn to show your furry friend a little sign of that love, whether it's a pet, a cuddle or a scritch. Because a pet's love for their human is among the most precious and loyal loves you will know.

T he day Midnight died, he almost didn't notice.

The sunbeam had been *just that good.*

Sunbeams were the perfect way to end a catnip jaunt through the room with the big white high-backed beds, the ones the two-legs sat on when they stared at their big flat box of colors and noise.

Catnip was fun. Made him feel like a kitten again, instead of the fifteen-year-old behemoth he'd become, with his short black fur stretched across his gloriously massive belly. Right ear permanently shortened by that scrap with a raccoon...oh, sometime back.

Midnight was never a cat to waste time on reminiscence. The present, that was what mattered. And if he was no longer so swift and bouncy as the kitten he'd been, well, catnip helped bring back some of his lost youth.

The catnip had buzzed through him. Made him bounce and roll and pounce pounce pounce on the dangly thing at the end of Little Warmth's stick. Of the three two-legs Midnight lived with, Little

Warmth was his favorite. She still giggled when they played, as she had when she was small and Midnight was a kitten. She had big blue eyes full of love, and long yellow hair Midnight got to bat at sometimes. And she still held him and sang to him and scritched all his favorite spots, just as she always had.

And after Midnight got to play catnip games with his favorite two-legs, that sunbeam under the giant rectangle window had been just perfect. The kind that made his fur ripple with pleasure as he settled down. Heat easing relaxation into his old bones as he rode out the tail end of his catnip buzz, purring himself to sleep.

So when Midnight rose from his nap in the lazy pre-dinner sun, he contemplated a snack and stretched the way he always did— forepaws sliding forward across the rough blue carpet until his shoulders pressed down that way that felt delightful. Then further still until he pushed his chest down past his belly and arched his hips just as high as they could go. Sleek tail high and proud. Then he dug his claws into the carpet to knead and stretch every tendon just so.

That was when Midnight began to notice that something wasn't right.

First, something was wrong with the carpet. It wasn't pulling against his claws the way it was supposed to. Why, he wasn't getting any of that good tendon stretch at all.

Second, he felt lighter. Lighter than he'd felt in years, even though he still had the expansive belly he was so proud of. So light he couldn't even feel that ache in his hips and knees that had been growing steadily for...oh, for some time now.

Third, he could still feel the catnip buzz. That was even odder than the lightness, because catnip was an established part of Midnight's routine, and Midnight knew his routines well.

Once every seven days, Little Warmth would scatter some catnip on the carpet in the room with the big box of colors and noise. Wherever Midnight was in the house, he would smell it. Spicy and enticing as a whiff of mouse, enthralling as a treat in the hands of a two-legs. So good to roll around in. Even better to taste, it danced on his tongue when he licked it. Like the taste of wild grass and power.

Something primal, as though the catnip spoke to some ancient version of Midnight, awakening it in the modern cat.

Little Warmth would watch and giggle while Midnight rolled and bounced, then she would stroke his fur and speak in the sweet voice she used only for him. Finally, she would take out the stick with the dangly thing and they would play until Midnight could play no more.

Then he would sleep in a sunbeam, and awaken sober and hungry.

But Midnight wasn't sober. He could still feel the buzz of the catnip making him bouncy. And he wasn't particularly hungry either.

Midnight looked around. The big, high-backed white beds that the two-legs sat on had some kind of white haze around them. Not like morning mist Midnight remembered from the days that the two-legs still let him romp around outside. Back before the raccoon. No, this mist had a slight glow to it. And it covered the pale walls too, and even the carpet. Everything had that haze.

And something was wrong with Midnight's nose. He should have been able to smell Little Warmth, and his food bowl, and that fake flowery smell that filled the house, especially around his sandbox.

But those smells were barely there.

Midnight needed help to figure this one out. He needed Little Warmth. He should have been able to hear her moving about, maybe in the room she slept in. She stared at other boxes in there. But the sounds, they were odd too. They echoed in a way he didn't like. As though he were in the tiny rain room where the two-legs tried to scrub away their smells.

Midnight didn't like any of this.

Except maybe the little buzz of catnip. That gave him some comfort. But still, he cried out long and loud for Little Warmth.

She didn't answer his first call, but that was not so odd. The two-legs, their ears weren't very good. So he called again. And again.

Finally Little Warmth came strolling into the room, carrying a tall, skinny, glass water bowl. That haze surrounded her too, thicker even than around the high-backed beds, but it didn't obscure her. As she entered, she was singing some little song that wasn't his so it didn't matter.

But she didn't come pick up Midnight or comfort him.

In fact, she walked straight past him to the sunbeam.

That was when Midnight saw his body for the first time. When Little Warmth crouched and reached to rub his body's belly, saying little nonsense things as she rubbed.

She figured out the truth at almost the same moment Midnight did.

And they both began to cry.

Midnight recovered himself quickly. Death was death, and nothing to be feared. He had brought it to his share of birds and field mice and tasty voles, back when the two-legs let him roam and hunt.

He had lived a full life, and he had always known death would come for him one day.

Truth was, Midnight had not been crying for himself.

He had been crying to feel such deep waves of sadness coming from his beloved Little Warmth.

Tears flowed down her unfortunately furless cheeks. Her nose sniffled and snuffled. Her voice broke as she held his body and tried to sing Midnight's songs.

Midnight went to her. Tried to put a paw on her leg to get her attention. That was his pick-me-up signal, but in the moment it only needed to say "Here I am. My body is not me. Here is your little Midnight."

But his paw passed through her leg with barely a pause. And Little Warmth didn't feel him. She didn't look up from the body of Midnight Past to the...whatever Midnight Present was.

He needed to try harder. He lifted both forepaws to her leg and bellowed his where-are-you meow.

Nothing.

And Little Warmth was crying even louder, uttering small broken words, her sweet face turning red.

She plopped down on her butt on the blue carpet and fell backward, weeping as she cradled Midnight's body against her bosom as she had so many times. So much sadness flowed from her now that it almost overwhelmed Midnight. He wanted to cry for her too. To cry for the sadness he could not abate.

But the first moment of shock had passed, and now the catnip would not let him weep. It buzzed through him. Forming a layer of bounciness between Midnight and the sadness. But it gave no comfort now. The buzz was wrong. Vile. Catnip was a thing of joy, a little gift from Bast to the cats of the world, to remind them that deep down every cat is wild. That, unlike dogs, cats had never been tamed into obedience. That cats lived with the two-legs because they chose to.

Catnip was bliss. And this was a time of sadness.

So Midnight tried to shake off the buzz as Little Warmth lay there, crying over his body.

He jumped over and over his favorite two-legs, trying to work off the buzz as she wept. But he was so light now that the leaping took no more effort than the landing, and that scarcely required him to bend his now pain-free joints.

He ran around her, and leaped, and pounced, and called out, but nothing seemed to break through those waves of sadness.

Finally, Little Warmth sat up, still holding Midnight's body as though he were still in it. She drew a few deep, shuddering breaths. Said a few things that sounded sweet but made her sob and squeeze her eyes tight.

That was too much.

Buzz or no buzz, Midnight put everything he had into one more meow. He reached deep within himself and let out a cry louder than the one that had chased off the Interloping Tabby some years back.

And for a moment—just a moment—Little Warmth stopped crying.

Her head came up, and she looked around the way the two-legs do when their weak ears can't tell where a sound came from. And then she said the one word he recognized.

"Midnight?"

But then she looked down at his body in her arms and shook her head, tears flowing down her face anew. She closed her eyes and shook her head harder. She said something else. Something dismissive sounding.

Little Warmth got awkwardly to her feet, and carried Midnight's body out of the room. He trotted along after her into the kitchen, where he could hardly hear her bare feet pad on the smooth floor that tasted fake and slick and lemon-but-not-lemon from the residue of the smell-ridder than the two-legs wiped across it.

Little Warmth picked up her tiny box from the cool stone counter, the one Midnight wasn't supposed to walk on, but did all the time anyway.

Midnight recognized the small, thin box she picked up. It was the one she played with and stared at more than any other box.

She held it to her ear and started speaking. But that was a two-legs thing. Whatever she was saying, it didn't matter. Not really.

Because Midnight realized three things.

First, Little Warmth had heard him call out, no matter how she now pretended she didn't.

Second, Midnight could no longer feel the catnip.

Those two facts had to be related. Running and jumping and pouncing had done nothing to work the catnip through Midnight, but that one call had used it up.

Midnight said a little word of thanks to Bast for giving cats catnip. And for the little bonus it seemed that herb brought over and above its bliss.

Catnip gave Midnight a way to reach across death to Little Warmth. And that was good, because of the third thing he realized.

Without the buzz of the catnip flowing through his system, Midnight could feel a tug inside his glorious belly. A tug that made him want to find a tree and climb, climb, climb. Instinct told him he felt the pull of the next world. That his time in this place was limited now.

Soon Midnight would have to pass beyond this world to the next, where he would wait for Little Warmth and guide her to what would follow.

But if catnip could keep that feeling at bay, then maybe it could help keep him here with Little Warmth....

But then Midnight remembered the way his paws passed through her leg, even with the catnip buzzing through him. He could not nuzzle her, or bathe her arms and chin properly. She could not stroke his fur, or scritch the places he liked, or cuddle him close.

He would be nothing more than...whatever he was. Between. And that would be wrong. The time had come for him to move on, and that tug was his reminder that what came next was waiting.

But Midnight had to say goodbye first. He could not leave his beloved Little Warmth so full of sadness. Had to see one more smile on her face before the pull of the next world grew too strong to resist.

He needed more catnip.

The problem was that Midnight didn't know where Little Warmth *kept* his supply of catnip. Yes, there were little bits in some of his toy mice, but that catnip was all old and used up. He needed the *fresh* catnip. He needed the catnip that Little Warmth would scatter for him every seven days, before they played their favorite game.

But Little Warmth hid that supply.

That was Midnight's own fault, and he knew it. He had seen only a few years of this world when he found his first supply. A little crinkly transparent thing full of catnip. He had smelled it on the cool stone counter not more than a few steps from where Little Warmth now held his body.

Young Midnight had smelled the catnip through the crinkly barrier. That was the first time he leapt onto the cool stone counter

in the kitchen. He'd needed only moments to chew through the crin-
kles to the catnip inside.

He'd found that supply in the morning, and still been bouncy
when Little Warmth came home hours later. Big Warmth and Deep
Voice were with her, and they were angry at the artistic way
Midnight had scattered the catnip across the counter as he rolled
in it.

But then, the two-legs had no appreciation for art.

Ever since, Little Warmth had hidden away the catnip, and
stored it in something stronger than the crinkly clear stuff. Midnight
had tried a few times to smell it, but his nose could not pick it up,
even when he was alive and all the scents were right.

They were all wrong now. He could barely tell the signature musk
of Little Warmth from the lemon-not-lemon of the kitchen floor or
the fake flower smell of the air.

But the tug in his belly was growing stronger, and he needed to
act fast.

Midnight ran back into the room with the big flat box of noise
and colors. Today's catnip was still there. Good. He was afraid he'd
slept—or died—through the screaming sucker, the one Little
Warmth used to catch up all the catnip after their games.

Midnight sprawled his massive body across the floor and started
rolling.

Nothing happened.

The catnip wasn't sticking to his fur. He wasn't getting the smell
the way he should have. A ripple of irritation flattened his ears and
worked its way down until his tail twitched back and forth harshly.

He tried licking the catnip.

Something.

It wasn't quite the same, and it wasn't as strong as he would have
liked. He couldn't quite taste it. But when his tongue passed through
the catnip—and it did, just the way his paws had passed through
Little Warmth's leg—he felt an echo of the proper buzz and a dimin-
ishment of the tug in his belly.

Midnight licked it all up. Every bit of catnip he could find. The buzz wasn't all it should have been, but it was something.

But what could he do with it?

And then he had an idea. Just a little puff of an idea. Hardly a dust mote worth chasing, but he had to try something.

Midnight sat in the middle of the scattered catnip and reach deep down into himself. He thought of his love for Little Warmth. He thought of his love of catnip. He thought of everything that was good in this world and he put every bit of it into the loudest, longest meow he'd ever given voice to.

He held that sound just as long as he could, and as he did he felt the buzz of the catnip leaking away and the tug in his belly starting again.

And it was stronger now. Urging him to run, to jump, to climb to what came next.

Little Warmth came running into the room, astonishment in her sweet blue eyes. Her face still red and puffy from all her crying.

Midnight's heart went out to her. He hated seeing the glimmer of hope underneath her confusion. Hated the wave of sadness that he knew would follow. Hated most of all that growing tug in his belly.

"Midnight?" she said again. And she looked around for him, saying little words he didn't understand, though he felt their hope. Perhaps she felt his presence. Knew that some part of him sat nearby, had called out to her.

Midnight's claws were working now, even though he could no longer knead the carpet. He needed to grip this world. To hold onto it just a little longer. To fight that need to move on.

Her shoulders slumped when she could not find him. Nor feel him. And she retrieved the screaming sucker and caught up all the catnip. Midnight followed her, fighting for every step as she put the screaming sucker away, and his hopes rose as she stopped and blinked for a moment.

Then she started up the stairs with a purpose. Midnight followed hot on her heels, prancing and high-stepping the way he had so very many times before. The tug seemed pleased that he was climbing something, but still it pulled him to move on.

When she got to the room she slept in, she went to the tall chest where she stored her fur substitutes. She pulled open the top drawer. Midnight knew that drawer. He'd gotten in there once when she'd left it open...oh, some years past. He knew it held soft things that carried more of her smell than any of the other fur substitutes she used to cover her unfortunately furless body.

She pulled out a small glass jar, and inside it Midnight could see the answer to all his hopes.

His stash of catnip! More than he'd ever seen before. Nearly enough to halfway fill one of his cans of food.

Little Warmth turned, but before she could take a step Midnight pounced. He pounced like the catnip was a bird and this was his last chance to catch one before being confined for life to the indoor world.

He passed straight through the catnip, mouth open wide. Trying to consume it all at once.

And in this between state he could do just that.

Midnight was vibrating now. The catnip jolted through his system like the joy of a hunt and the pleasure of a scritch and the warmth of a sunbeam and a full belly all at once, and then some.

The tug went away. As though it were gone completely, but Midnight knew better.

Midnight ran in front of Little Warmth, who was now walking back toward the stairs.

He reached down into his depths as he had before, and poured all of his love for Little Warmth into two things: one last purring meow (and the purr came easily through all that catnip), and one last attempt to leap into her arms.

"Midnight?" said Little Warmth, dropping the jar of catnip...

...and trying to catch him.

And for that one moment. She could.

For that one moment, that one final moment, Midnight was once more purring in the arms of his beloved Little Warmth. She was laughing and crying all at once and trying to say his name.

But before she could finish his name, the moment was past and her arms moved through him.

The tug came back with a vengeance. Too strong for Midnight to resist now. He had no choice but to follow it through the wall to a great oak tree that had never been in his backyard territory during life. The Tree Between Worlds.

And with one last laughing crying smile from Little Warmth to bolster him, Midnight began to climb.

LIFEBLOOD

ALEXANDRA BRANDT

Alexandra Brandt's debut fantasy short story, "We, the Ocean," from Fiction River: No Humans Allowed *was featured on the* Tangent Online *2017 Recommended Reading List. She has sold stories to other volumes of* Fiction River, *as well, including* Wishes *and several upcoming volumes. She writes fantasy, sci-fi, and superhero short fiction, including her portal fantasy series,* Wyndside Stories, *which also has stories in several anthologies and collections. When not writing fiction, she writes nonfiction copy for a medical practice.*

"I'm a huge sucker for superhero stories," Alexandra says, "and you can find references to my childhood obsession with the X-Men in this one." She says that she'd been thinking about this particular character, and the kinds of ethical dilemmas that she might face, for quite some time. "When I realized her story was actually a story about love (although maybe not the kind of love you would expect), I found the perfect opportunity to finally tell it for this anthology."

In this tale, Anolia not only comes to grips with the concept of selfless love, but she also explores her own reliance and dependence on the others in her lives in a uniquely interesting way. Just like love itself is layered and complex and underlies the motivation of characters in this story, the narrative itself, told from Anolia's point of view, is similarly woven.

You learn to live moment by moment in a world like mine. Time as an entity begins to lose meaning, and even marking the hours by the old pink plastic wall clock—a relic I brought with me from my old life—seems merely born of nostalgia. I forget to care what the numbers mean. The TV stands silent, most days.

When I first made my choices, at the beginning, painting these walls butter-yellow and filling them with bookshelves from my home seemed like a good idea. But the books would gather dust, now, if they weren't required to be sterile by hospital standards.

Inexplicable, really; it's not as if a non-sterile environment would endanger me. No, when death takes me, it will not be by disease.

I fear weariness, more than anything else. That, and losing myself.

My whole world runs by the machine.

Every day...*is* it every day?...they hook me in, and I wonder who will be the new person in the other half of the apparatus, the next dying soul they've wheeled in, silently, sedated—although not for long, once my blood hits theirs—all unknowing that the miracle cure upon which they've hung all their hopes is hooked in to a pod they'll never see: a living, breathing woman. Well, half-living, at least.

After silent hours of watching my lifeblood cycle through the tubing in the pod wall, watching someone else's tainted blood cycle back to me, feeling my entire body fight someone else's war...after that it's bed and fluids and a carefully balanced meal, then rest, then mandatory exercise, then more fluids, and the machine once more.

It's a world I created for myself, years ago.

If I weren't so tired, I imagine I could feel the same satisfaction —even joy—I once felt, knowing that at last my gift was truly a *gift*, and that the world would be better because of it.

I do miss that.

And then there's you.

Sometimes you make me remember, too.

"Elena," you told me, when I asked your name. When they decided I needed a physical therapist, when we realized my muscles were beginning to atrophy from machine, then bed rest, then machine again.

I have never been good at noticing what my body needs. Perhaps it stems from the years when I thought universal immunity meant universal invincibility.

Now, since coming here, I have begun to notice acutely what my body is doing on the *inside*. The fierceness with which it fights all battles of blood. This has, after all, become the purpose of my life.

But my gift can't reverse damage already done, damage brought about by sheer negligence.

So there you were, standing in my hospital home in your sky-blue scrubs, your brown eyes wide, wider than my little nephew's on the

Christmas we all spent together in a "real, honest-to-God *ice castle*," about a month before I made that final decision to put my body, and my life, where my heart knew it had to go....

Anyway. Your eyes reminded me of Kevin, of that day, and I loved you for it.

But of course your wonderment was all about the machine, and about me, miraculous me. I know you'd had the fear of God put in you with the dozens of nondisclosures and legal agreements before they even let you know I existed. But here I was, and there you were, and you called me, Anolia Green, a "real-life superhero" without realizing I'd heard you.

I loved you for that, too.

It made me believe all over again.

Not believe that I was a superhero, of course. But believe in my *purpose*.

Which is a strange thing to say, considering everything that's happened since.

Or perhaps not so strange after all.

The second day, while you helped me through the first exercises, I decided to tease you a little. "I'm not a superhero, you know," I said, and watched you duck your head and blush, realizing I had overheard you. "It's just a weird, one-in-a-million chance genetic mutation." This is what Dr. Hart and I had figured out, over ten years ago now, when we were still friends and taught at the same school, albeit in very different subjects.

At my words, you outright laughed. It was a beautiful laugh. "Haven't you ever heard of the X-Men?" you asked me.

Well, yes. But...

And while I still continued to try to explain how my situation was entirely different from a comic book world, it seemed I couldn't help but smile.

I think I had forgotten what smiling felt like, honestly.

I started paying attention to the time after that. Ten a.m.—that's when you came in, Monday-Wednesday-Friday and some Saturdays. I might not have noticed the days of the week if you hadn't started telling me. None of the other nurses—there were two—ever volunteered information like that. Of course, they never made me smile, either.

They were always pleasant enough. But of all the people I saw—even Dr. Hart, on those rare occasions—you were the only person who actually seemed to see *me* when you looked at me.

And you kept calling me a superhero, too.

"You know one of the X-Men can cure disease with a touch," you told me; it must have been in those early, happier days, although I don't remember exactly when. "His name's Elixir. How does that sound for a superhero name?"

I snorted, playing along. "I can't take a name some other hero already has. That's just bad form." Other names were brought up and discarded. "Panacea?" "No." "Lifeblood?" "What kind of a name is that?" "Dr. Caduceus?"

"I'm not that kind of doctor," I told you. (And as it turns out, the medical symbol is actually the Rod of Asclepius anyway. Who knew?)

Needless to say, I did not get a superhero name, and I preferred it that way. I didn't need or want to be a hero.

But I wonder if even *thinking* about it marked the beginning of the end.

The change happened in you first, but it was weeks before I noticed. You started looking at me with concern in your face, more and more every day. Even while I thought I was doing much better with my strength and mobility.

I was tired, of course. But I am always tired. It's just the nature of things.

Something in your attitude was shifting. You muttered to yourself, under your breath so I couldn't hear. Sometimes I would catch you looking at me and shaking your head, when you thought I couldn't see.

"You don't do much when I'm not around, do you?" You finally asked me one day. "You never even watch TV or read any of those books in your room."

I didn't really know what to say to that, so I shrugged. "You know how it is," I think I muttered at the time. I felt a vague wave of guilt, but thinking about things like that made me feel even more tired. So I ignored your prodding about it until you went away after our session.

But you came back with even more concerns. "Anolia, don't you ever get to leave the hospital?" you asked next. "How long has it been since you went outside?"

Years, I thought. But I didn't tell you that. "It's not like a prison," was all I said. "I'm here voluntarily. I just don't have the time or energy for..." Well, anything. Not since I started going into the machine every day, instead of a few times a week.

When had *that* started?

I couldn't even remember.

I said nothing of this to you, of course. I didn't want to have to defend my actions and choices. I was doing the right thing, and that was what mattered.

But is this what doing the right thing should feel like?

You asked me, "Anolia, are you truly *happy* with your life like this?"

And I couldn't find an answer.

At some point, when the questions become too many, when you can't stop thinking about them no matter how hard you try....

At that point, something must change.

For me, it meant picking up the hospital phone I hadn't touched in...months? Years?...and asking for a computer with Internet access.

I'd had one, at the beginning, and now I didn't. It was very strange, when I bothered to think about it. What had happened to it? When had it disappeared?

The nurse at the other end of the line was startled by my request. Dr. Hart was startled. They didn't have one on hand for me, they said. They'd have to get one special and it wasn't in their current budget.

I was tired enough to be tempted to let it go, but something in me made me stick to my request. I wasn't their prisoner, I reminded them. We were working together on this, and I wanted a computer again.

It took over two weeks, and a few more gentle reminders from me, before they finally brought me an adequate laptop, older model, with a barely adequate Internet connection.

I started looking for articles about Dr. Matthew Hart, because the question that seemed to surface in my mind most often was this: What exactly am I doing here?

I thought I'd known the answer. But it seemed I needed validation.

Unfortunately, I didn't receive what I needed.

You see, I still remember Matthew—Dr. Hart, that is—excitedly bringing me articles, right at the beginning, that had mentioned his partnership with LiveBio Lab for this experimental new treatment for rare and incurable diseases. People were lining up for the treatment; the waiting list was years long.

Those articles, in conjunction with some problems in my personal life at the time (heated arguments with my then-husband), had spurred me to decide to move in to the hospital full-time and do the transfusion treatments (pre-machine) once a week instead of a few times a month. We were seeing success. We were seeing lives changed.

Now, with the machine not only fixing the clunky transfusion process, but also running daily, I expected to see even more of these stories.

But I did not.

Instead, I saw nothing at all. Just a brief statement that LiveBio

Lab stopped seeking grants for medical research about six or seven years ago.

I said nothing of this to you when I saw you.

Instead, I picked up the hospital phone again and called Matthew. Dr. Hart himself.

It took about a day before I could get through to him, despite the fact that he worked in the very same hospital that composed my whole world.

Still, he came to me in person. I told him it was a pleasure to see him again, which might have even been true. I showed him what I'd found on the Internet—or lack thereof—and asked him about it.

Foolish person that I was.

His response seemed frank enough: he said he'd discovered the lab couldn't get grants without revealing my existence, and that would cause all kinds of trouble, including endangering me.

He didn't say why, precisely, but his argument did seem logical.

"So we have to do everything privately now," he said, "and all the money we earn from the treatments goes right back into building our research lab and funding the state-of-the-art equipment we need and so on."

I had some more questions about that—

"The main thing, Anolia," he reminded me, "is that we need to find a way to isolate your blood from your body without killing its properties, and we still don't have that." And yes, that *was* the thing that had stymied us so far, keeping us from being able to turn my unique mutation into an actual medication for the masses.

But I already knew all *that* information.

In fact, I realized, after he shook my hand and left...he hadn't really told me anything new at all.

What's more, he'd taken my laptop with him.

And I didn't get it back.

———

That's when I started relying on *you*, Elena, and for that I am sorry.

I hate to think that I caused you trouble.

But I know I did.

You were eager to help. *So* eager, in fact, that I wonder now if you hadn't already been doing a little side research of your own, regarding my situation. Some judicial snooping around the hospital files.

The information you brought back to me was not reassuring.

Patients with incurable diseases and conditions were still coming to us, yes. The waiting list was still years long, although immediate needs did get first consideration...for a price.

This experimental, semisecret, non-FDA-approved cure—Dr. Hart was charging over one million dollars per patient. All that money for a few hours with the machine, with me, fighting a battle of blood.

This was not what I had signed up for.

For the first time, I thought: *I need to get out.*

The trouble was, when?

When do you decide, that's it, the next person who has signed up for this miracle treatment *because they are dying* doesn't get the gift of life?

There is always a next person, and a next person.

"I can't do it," I finally told you. You were holding my hand as I sat on the bed, tired from the therapy and from the machine. My clock had vanished, somewhere in the past week, and I was suspicious that Dr. Hart and the other nurses had actually upped the frequency of my times spent in the machine.

But it was hard to tell when I couldn't even tell what hour it was anymore.

I'd had blackout blinds put on the windows a few years ago, when I started needing more naps...a mistake, since now I was generally too tired to walk over and raise them.

And I couldn't even rely on *you* to keep me on track, because they had reduced your days with me to once a week.

I think.

So I *think* I'd been wrestling with this impossible question for about a week as well. And when your hand tightened on mine, I know you didn't like the conclusion I'd come to in your absence.

"I know, I know," I said, squeezing my eyes shut against the look on your face. "I don't approve of his methods. I'll try to negotiate with him about that. But I can't just leave forever...I can't even ask them to change all this to suit me better..." I gestured to my room, to the door that adjoined the chamber with the machine. "Because there are so many people, Elena. So many with horrible diseases that are killing them...not just cancer. Not just AIDS. Diseases and conditions that aren't getting researched because they're so rare, which means they may never get a cure. How can I abandon them? How can I question the methods, when the results are actually saving lives *every day?*"

That was the crux of my problem. It was the reason I had left my own family—left *Daniel*—to do this thing in the first place.

You kept holding my hand, but you were shaking your head the whole time I spoke. "Anolia, whatever your old friend is using that money for, not even half of it is going into the research lab," you said tightly, when I finished talking. You pulled a flash drive from your pocket, although of course I had no computer to use it on. "Can you let him exploit you, and take the money of desperate people, when it's ultimately only a stopgap and he's not even *trying* to work toward the greater good?"

Ah.

It's strange.

Hearing those words from you may have destroyed my already-wavering faith in Matthew Hart, but it restored my hope.

It meant I could leave without guilt. If I left, it *would* be for a greater good. I could still use my gift like a real hero would.

I'd have to either try to find someone incorruptible, or find a way to found my own research lab. I could do that. I could make it work. I could ensure it was moving toward a future where *everyone* was cured, not just the people with desperation and deep pockets.

Leaving was the right thing to do.

It made me feel giddy, knowing this.

"You could start living again, Anolia," you said to me, softly. The light in your eyes told me how much you cared about this. About me.

"I've been thinking about this a lot," you continued. "I don't think they will let you go easily. Think about all the changes they've been making over the years. Designed to keep you tired and compliant. So you don't ask questions or demand things. Just think about this past week, if you need proof of that."

A sobering thought indeed.

You put something into my hand. "I've been doing a lot of research. There is a particular human rights group that handles strange cases like yours. They can get you out *and* help you stay under the radar until you figure out what you want to do with your life." I looked; it was an object that nominally resembled a cell phone, only much smaller. "You just hit that button to call, and—"

The outer door opened, and we hastily hid the device within my hospital cot. One of the regular nurses, Joan, came in briskly. "We've got an eleven-year-old girl coming in with an emergency," she told us as she began to hustle you out. "Physical therapy time's over."

I wondered at the timing, but...an eleven-year-old girl. Joan could be lying. But what if she wasn't? I couldn't risk being the reason a child died.

I said nothing as you were pushed out the door. I said nothing as I entered the machine, perhaps for the last time.

But it wasn't the last time, because Dr. Matthew Hart himself visited me next.

"I'm concerned," he said without preamble. I was resting again in my room, now void of clock, phone, *and* TV. The books hadn't been touched...yet.

Matthew sat down beside my bed. "Someone has been getting into LiveBio's protected files and financials. Do you know anything about that?" His eyes bored into mine, and I wondered if I could lie to someone who'd known me for over fifteen years. "You've been behaving very...unlike yourself...recently," he continued. "What's changed? We're still doing everything we set out to do. Together." He put his hand on mine, but there was none of your warmth there. He didn't care about me the way you did. I knew that then, and I know it still.

"Where's the money going, Matthew?" I asked quietly, withdrawing my hand. "If it's going to further research, that's one thing. Of course I want to save lives. But I also want to build toward a future where a *real* cure exists. Not just me and my limitations. We both agreed this was about the *future*. A future without disease."

"It is," he said, leaning forward. "I told you, that's what this lab is working for—"

"Then," I raised my hand, a tired gesture that still managed to interrupt his flow of words. "Why...have I, ah...heard that half of the money is going elsewhere?" I was careful not to mention you, in what turned out to be a pointless gesture.

He could have outright denied my accusation, and I would have known he was a liar, and strengthened my resolve to get out then and there.

But instead he said, "Bribes, of course. Protecting you, protecting our mission. I've had to pay a lot of bribes to keep this from being taken out of our control. Or getting shut down."

He sighed heavily. "I'm not proud of it, but it was absolutely necessary. This was—and is—*always* about our future without disease, Anolia. Always." He sat back, watching my face as I processed his words. "And you can ask your little informant to verify, too." He stood up. "Thanks to you, I'll probably have to pay *her* another bribe to keep quiet about her digging."

My head was reeling as he left. I couldn't think. Was bribery a justification? How could I know what was right? What was good?

And what about Elena? What about *you*?

It is a point in your favor, Elena, that I didn't even consider that *you* would be taking bribes from him. I thought that was stupid.

But I did wonder, then, if you had been lying to me; if you had known the money was for bribes, which were all about keeping the research alive, and you had just withheld that information so I would decide to leave.

Or maybe you hadn't seen the bribes as a necessary part of the project.

In some ways, I could agree with that. But from a strictly utilitarian standpoint—if I wanted to do the greatest good for the greatest amount of people—maybe it was a necessary evil. I didn't know.

But you still should have told me...and I still should have asked.

Instead of jumping at the chance to escape. Selfishly.

True to Dr. Hart's word, you showed up the very next day, proving that he indeed knew the identity of my informant. "I don't know why they scheduled me today," you started, but I interrupted you.

"Was the money really for bribes to keep the research safe?"

You were taken aback. "Well, yes," you said. "But does that matter? It's wrong. You can't be sacrificing your life and happiness for something like that. Right?"

I didn't *know*.

It wasn't about ethics alone. There were still lives at stake. And a future I believed Dr. Hart was still genuinely working for.

And it couldn't be about my feelings, my happiness, my life.

You knew that. We'd talked about it.

The silence grew, and as it did you became more and more incredulous. "You can't be thinking about *staying* now," you said. "*Can* you?"

"I have to think about lives saved," I whispered, looking at my hands. "I can't just think about me."

You took both my hands and looked into my eyes. "I love you, Anolia Green," you said simply, and my heart grew so full and warm, despite my misgivings, that I couldn't speak.

I don't know what you saw in *my* eyes, but I think it was enough.

You said, "I love you, and I can't stand watching you die by inches."

And the warmth fled.

Oh, Elena, I know now that you spoke those words truly from the heart.

You couldn't have known they were the wrong ones.

And yes, I realize now they were nothing like Daniel's words to me ten years ago...but they hit all the same places. That you loved me, I didn't doubt for a second. But Daniel, my husband, had loved me too.

He had loved me, but selfishly. He hadn't been willing to let me do my life's work, not when he realized the true extent of it. It took me away too much. It left me periodically tired, when I did the transfusions a few times a month, although nothing like now. But what's more, I was always thinking about it. Talking about it. Talking about Dr. Hart, too. Daniel became less and less tolerant, not caring about the lives we were saving.

He said he was concerned about me, but back then I had been fine, really. I knew it wasn't about me, it was about him. It was about our love, and how he perceived that relationship.

I couldn't sustain a love based on selfishness, so I broke it off. And told Dr. Hart I wanted to join the research efforts full-time.

I wanted to prove that love could, and should, be selfless.

And then there you were, telling me you couldn't watch me like this, and it felt like the opposite of selfless love all over again.

I didn't know how to tell you that, properly. "I'm not dying," I said, withdrawing my hands from yours. "I'm living in the way I think is right." I looked away from the hurt in your eyes.

Of course I should stay here. I couldn't just be thinking about what you or I wanted out of life.

"Anolia, you can't..."

I shook my head. "Don't," I said. "Don't make this worse." I kept my eyes trained on my lap until you moved away.

I didn't look up when you opened the door to leave, but I did hear you say quietly, "I'll be back next week, Anolia Green."

But you weren't.

I didn't see you again.

And when I asked Dr. Hart, and he said you had taken a bribe and left, *I didn't believe him*, Elena. I looked in his eyes and I knew he was lying.

And I didn't know what it meant, but I feared.

Oh, I still fear what it means.

The knot won't leave my stomach, Elena. I remember all the words I never said to you. Every time Joan makes me do the exercises *you* devised for me, the knot tightens.

I wonder how much money Dr. Hart is paying Joan to keep her mouth shut.

I wonder a lot of things, when I have the energy to do so. Time loses all meaning; the nurses never open the windows for me when I ask. I've spent spend much of my time in a haze punctuated by brief moments of clarity.

But I do know this, in those moments. I realize it now: Matthew Hart may think he is working toward the greater good, but he does not do it out of *love*. If he believed in it, truly, if he was doing it out of compassion for the world, he would never stoop to these methods.

He has forgotten how to love, and so have I.

Or I had, until you.

You weren't loving selfishly...and I wasn't loving selflessly either. Self-sacrifice does not equal love, not when you have forgotten what it is like to be human in the first place.

Not when you've forgotten how to love yourself, too.

I remembered the device you gave me, Elena. I found it stuck in my bed today, and remembered what you said. I pushed the button.

I am free.

I'm going to start my own project. Project Lifeblood, I'll call it. I have a shot at this, and I'll do it on my terms. In the meantime, I'm working with these people to do some sneaky, small-scale healing for HIV-positive people, especially the ones without funds to treat themselves.

This group you found, their resources run deep. If anyone can find you, they can.

I count the days until I see you again, Elena.

WHO LOVES THE UNLOVED?

LAURA WARE

Laura Ware's column, "Laura's Look," appears weekly in the Highlands News-Sun *and covers news items or ideas she can talk about for 600 words. She published a collection of her earliest columns in 2017.* Her short stories *can be found in a number of* Fiction River *anthologies, including* Past Crime (Special Kobo Edition), Last Stand, Editor's Choice, Reader's Choice, *and* Feel the Fear. *Her novels include* Dead Hypocrites, The Silent Witness, Redemption *and* Two Weeks in Guyana. *Her essay entitled "Touched by an Angel," was published in* Chicken Soup for the Soul: Random Acts of Kindness *in 2017.*

And as for inspiration for the story, Laura provides two answers to that.

First, she cites a tale about how columnist Erma Bombeck once shared a letter she received from the mother of a criminal in her book, Motherhood: The Second Oldest Profession. *"The letter," Laura says, "is haunting to read."*

The other answer she provides is more personal in nature. "I am close to someone who broke the law and served time in prison for it. I love them dearly, though I don't approve of what they did. I know I am not alone, and I thought someone needed to point out that these men and women are also loved and cared about. It's not always easy, but at least in my case it's worth it."

One of the things I have often reflected upon, whenever hearing of a terrible or violent crime, is how the person who committed that crime was once an innocent baby who, at one time, was most likely wrapped in the loving embrace of the parent or person who cared for them while they were helpless. There are victims of the crime; but are the people who love the person who performed those acts not also victims in a way?

The love of caring for and raising another person doesn't disappear when that child grows up and when that child engages in deviant behavior.

I think it is important that an anthology about love include this type of undying love, from the perspective of a mother who has to face the conflict between her undying love for her child and her belief in what is good and right.

Laura portrays this struggle in a touching and realistic fashion through Michelle Travers, the mother in this tale.

T here were certain moments in her life that Michelle Travers felt were burned into her very soul.

There was, for example, her wedding day. If she closed her eyes she could see the small church auditorium in front of her, the pale blue carpet between the oak pews littered with pink rose petals. Her bouquet was filled with white tea roses, their faint scent adding to the magic of the day. She recalled her father's large warm hand patting her hand on his arm just before they started down the aisle, towards her beloved Edward. The music of "The Wedding March" swelled just before she took her first step, and she thought her heart would burst from the happiness she felt.

Then there was a different day. A day in their doctor's office. Michelle remembered the cherrywood shelves groaning under all the books. On the doctor's side of the desk stood a mug of mint tea, a tea she couldn't stand since that day. The doctor himself, a middle-aged man with brown curly hair, wearing a white lab coat over a blue polo shirt and navy slacks. His voice, kind and sympathetic as he delivered the news. Aggressive prostate cancer. The same kind that had killed Edward's father and grandfather would now take him far too soon.

The funeral eight months later was another moment. Michelle had not known that someone could cry so many tears as she wept. Her son, Eddie Junior, uncomfortable in his black suit and stunned at their loss. The polished mahogany casket in front of the auditorium that held the body of the man she loved more than anyone on earth. Flowers. So many different kinds and scents. Afterwards, a dinner the church ladies had put together of ham, scalloped potatoes, and coleslaw that she struggled to eat.

And now, this moment. Michelle stood in her kitchen, leaning against the steel sink, the open dishwasher to her right. Her cooling coffee sat on the gray granite countertop across from her. Caper, her black terrier, sniffed around her feet looking for fallout from her loading the dishwasher.

But all that was minor compared to the six words her son had just uttered on her cell phone, his voice hoarse.

"Mom, I've been arrested. For murder."

It had to be a mistake. *Had* to be.

Michelle managed to get to the county courthouse the next morning after a night of tossing and turning. And *that* was after she'd managed to get hold of a lawyer whose name she got from Frank Weld, one of the elders of the church (and telling him why she needed the name had been stressful and humiliating in and of itself).

As agreed, the lawyer, a man named Jerry Colson, met her in front of Courtroom B. She spotted the man, dressed in a blue pinstripe suit, his graying black hair and wire-rim glasses fitting the description she'd been given.

Steeling herself, she marched across the marble floor. "Mr. Colson? I'm Michelle Travers."

"Mrs. Travers," he said, shaking her hand. "I've spoken to your son. We will be requesting bail, but I must warn you there's a strong possibility we won't get it."

"I don't understand." She felt exposed in this wide hallway. She noticed three people sitting on a bench next to the large, dark wood doors that led into the courtroom. A couple about her age, along with a younger woman. The women were blond and, to Michelle's unpracticed eye, appeared to be related.

"Mrs. Travers?" Colson spoke gently.

She shook her head to clear it. Fatigue was making it hard to concentrate. "I'm sorry."

He studied her, then glanced at his watch. "We need to go in now, but afterwards, there's a small café about half a block away that serves decent coffee. If you don't mind my saying so, you look as if you could use some."

Michelle blinked. "I'm sorry, are you asking me out?"

His eyes widened. "Not at all! I thought we could discuss the case a bit. I have a little time after this hearing, and since you hired me I thought I would keep you abreast of things."

She felt her cheeks warm. "Of course. Maybe Eddie can come with us after we post bail."

Colson's mouth opened but he seemed to think better of what he was going to say. Instead, he waved her towards the courtroom. "Please, let's go in."

Michelle had seen courtrooms on television and in the movies but had never been in one herself. The room was smaller than she imagined, only four rows of oak benches with an aisle separating them into two sections. The carpet was a gray patterned commercial-use type that she supposed hid dirt well. Despite the puff of cool air she felt as she passed near a wall vent, the room was a little warm, apparently fighting a losing battle with the Florida heat.

The trio who had been sitting outside the courtroom passed her to take a seat on the right-hand side of the room. The older woman clutched a tissue, and her reddened eyes told Michelle she needed it.

She let Colson go by her through a low gate that separated the spectators from where the judges and lawyers sat. He walked over to a table on the right and began speaking in low tones to a dark-haired woman in a red skirt and white ruffled blouse.

Uncertain, she stood in the aisle. Colson glanced her way and then pointed to the benches on the left-hand side. With a nod she found a seat on the bench that was second from the front. Clutching the straps of her big black purse tightly, she prayed to wake up from what had to be a nightmare.

At nine a.m., a man who stood in front of the judge's bench called out, "All rise! This court is now in session, the Honorable Judge William Smithers presiding."

Michelle got to her feet as a tall thin man in black robes came into the courtroom. He took his seat and, in a deep voice, instructed everyone to be seated.

For the first twenty minutes, Michelle waited while case after case was called. At some point Colson had taken a seat with a few other men and women in what Michelle assumed was the jury box.

When a case was called, one of these people would come and stand at the table to the left with a defendant. Once their case was dealt with, the lawyer would either leave the courtroom or go back to the jury box.

Finally, a door in front of Michelle and to her left opened. She got her first look at Eddie since he'd called her the night before.

He was dressed in an orange prison jumpsuit that appeared tight on his muscled frame. A scrape marred his tanned cheek. His hands were cuffed in front of him as a uniformed officer escorted him to the table. Colson was there to meet him.

Eddie didn't look her way and her heart sank. She listened as the man in front of the judge's bench rattled off a case number she forgot when he intoned the charges. Sexual assault. Murder in the second degree.

The judge spoke to the woman in the red skirt. "What is the prosecution's attitude about bail?"

"We request no bail due to the nature of the crime," the woman answered. Michelle hated her.

"Your Honor," Colson said, "My client has no previous record. His mother lives here in town. He doesn't own a passport. He is not a risk."

"I disagree," Judge Smithers said. "He is accused of a severe crime, and I've seen men jump bail on lesser charges." He picked up a piece of paper. "We will revisit the bail issue at arraignment in two weeks time."

Michelle was stunned. No bail? She wanted to say something, to protest, but the judge banged his gavel and they were leading her boy away from her.

She scooted off the bench and went past the first row, the low wooden barrier keeping her from going further. "Eddie!"

The gavel banged again but her son turned. She was shocked to see him frown and shake his head at her. She reached towards him, but he was too far away. With a shrug Eddie turned away from her and was escorted out of the courtroom.

Her vision blurred as tears burned her eyes. A light touch on her shoulder made her turn to see Colson standing next to her. "Let's go get that coffee," he said.

She turned to leave and noticed the trio of people were standing in the aisle, glaring at her. Puzzled, she looked behind her and wondered if they were staring at someone else.

At Colson's urging, she walked to the aisle and started to exit the building. As she passed the trio, she heard the young woman hiss, "He's a monster."

Annoyed, she started to turn back to confront the rude girl but Colson urged her on. She heard a man's voice behind her talking, but she only caught a part of his statement: "...won't bring Maddie back."

Michelle recalled that name. Wasn't Eddie dating a Maddie? And she was blond, too, like those women.

As she left the courtroom Michelle wondered if she'd just run into the alleged victim's family.

The café was small, with half a dozen round tables jammed inside. The pale yellow walls were covered with artwork from local artists. Here the air conditioning was working just fine and Michelle felt a chill on her bare arms as she and Colson walked through the glass door.

The lawyer led her to an unoccupied table near the rear of the building. "I'll get us some coffee. And would you like something to eat? They have cinnamon rolls that are wonderful."

She'd smelled the rolls when they walked in. The scent reminded her that she'd skipped breakfast that morning. "They smell fabulous. But I can pay..."

"Please, indulge me," Colson said with a smile. "My grandmother, God rest her soul, would be appalled if I allowed a lady to pay when I could do so."

"That's...a bit old-fashioned," Michelle said.

"Perhaps, but it is my policy," Colson said. "And you will be paying, Mrs. Travers. This could well be a difficult case."

Her heart sank at his words. "But Eddie isn't guilty."

"Why don't I get us that coffee and pastries?" Colson said. "How do you take it?"

"Two sugars and a splash of cream," she said.

Watching Colson go to the glass-topped counter to place the order, she tried to read his body language. She'd noticed how he changed the subject when she brought up Eddie's innocence, and it worried her. Did he think her son was guilty?

Maybe. But then again, he didn't know Eddie. *She* did. He didn't know how Eddie participated in church, leading singing and prayers. He had no clue about how kind he could be, remembering to call her several times a week and surprising her from time to time with flowers, since Edward Senior had died.

She'd explain that to Colson. Then he'd understand.

A few minutes later Colson returned with a red plastic tray. Steam rose from two brown mugs on the tray, and two cinnamon rolls the size of small saucers took up the rest of the room.

Colson sat down and handed over a mug and roll. "Here you go."

"Thank you," Michelle said. She took a sip of the coffee, the hot liquid burning her tongue. She didn't care, she wanted the caffeine jolt.

After taking a bite of his roll and a sip of his coffee Colson wiped his mouth with a paper napkin. "Now, I want you to know I've spoken with the District Attorney about this case. She might be willing to offer a plea bargain."

"A plea bargain?" Michelle asked. "But he's innocent."

Colson sighed. "Ma'am, I understand why you say that, but I don't know that for sure. The state seems to feel they have a case."

"It's a mistake," Michelle argued. "Eddie would never...he'd never to what they're saying he did."

Colson pinched the bridge of his nose. "I will consult with your son, of course, before I take any deal."

"Eddie isn't paying you. I am," Michelle said. "Don't I have a say in this?"

"That would be between you and your son," Colson said. "But

you are hiring me to represent him, and I can only offer you my best recommendations."

Michelle shook her head and took a savage bite of her cinnamon roll. "I'll talk to him," she mumbled around her mouthful of pastry.

"That would probably be best," Colson said. "I hate to bring this up, but there is the matter of my payment."

She wiped her fingers on a napkin. "I have it right here," she told him, picking up her purse. Thanks to Edward's life insurance, she had a little bit of a nest egg. For Eddie, she'd spend it all if she had to.

She handed over the check she'd scrawled out sometime that morning. "Do what you have to so Eddie can come home," she said.

Colson took the check and slipped it into a jacket pocket. "Please talk to your son, Mrs. Travers. And believe me when I say I am going to work in his best interests."

Because Sebring was a small town where murder was uncommon, the news of Eddie's arrest made the front page of the local paper the following day.

Michelle decided to read it while she was eating a breakfast of coffee and buttered toast. She got halfway through it before she pushed away the half slice of bread, her stomach clenching.

According to the article, neighbors had called the police reporting loud screaming coming from a home belonging to Maddie Acosta. The cops found Eddie in the house with the body of the victim cooling in the bedroom. Eddie had tried to run but was apprehended by the police and arrested.

The phone rang. Michelle decided to let the answering machine pick it up. It turned out to be a reporter for the paper wanting to talk to her. She shuddered.

It was Tuesday, and her Ladies Bible Class was meeting at the building at ten o'clock. Michelle decided she wanted to be out of the house, away from the telephone. She grabbed her Bible and her tablet and headed to Lemon Avenue Community Church.

She got there with a couple of minutes to spare. There were about fifteen women in the rectangular fellowship hall. A small kitchen was located at one end, to the left. Gray banquet tables and white folding chairs were set up in a classroom style. A white board dominated one wall.

The teacher, a younger woman named Annie Mullins, greeted her with a smile and a wave. Feeling a little better, Michelle put her things on one of the tables and headed back towards the kitchen to grab a cup of coffee before class.

Three women were talking on low voices by the small coffeemaker in the kitchen. As Michelle entered one of them was saying "...they spoiled him rotten."

Michelle froze. One of the women who was facing her paled and whispered something to the other two. They immediately fell silent, but Michelle could clearly see the copy of the newspaper in the hands of the woman who'd said Eddie was spoiled.

The woman who'd spotted her smiled, which did nothing to hide her discomfort. "Hello, Michelle. Want some coffee?"

Michelle found herself close to tears. "No, thanks," she stammered. She hurried out of the kitchen and grabbed up her purse, Bible, and tablet. Without a word she left the building, managing not to cry until she got to the car.

For now, Eddie was in the county jail, which was located near the courthouse. Michelle decided to go the day after the disaster at Ladies class. She was worried about Eddie. Hopefully he didn't get the paper in there.

She found herself in a long drab room that was bisected with a clear plastic divider. There were booths where one sat and talked to their loved one via a phone. The room smelled of sweat and Lysol.

Taking a seat in the hard plastic chair, she wished for her cell phone to look at while she waited. But per the instructions she found on the Internet she'd locked her purse and phone into the trunk of her tan Toyota Camry. She just had her keys and identification.

It seemed to take forever but finally Eddie was sitting in front of her. His expression was unreadable as he lifted his receiver. Michelle did the same. "Hello, sweetheart."

She watched as he swallowed before speaking. "Hi, Mom."

Blinking back tears, she said, "It's going to be all right, baby. I'm going to get you out of here."

"Mom..." Eddie took a deep breath. "I talked to the lawyer yesterday. The DA is offering me a deal. I could be out of prison in fifteen years. It wouldn't be life. Or worse."

"You shouldn't take it," she said quickly. "I told him I wanted him to fight for you."

"He *is* fighting for me. Mom, I'm going to take it."

"But you're innocent," she protested. "You shouldn't be here."

He glanced down at the counter in front of him. She saw he was shaking. Placing a hand on the divider, she said, "Look, I'll find another lawyer. One who will fix this."

"No, Mom."

"What do you mean, 'no?' This is your life we're talking about."

"I know," he snapped. He looked up at her and she saw how stormy his eyes were. "Mom, I'm gonna plead guilty."

"But...but you can't lie!" She was stunned.

He swallowed again and then muttered, "I won't be."

Michelle felt as if everything in her had frozen. For a moment, all she could do was stare. Then she shook her head. "No. You wouldn't. You weren't raised that way—"

"I did it, Mom," he said. "Do I have to get into the details to convince you? I'm guilty."

Michelle struggled to think. "But...*why?*"

He licked his lips. "She led me on, Mom. Then she changed her mind, said I wasn't good enough for her. I think she was cheating on me, too."

"That's not a reason to...to..." Michelle couldn't say it. Her grilled cheese sandwich twisted her stomach into knots.

"I lost it, okay?" Eddie said. "I'm a screw-up. I lost it and I'm gonna lose everything. At least this way I could get out of jail before I'm forty-five."

Michelle pressed a hand to her mouth. This wasn't happening. Couldn't be happening. "What...how...what did we do wrong?"

He rolled his eyes. "This isn't about you or Dad, okay? There's stuff you don't know about me, Mom. Maybe you'd better cut ties if you don't want to find it all out."

"Eddie!"

"I mean it," he said. "It's not gonna be pretty. And I can tell you hate me now. So maybe you should just stay away."

"I..." she was shaking. She couldn't think, needed time to figure this out..."I have to go."

"Okay," he said. He hung up the receiver and stood up before she could say anything else.

Before she could say she loved him.

Michelle asked a guard for directions to the nearest restroom. Once there she got into a stall, dropped to her knees, and emptied the contents of her stomach into the toilet bowl.

When she finished she sat back, panting. This was all wrong. It wasn't supposed to be like this. She'd raised him right. To do that...

Leaning against the side of the metal stall, Michelle wept.

Frank Weld was retired and lived with his wife, Betty, in a small house ten minutes away from downtown. It was a white frame with dark green trim. Rosebushes grew in the front yard, pink, white, and red blooms nodding in the sun.

Michelle hesitated at the door. Frank had said to come on over, but was she imposing? What if he was like the women in class the day before?

The green front door swung open and revealed Frank. The

balding older man wore a navy blue T-shirt and white cargo shorts. "Come on in, Michelle."

Still she wasn't sure. "I don't want to impose..."

"You're not," he said. "This is about Eddie, isn't it?"

She nodded as he led her to an oblong table that stood next to the sliding glass doors that led to an airy back porch. Betty was sitting at the table, sipping a glass of what looked like iced tea. She smiled as Michelle entered.

Michelle took the offered chair, across from Betty. Frank sat at one end of the table. He tilted his head towards Betty. "Is it okay if Betty stays?"

Betty had been in Ladies class but not one of the whispering women. Michelle shrugged. "I suppose. If you get the paper, I'm sure she knows about it already."

"I read it online," Betty said. "An awful thing for your family, Michelle."

"Before you start telling us why you needed to talk to me, would you mind if I opened with a word of prayer?" Frank asked.

"Of course not," Michelle said. She took Frank's and Betty's hands and listened as Frank prayed for her and for Eddie. She noticed he didn't ask God to get Eddie out of jail, but to give him strength to stay faithful.

When the prayer was finished, the couple looked at Michelle, waiting. She decided to take the plunge. With a deep breath, she murmured, "He says he's guilty."

Betty gasped softly. Frank shook his head. "I was hoping he wasn't, but I thought from the article there might be a chance. I'm so sorry, Michelle."

She started to cry. "What did we do wrong? Ed and I tried to bring him up right, tried to teach him the right path...he became a Christian..."

"Michelle. Michelle, look at me," Frank said.

She lifted her tear-stained face to the elder. When he had her attention, Frank spoke with conviction. "This is not your fault."

"But..."

"Eddie is an adult, not a child. He made his own decisions, and now he's got to live with the consequences," Frank told her.

Michelle wiped at her face. "I heard one of the women in class say we spoiled him..."

Betty clucked her tongue. "Michelle, that was unkind of her. And it was gossip. Who was it?"

"I'd rather not say," Michelle replied. "I don't want to get anyone in trouble..."

Betty sighed. "I think we should talk to Annie. She can explain to the class how they should act...it sounds as if some of them need that lesson."

Frank nodded. "I'm not saying you were a perfect parent, Michelle—none of us are. But you did the best you knew how to, you and Ed. It's not your fault Eddie tossed it away."

"He thinks I hate him," Michelle said. "When he told me...I was shocked. I had to leave."

"But you don't hate him, do you?" Betty asked.

"I'm so angry at him," Michelle admitted. She looked down at the table, noticing a couple of stray bread crumbs. Using a finger she began moving them around. "In fact, I could shake him."

"That is a normal response," Frank said. "Michelle, you have to make a choice. If you decided to disown Eddie, there are a few people who would think you were doing the right thing."

"But you wouldn't," Michelle said.

Frank got up from the table and left the room. He returned almost immediately with his black Bible in his hand. "You remember the story of the prodigal son?"

"Of course," Michelle said. "A man's son takes his inheritance while his father is still alive and wastes it on riotous living. He repents and returns to the father, who welcomes him back with open arms."

"Think a minute, Michelle," Frank said as he opened up his Bible. "The Bible says the father saw his prodigal while he was still a ways off. Do you think that was the first time he looked for him?"

"I have to admit, I hadn't really given it any thought," Michelle said.

"Then consider this," Frank said. "Did the father stop loving the son until he came back? Or did he continue to love him throughout that time he was away?"

"He still loved him," Michelle answered. She wiped at her wet face. "Can I have a tissue?"

Betty got up and returned with a box of tissues. "Now, you understand either way this will be a hard time for you. People will talk, as you learned."

Michelle blew her nose. "And what do I do about that?"

"Consider the source," Frank said. "And know in your heart the truth of the matter. People are going to say terrible things about Eddie. Some, from what you said, might be true. Talk to me and Betty. We aren't going to judge you."

"Not everyone will know what to say to you," Betty added. "Please be patient with us."

Michelle twisted the tissue in her hands. "I'll try."

"So." Frank sat back in his chair. "Let's have some iced tea and you tell us about the situation."

It took Michelle several days before she felt comfortable enough to return to the jail. During that time she prayed about the situation often, to the point she wondered if God was sick of hearing about it.

She sat with the Welds during Bible study Wednesday night and got through it without a meltdown despite the stares and whispers.

Now, back in another hard plastic chair, she waited for Eddie. While she did, she prayed some more. It couldn't hurt.

When Eddie saw her, his eyes widened and he stopped walking. He then hurried to the seat across from her and picked up the receiver. "You came back."

"Of course I did," she told him. "I love you, Eddie, no matter what."

"But Mom," he protested. "I know I'm a disappointment to you."

She gripped the receiver tightly. "Eddie, listen very carefully to me. Yes, I am disappointed in your behavior. But you are not a disappointment."

His gaze dropped to the counter in front of him. She watched a tear drop into the hard surface.

She softened her tone. "You're my son, and I will always love you. Yes, I want to help you get back on the right path. But no matter what, I will love you."

He lifted up his head and she saw him work to conceal his vulnerability. "Mom, I'm tough. I can make it fine."

"I know you can," she said. "But know that at least one person in this world will always love you."

"Even if I plead guilty?" he asked.

She'd prayed about that too, and she had a ready answer. "Yes. But come back to the light, Eddie. This doesn't have to be the end."

His free hand clenched into a fist. "I don't know if I can come back. Not after what I've done."

"Trust me, you can," she said. "And I will welcome you back when you make the journey."

There was a long moment of silence. Then he said, "Thank you."

Michelle blinked back tears. No, this wouldn't be easy. Given his crime, Eddie was not the most lovable person on the planet. And people would talk.

But unlovable or not, he was her son. And she would never give up on him. No matter what, she would always love him.

She hoped he would never forget it.

HENRY AND BETH AT THE FUNERAL HOME

JOE CRON

Joe Cron's diverse writing career comprises novels, short stories, essays, and theatrical productions, spanning some four decades of professional work. His short stories "Case Cracked" and "The Untimely Demise of Rachel Tamson" have appeared in earlier volumes of Fiction River. *Joe's most recent novel,* Alden Bridge, *has been praised by readers as a "wonderful tale of unconditional friendship and coming-of-age" and "his best work." You can visit Joe at joecron.com.*

When asked about the inspiration behind this story, Joe says that seeing the phrase "feel the love" resulted in so much exploding in his brain. "Warmth, humor, and romance, but also simple familiarity, the acceptance of flaws, and endurance through time." He said that he wanted to write something that captured, "through nothing but a snapshot of a conversation, those elements and perhaps more, shared between a couple with an undeniable and unbreakable bond forged over a lifetime."

The setting and the richly peppered nuances of dialogue do the perfect job of capturing all those things in this moment shared between Henry and Beth, which illustrates that lifetime bond of love in all its imperfect ways.

Henry Aberdeen sipped from a plastic glass of lemon-lime soda in a love seat at the Sternberg Funeral Home. Two glasses, actually, nested one inside the other, because the first one cracked and leaked when he picked it up. Sitting next to him, likewise holding a soda glass, but only one, was his charming and beautiful wife, Beth. To his immediate right, a small accent table. A little farther to his right, a brown casket where their long-time friend, Gerald, lay. Like Gerald, the Aberdeens were both in their mid-eighties, both slim—some would say frail, but Henry would argue they were in impressive shape for their age—and both in their usual, tasteful, dark blue visitation outfits.

Everything in the room was some type of predictable but disappointing brown. The beige walls were lined with simple, armless, uncomfortable wooden chairs; Henry was thankful there were also two nicely padded love seats on opposite walls near the casket. The carpet was dark brown, with a lighter brown diamond pattern in it, and the windows were all covered in medium brown curtains. Lots of funeral homes covered the windows like that, and Henry always wondered why. Seemed it would be more soothing to view a little bit of nature at a time like this, especially after they went to such lengths to wrap the place in earth tones. And why wouldn't they open the curtains? It wasn't like they were in danger of a renegade circus act running up to the windows or anything. No band of escaped convicts in orange jumpsuits jogging by to disrupt the mood.

There was plenty of color near the casket, owing to several huge, gaudy flower arrangements, and a number of smaller ones. Henry preferred the smaller. They were more elegant. A nice, simple expression of condolence. It was the thought that counted, not the size or expense of the presentation.

Henry and Beth had been to plenty of visitations over the years. Many were for people Henry considered more acquaintances or occasional friendships. Not this one. They shared a long, storied history with Gerald and his wife, Diane. She survived him, and was standing near the middle of the room in a black pantsuit, chatting and crying and giving courteous hugs to the two dozen or so visitors in attendance.

"Should we tell her?" said Henry.

"Tell her what?" said Beth.

"That you had an affair with Gerald."

"That'd be rich."

"What do you mean?"

"I don't know, I guess just that it would throw her for a loop before she goes. She's not far behind him, you know."

"You mean send her straight to her coffin, more like."

"Yup," said Beth. "The perfect murder."

"You'd have to do it today, in public. If you just went to her house and told her, everyone would know it was you."

"True. Still, a natural death. They couldn't pin it on me."

"But everyone would know."

"Yeah, but would that be bad? Half the people in this room would thank me."

Henry chuckled. "Probably."

"You?"

"What?" said Henry.

"Would you thank me?"

"What's that supposed to mean?"

"I know you like her."

"Liked. Past tense. I only have eyes for you."

"Yeah, I bet you say that to all the girls." Beth was silent for a moment. "She makes a hell of a lasagna."

"Good God, yes."

"That stuff would give you an orgasm just smelling it."

"We should talk her into making us one before she dies. Take the lasagna, then tell her about you and Gerald."

"Or six. We could freeze them."

Henry waved a hand faintly toward a very overweight man in a chair across the room, holding a plate in one hand and a half-consumed piece of coffee cake in the other. "See Randy? I bet she makes some for him."

Beth laughed softly. "He's got some frozen, for sure."

"Absolutely."

"When the police raid his house and open the ice chest, one side will be all body parts and the other side is all Diane's lasagna."

"Right. Then they go to his room and there's a shrine, with pictures of lasagna all over the walls with pins and string and stuff, and a little table with candles and an empty lasagna pan."

Beth was still laughing. "And the recipe in a frame."

"As if."

"That's true. If anything killed Diane, it would be that her lasagna recipe got into the wrong hands."

"You're one to talk," said Henry. "Your recipe book is an impenetrable fortress."

"You'd be the one suffering if anything happened to it."

"Agreed, but it's not the end of the world if someone made photocopies. You act like if somebody in Indonesia were capable of making your peach cobbler, all is lost."

"Well, they're my creations. I'm just protecting my patent. Maintains the mystique."

"Yeah, but then you gave one to Gary's mother. Stroganoff, I think. Could've knocked me over with a feather."

"Special case," said Beth. "She was grieving him. I was trying to help."

"I suppose. At least Gary won't get to eat your stroganoff any more. I never liked him."

"No, me neither."

"What? What do you mean, you never liked Gary? You married him, for cryin' out loud."

"Oh, *that* Gary. My first husband." She grinned and nodded. "Yeah, I liked him."

"What do you mean, *that* Gary? How many Garys do you know?"

"Well, there's—"

"Scratch that. How many Garys do we *both* know?"

"Just the one, I suppose." She sighed. "He was something else. That trip to Fiji was amazing."

"What?"

"That swimsuit, and the beach, and the mai tais..."

"Beth."

"What?"

"Snap out of it. That was me in Fiji."

"It was?"

"You and me went to Fiji. That wasn't Gary."

She paused. "Well, it certainly was amazing."

"It certainly was."

"I love you."

"I love you too, sweet pea."

There was a brief lull, and they each took a sip of their sodas, then Beth picked up the conversation again. "So, should we tell her?"

"Tell her what?" said Henry.

"That I had an affair with Gerald."

"You had an affair with Gerald? That'll be the day."

"Well, *now* I can't. He's dead."

"When on earth did you have an affair with Gerald?"

"What's wrong with you? Back before we were married."

"That was Gerald?"

"Yes."

"No way. That was Mark."

"Oh, good heavens, no," said Beth. "I was married to Mark. Husband number two. Married to Mark, and having an affair with Gerald."

"Honestly?"

"And you were married to your second, Brenda."

"Jeez, don't remind me."

"And I'm your third."

"Good Lord, I know that."

"Well, just in case you forgot."

"How could I forget that?"

"It happens."

"Never," said Henry. "Third time's the charm."

"That's for sure."

"Second time was more of a hex, really."

"Not as bad as your first."

"Becky? What was wrong with her?"

"Horrible cook."

"It's all about the food with you, isn't it?"

Beth curled a wry smile. "Not all."

"Well, okay. Touché."

"And it's all about the 'B' girls with you, isn't it?"

"What?"

"Becky, Brenda, Beth."

"Total coincidence."

"Your doctor is Belinda. Should I be worried?"

"If it keeps you on your toes. A little competition never hurt."

"Liar. You wouldn't do that in a million years."

"No need. Not when you already have the best."

There was a short silence, and another sip of soda for each of them.

"It makes me happy, you know," said Beth.

"What does?"

"That we found each other."

"Beth, we've known each other since grade school."

"I know, but we didn't really find each other, or recognize it, or admit it, or whatever you want to call it, until...when were we married?"

"Thirty-six years ago. I was fifty, you were forty-eight."

"Positive?"

"Yup. You've always been two years younger than me."

"No, smartass. The year."

"Yes. I told you then I was going to live to a hundred, so I could be married to you for at least half my life."

Beth smiled. "And how's that coming?"

"I'm still kickin'."

"Did you take your pills this morning?"

Henry had an awful, sinking feeling in his gut at the realization that he probably hadn't. Beth was not going to be happy at this, and he felt bad both for making her angry and for knowing he was about to receive a well-deserved berating.

"Ah, crap," he said. "I don't remember. I don't think so."

"Dammit, Henry, you've got to do that!"

"I know, I know."

"They aren't optional. They aren't a hobby."

"I know."

"You have to take them," said Beth. "You can't skip."

"Well, what else can I do?"

"You'll have to take them when we get home."

"But that'll be what, six?"

"We'll leave a little early. We can make it five o'clock."

"Then what?" said Henry. "Take my second batch at two in the morning?"

"If that's what it takes. You need those medications. All of them."

"All right, all right. I can set an alarm."

"Then we'll push tomorrow's out a little bit, and get you back on schedule the next day."

"Okay. Sorry."

"Don't apologize to me," said Beth. "It's *your* life you're playing with."

"Not really. We're in this together."

Beth's reply had an air of finality. "Well, then, act like it. Take your damn pills."

With that, Henry knew Beth wasn't upset with him anymore, and he was free to be playfully defiant with his next comment. "Fine, I will."

"Fine, you'd better," said Beth.

"Did you take yours?"

"You bet I did."

"Well, all right, then," said Henry. "Speaking of going home, is there enough gas in the car to get there?"

"Should be."

"And we don't have anywhere else to go this week, right?"

"Not that I know of. The budget is tight, but no more expenses right away."

"Okay, good."

Beth's tone got more thoughtful. "Henry, has it ever bothered you that we have to watch our money so closely?"

It honestly never had. Beth only worked part time and left that decades earlier, and Henry retired the moment they thought they could make it without his regular job income. He knew full well it meant meticulous budgeting for the rest of their lives, but choosing to have the time with Beth over more comfortable finances was a no-brainer.

"We're fine," he said.

"I know, but haven't you ever really just wanted to be rich enough to not worry about it every day?"

"I don't worry about it."

"Good. Me, neither."

"Are you sure?" said Henry.

"Yes."

"You know I don't need to live like Dirk McKaskill."

"Who's that?" said Beth.

"You know him, the guy, the owner of the Ranson Gaskets plant."

"Oh, right, the huge, stainless-steel house guy."

"We were there once for my company Christmas thing."

"Jeez," said Beth, "could that place have been more ostentatious?"

"Spent the whole time standing up 'cause I was afraid to touch anything."

"Who wants to live like that? Who wants to live in a house full of stuff you can't use?"

"Exactly," said Henry. "He probably tells the maid to turn the pages of his Neiman Marcus catalog so he doesn't have to come in contact with plebeian items like paper."

"Right," said Beth. "And has the chef analyze recipes in the lab so he can serve the exact balance of herbs from Madagascar so his poo smells like hyacinth."

"Yeah. No, thanks."

"Me, neither."

"My poo can smell like regular turds, thank you very much."

"And they do."

"Damn right." Henry's tone became more serious. "Look, I know we have to plan carefully all the time, but planning isn't the same thing as worrying."

"Not at all," said Beth. "I just want things to be right for you, and it wouldn't be right if you were spending your retirement years worried about money."

"We'll do whatever we have to. I'd live on ramen noodles in a refrigerator box as long as it was our box."

"I love you," said Beth.

"I love you, too, sweet pea."

"You think Dirk McKaskill eats ramen noodles?"

"Are you kidding me? Dirk McKaskill has never even seen the word 'ramen' in his life."

"Probably not."

"Dirk McKaskill wouldn't even rent his developments to people who have ever heard of ramen noodles."

"That's for sure."

"Speaking of which, did the rent get paid?"

Beth was silent for several seconds.

"Really?" said Henry.

"I meant to," said Beth.

"Oh, for cryin' out loud."

"I got it ready," said Beth. "It's in the envelope."

Henry could feel his irritation bubbling up, and he knew it was going to make Beth feel bad, but it put them in a difficult spot, and he couldn't keep from expressing his frustration. "Well, that doesn't help a lot, does it?"

"I'm sorry."

"It had to go today."

"I know."

"If it's not today, we pay an extra fifty bucks!"

"I know that."

"We don't have that to give."

"I'm sorry, Henry."

"What can I do?" said Henry. The scolding was over, and he was moving on to trying to fix the problem, but he still had a fair bit of consternation in his voice. "If I bug you about it, you think I don't trust you, but if I don't say anything, you forget."

"I can't help it."

"Well, we have to figure something out. This isn't working very well."

"I will. I can post a reminder somewhere. Something by the door or something."

"If I do that for you, is it okay? Can I do that without making you feel like I'm nagging you?"

"Yes, that would be good."

"All right, then," said Henry. He was calm now. "Don't worry about it. We'll figure it out. Where's the latest postal pickup?"

"The Frontier Avenue Station is five o'clock."

"Well, we can make that, actually, if we leave pretty soon. We're leaving early, anyway; we'll just back it up a little more so we can get the rent check and drop it at Frontier."

"I'm sorry."

"It's okay. We caught it okay. And if it costs us an extra fifty bucks some time, well, I'll just do some odd jobs for Dirk McKaskill."

"Such as?" said Beth. Henry was relieved that a touch of lightness was back in her demeanor.

"Maybe," said Henry, "he'd hire me to just sit on the floor next to him so he could look down on me."

"Or maybe you could thumb his nose for him. You could be his designated nose thumber."

"Sure. I'll have some cards printed up: *Henry Aberdeen, Professional Nose Thumber.* Decent retirement income to be had there."

"It's an unfulfilled niche."

Henry drank the last of his soda and placed his empty, nested glasses on the table next to him, then looked around the room some more.

"So, should we tell her?" said Henry.

"Tell her what?"

"That you had an affair with Gerald."

"Yeah, right."

"No, I suppose we shouldn't. That'd be cruel."

"Incredibly mean," said Beth. "She'd believe it."

"Of course she would. Why shouldn't she?"

"What are you talking about? You think Gerald and I had an affair?"

"Ha ha, very funny."

"You're delirious. I never had an affair with Gerald. Get serious."

"Really? What do you think you were doing before we got married?"

"Having an affair, but not with Gerald."

"Who, then?"

"Roger."

"Roger, the art professor?" said Henry. "You had an affair with Art Professor Roger?"

"It didn't last long, but it was a blast. Some people thought he was a little stuffy, but they've never been to Fiji with the man."

"Fiji?"

"Pulled out all the stops, that one. Wild man."

"You're the one who's delirious, my dear. That was me with you in Fiji."

"That was you?"

"Yes. You and I are who went to Fiji together. It was our honeymoon."

"Are you sure?"

"Positive."

"Well, then," said Beth, "all I can say to that is, well done."

"Thank you."

"I always wanted to honeymoon in Fiji."

"Yes, I know, and you did."

Beth turned her head to look at Henry. "You do know that I've always felt like our whole life together is a honeymoon, don't you?"

"I do, my love. Me, too."

"And I've never wanted an affair with anyone but you this whole time."

"I know. It's odd and wonderful. Everything we did before we married seems like another life. I look at people, even people right here in this room, and see some who struggled and divorced and were never sure, and it feels completely foreign to me. I have no concept of what's it like to not be sure. It might sound weird, but I kind of don't even think of you as a separate person."

"I know exactly what you mean," said Beth. "I'm not just Beth. Haven't been for thirty-six years. I'm Beth and Henry. Whatever we've been through, whatever we go through, there's never been a time when I considered we could be anything other than Beth and Henry."

Henry took Beth's hand softly in his. "Could be."

"What?"

"Could be something else."

"What are you saying?"

"Could be Henry and Beth."

"Ha. In your dreams."

"Just sayin'."

"Whatever lets you sleep at night."

"And you did have an affair with Gerald."

"What's that got to do with anything?"

"You said you didn't."

"Why would I say that? Of course I had an affair with Gerald. Me with Gerald and you with Diane, right before we decided to marry each other."

"That was Diane I was carrying on with?"

"Of course, silly. You don't remember the dinner party? The party to end all parties? You, me, Brenda, Mark, Gerald, and Diane all screaming at each other at the top of our lungs?"

"That does ring a bell," said Henry.

"And we had it all out," said Beth, "and Gerald and Diane decided to stay together?"

"Right. So she knows about you and Gerald."

"Knows? Hell, yes, she knows. There were times I thought that's all she knows."

"No need to tell her, then."

"Good heavens, no. I mean, it was ages ago, and I'm glad we all got over that stuff, but what a thing to bring up again with Gerald dead."

"Right. No need for that."

"Nope." Beth lifted her glass to her mouth and drained the last drops of her drink. "Let's get you home to take your pills and we'll pay the rent."

"Sounds good."

Their hands were still together, and Beth gently squeezed Henry's. "Then we can relax with a mai tai," she said, "and maybe one or two other things we did in Fiji."

"Fiji?"

"Oh, yes."

"What are you talking about?" said Henry. "I've never been to Fiji."

TRUTH AND LIES

DAVID H. HENDRICKSON

David H. Hendrickson's first novel, Cracking the Ice, *was praised by* Booklist *as "a gripping account of a courageous young man rising above evil." He has since published five additional novels, including* Offside, *which has been adopted for high school student required reading, and forthcoming,* Bottom of the Ninth.

His short fiction has appeared in Best American Mystery Stories 2018, Ellery Queen's Mystery Magazine, Heart's Kiss, *multiple issues of* Pulphouse, *and numerous anthologies. One of* Fiction River's *most popular contributors, his byline has appeared in seven of our volumes, with more to come. He is a multi-finalist for the Derringer Award, and his story "Death in the Serengeti," which appeared in the* Pulse Pounders: Adrenaline *volume of* Fiction River, *was honored with the 2018 Derringer Award for Best Long Story.*

When asked about the unique approach Dave took to this Feel the Love *story, he says: "I couldn't help thinking about the impossible-to-resist attraction to so many of the lies we tell ourselves. We can't stop loving them in spite of all our suspicions."*

The story is, at first, allegorical, but, like the lies that we choose to surround ourselves with, to believe and also to, in an obscure way, love, over the cold and hard truth that is so easily cast aside, it becomes more and more real.

I love Lies. She smells of roses. Dozens of red, red roses. Roses with nothing but petals.

No thorns.

She makes a bed of them for me to lie down on. She lies down beside me, holds me to her breasts, and coos sweet nothings into my ear. She strokes my cheek with the softness of a single, delicate fingertip. If she finds a tear there, Lies wipes it away. She wraps her arms around me, and in her embrace I am all I have ever hoped to be.

She tastes like honey. Sweet. Never bitter. Her skin, soft as feathers.

She wears short skirts. High heels. On occasion, fishnet stockings. Bright red lipstick on her soft, moist lips.

It's no secret. She has a tawdry reputation.

But what do I care? I am never happier than when I am with Lies. I wish I never had to leave her.

But when Truth arrives, wearing her starched white shirt, dark blue tie, and impeccably tailored Armani suit—black with a dark blue pocket square to match the tie—and sternly clicks her black Italian shoes, my beloved Lies must flee. She cannot bear the presence of Truth.

Neither can I.

Truth pretends to be my friend, putting an arm around me, giving my shoulder a squeeze, and smiling. But it's a hard, cold smile, one with no love, joy, or merriment in it. The smile of a sadist. A smile that condemns me to despair, condemns me to my own personal Hell.

"I'm doing this for your own good," Truth says, and grins her almost perfect smile. Perfect except that with its icy coldness it appears ready to crack like a sliver of a glacier cascading into the sea. Perfect except that her bright, white teeth are just a little too sharp. Perfect except that her black eyes stare at you, unblinking, and if you dare return the stare, you are drawn into their darkness as if they have no end.

I don't believe for a minute that Truth has interrupted my time with Lies for my own good. Truth says that she will set me free, but she cares nothing for me or my freedom. She hates Lies, and when she sees the two of us together, so very happy, Truth cannot stand it.

For my own good? Hardly. Truth is a sadist, ever seeking to inflict her pain, upon the likes of me—of everyone!—and upon Lies herself, who she sends scurrying into the shadows, unable to withstand her glare. It's a lust for pain that Truth can never fully satisfy.

And so she persists, each time driving Lies away.

My oldest memory of Truth and Lies was as a short, pudgy little child. Was I four, or five, or six? It does not matter. What matters is that I believed in Lies so fully, so absolutely, and she made me so very, very happy.

She came to me then in the form of Santa Claus. Laugh all you want. Mock me if you will. But I was happy! It was Christmastime and I helped my mother decorate the tree beside the staircase, dressing it with lights and bulbs of all colors and strings of silver tinsel. I squealed with delight when together we climbed the wooden stepladder and she helped me mount the glowing angel atop the tree. For weeks the house smelled of pine and home-cooked cookies: oatmeal and raisin, chocolate chip, and sugar.

I was an only child and thus had my own upstairs bedroom, small and cramped with cheap, second-hand furniture, the wood chipped and discolored with dark blotches sprinkled across its light brown hue. But it was mine. And in that little bedroom, musty with all its little boy smells, I had a dresser against one wall, a desk against the opposite one, and my bed in the middle. And I sat at that desk and wrote my letter to Santa Claus.

Unbeknownst to me, it was really to Lies.

Dear Santa, I printed in awkwardly drawn, scrawling letters. *I have tried very hard to be good.* I went on extolling my virtues that year while explaining the reasons behind my failings, certain that Santa would find merit in the one and understand the other. I then begged that he would bring me the red Schwinn bike I coveted, the one centered on page 235 in that year's Sears catalog. I even included the page number for Santa so there would be no mistake. I watched *Captain Kangaroo* on TV—never missed a show—and even the Captain agreed that there was no bike like a Schwinn.

I told Santa how I would use my spare baseball cards, the duplicates of bad players—worthless to me despite the intoxicating residual smell of the pink, flat stick of gum that came with each pack and even today takes me back to those cherished days—and I would do like Robby Comeau down the street and attach them to the spokes of the wheels so they would go *thwack, thwack, thwack* as I pedaled proudly down the sidewalk.

And when Christmas morning arrived, I flew down the steps so fast I almost tripped and fell, surely breaking my arm or wrist or neck, but I arrived safely at the landing, and there beside the wonderfully decorated tree was the most poorly disguised gift of all time, red and green wrapping paper around what was undoubtedly the red Schwinn bike from page 235 of the catalog.

I tore that paper off, shrieking with euphoric delight.

"Santa got my letter! Santa got my letter!" I yelled at the top of my lungs, as my parents looked on, my father's arm around my mother, and they shared my joy.

I was happy, so very happy, with what Santa—what *Lies*—had brought me.

It was pure bliss until Truth, in the form of Robby Comeau's older brother, informed me what a fool I was. It was *my parents* who had bought that bike, not Santa Claus.

There was no Santa Claus. No magical appearance from him on the night before Christmas in answer to my carefully constructed letter. Only stupid babies thought that.

A fistful of joy and all of the magic was ripped out of that red Schwinn bike.

By Truth.

Robby Comeau's older brother was right, of course. There was no Santa Claus. And I was just a stupid, little baby, who couldn't help crying at what I'd learned.

But I had been *so* delighted!

Truth hadn't been able to bear my happiness. She'd had to unmask Santa Claus—unmask *Lies*—as a fraud.

For my own good? Because it was time to *grow up*?

Already, I hated Truth.

Don't be a baby, I'm sure you're thinking. It was just Santa Claus. Every kid goes through that.

I don't disagree. I never said I was unique. In fact, I say the opposite. I am everyman. I am everywoman. Only the rarest exceptions walk among us.

We are all told we are special. We are all told we can be anything we want to be. Those are some of the sweetest nothings that Lies whispers in our young, gullible ears. So intoxicating, so hypnotic.

"You're special," we hear, and Lies kisses our forehead and rumples our hair as we hear those words. Words we want to hear. Words we *must* hear, for to think anything different—*"You'll never amount to anything! You're useless!"*—would be intolerable. No, we must hear, "You can be anything!"

When I first heard those words, I decided that I wanted to be an astronaut. I dreamed of floating weightlessly in space...of looking down upon the pale blue globe we call Earth...of walking on the moon, bouncing with every step like Neil Armstrong...of maybe even living on Mars and every night cleaning its dry, red grit from my spacesuit.

I dreamed it all until in the sixth grade nearsightedness forced me to get my first set of glasses, and Truth gleefully told me—I could sense the mocking glee even as the most fraudulent sadness covered her face and heavy-lidded eyes—that astronauts must have perfect twenty-twenty vision. Not a one wore glasses.

And so my dream of becoming an astronaut came crashing down to Earth.

I *couldn't* be anything I wanted to be. That lie was exposed.

But I was still special, wasn't I? Surely, that much still had to be true. I was special but had simply been misguided in my initial choice. No, I wouldn't—couldn't—be an astronaut. I'd instead be a point guard in the NBA.

And when I couldn't even make the junior high team, still short and pudgy and strikingly lacking in even the most modest athletic skills, I decided I'd become a leading actor in the movies. And after striking out with the Drama Club—"hopelessly wooden delivery" is the phrase I still recall, I decided, briefly, to become the President of the United States.

No sooner did I decide on a new "anything you want to be" choice than Truth squashed it beneath her Italian-shoed foot like a cockroach on cracked concrete, grinding the sole of the shoe over what remained of that dream long after the initial satisfying crunch.

Eventually, I fell in love with the guitar. At the age of seventeen, still short and pudgy and with a forehead dotted with acne, I fell for a Fender Stratocaster just like the one Eric Clapton used to play "Layla" while with Derek and the Dominos. And for the first time, Truth couldn't slap me down and stomp me underfoot.

I wasn't half bad and I was in love. I'd play that Fender until I got blisters on my fingers and then I kept going. I didn't play that guitar to impress others or to get girls, which was impossible because I was still distinctively unattractive.

I played it because of love. Love of music. Love of the instrument. Love of creating sounds that could maybe, some day, please-God-let-it-happen move people.

Soon, only the most highly trained ear could distinguish my "Layla" guitar solo from the master's. Same with "Stairway to Heaven" and "Free Bird." I learned 'em all.

God help me, I was in love.

I believed I was special. And while I might not be able to pursue the most fanciful of goals—astronaut to Mars, point guard in the NBA, the next Dustin Hoffman, or the President of the United States—I believed that now I could be whatever I wanted to be because I had found my true calling. I would be a musician, a guitarist, who would create art people would appreciate, enjoy, and remember.

This was within my reach. I was, after all, special.

And so I spent decade after decade pursuing that dream. Traveling the country. Getting ripped off by one bar owner after another. Getting ignored by one drunk after another. Living hand to mouth. Missing so many meals that I was still short but no longer pudgy. I took on the near emaciated look of the severely addicted, though I never once touched any drug.

I kept going long after every chord of common sense screamed in a cacophonous howl that I was wasting my time.

In the end, I wasn't special. Not at all. I was a dime a dozen. If that. Whether performing alone or part of a band. Whether the front man or back in the shadows.

In the approximate words of more than one bar owner after he stiffed me my fair due, "There are a million, billion guys like you. As soon as one of you drops dead, another ten come along to take your place. It don't matter to me. It don't matter to no one."

Believing that I was special, believing that I could be what I so desperately wanted to be—*believing Lies*—I gave my all. In the process, I forfeited all attempts at true love. I even wrote a song about it, "You're Never Home, and I Got Lonely." Not a half bad song and with a catchy guitar riff in the middle, if I may say so myself. But other than a whole lot of drunks in a whole lot of bars, hardly anyone heard it. And seems like no one remembers it at all.

No, don't get me started about true love. Don't you *dare* get me started.

And what did I end up with when it was all said and done?

I'm broke. In every which way. Financially, to be sure. I'll never pay off the hospital bills. But my body is also broken. Hands and fingers now arthritic. The ringing of tinnitus roars in my ears all day like an aural stabbing, the payday for years of turning the volume up to the max.

Nobody remembers me or my music. Whatever joy I gave those who heard me play is forgotten, and perhaps never even existed in the first place.

I wasn't special at all.

Not one bit.

"Only the very select few are special," Truth says to me in a tired tone usually reserved for speaking to simpletons. "That's what makes them special."

Over and over, she says those words, mocking the gullibility of my youth when I believed that I truly was special, and even worse, that same gullibility that continued as an adult.

I'm a fool. At last I know it.

"Acceptance is the first step," Truth says, not fully suppressing a smirk. Then she adds with that duplicitous gleam in her eye, "I'm only trying to help."

The end is near. I've run the full gamut. I lie in my deathbed, gaunt almost to the point of skeletal, my breathing agonized and wheezing, like an accordion being drawn slowly in and out. My ragged clothing is drenched in sweat, both old and new. The sheets reek of urine.

I am, of course, alone. Alone except for Truth.

Would that I be alone.

"You've wasted your life," she says. "You're going down into the ground. Worm food. Ashes to ashes. Dust to dust. Nothing more remains. Your light will be extinguished, and no one will remember."

And then finally, she leaves, whether as one final parting mercy or, far more likely, because there's no more sadistic sustenance to suck out of my marrow.

And so I call for Lies to come join me. I plead. I've never needed her more.

Lies, I beg of you, come to me now, I cry out in a deathlike rasp, my mouth and lips dry. Tell me that I was special, even if I was not. Tell me that I will be remembered, even if I have already been forgotten. Tell me that I had worth even if that was no more than a dime a dozen.

I was special! I need to hear it! You can't whisper those words to me when I am young and then fall silent now!

And then I feel her presence all about me. The smell of her roses.

The stroke of her feather-soft fingertips upon my cheek. Her kisses upon my ears.

Thank you! From the bottom of my heart, thank you for not abandoning me now.

I love you, Lies. I have always loved you. I have worshipped you all my life.

Lie down beside me now. Forgive the rank smells of death. I can do nothing about them.

Here. Right here. Yes.

Hold me. Forgive me for shaking.

Yes, that is good. Yes.

Now whisper into my ears those sweetest words of all. Tell me that something other than darkness awaits me. It need not be eternal bliss. Perhaps a chance to live it all over again, and next time get it right. Next time, I can be special. Or eternal bliss. That would be best of all. Of course, eternal bliss!

Anything but the darkness.

Yes, I can see the bright light coming for me.

Thank you, my sweet, sweet Lies. Thank you.

It is coming closer now. Closer and closer still.

Bless you for giving me this one last relief. Anything but the darkness.

Lies, I have always loved you. You are the sweetest and fairest of them all.

I will always remember you. Somewhere in your loving heart, Lies, please remember me. Even if you won't, please say that you will.

WITH LOVE IN THEIR HEARTS

ROBERT JESCHONEK

Robert Jeschonek has an eye for the unusual. His futuristic tales are unique and strange, yet always full of heart. His decidedly unique style of fiction appears in the tales "In the Empire of Underpants" in Fiction River: No Humans Allowed, *in "Piggyback" in* Fiction River: Feel the Fear, *and in six other volumes of* Fiction River. *You can also find his envelope-pushing fiction in* Galaxy's Edge, Escape Pod, Pulphouse, StarShipSofa, Tales from the Canyons of the Damned, *and many other publications. Apart from these stories, he has also written official* Doctor Who *and* Star Trek *fiction as well as* Batman *and* Justice Society *comics for DC Comics.*

"If there's one thing humans excel at," Robert says about the story, "it's rationalizing behaviors that go against their moral compass. If doing something dark will satisfy a need, we have a seemingly infinite number of ways to justify it, to come up with workarounds for laws and morality that enable us to keep our consciences clear while still getting what we want at the expense of others." This is the type of flexibility that has helped humankind survive and ultimately dominate the Earth. Robert wanted to explore that in this story.

The story opens with a startling juxtaposition; the statement of love towards an enemy in the heart of a violent attack. The tale continues to make the reader reflect on the concept of love, and the various ways love can be incorporated into a life's mission, exploring the idea of "a love that kills" in an entirely new way.

I love you!" Hissing the words through the blood in my mouth, I lunge at my opponent. And I *mean* those words with all my heart —I *have* to—even as I swipe my dagger across his chest.

As he dances back out of reach, a line of red opens up where I cut him. His dirty, bearded face clouds...then quickly clears. "I love you *more!*" He smiles as he leaps at me with both fists forward, aiming them like a battering ram at my face.

Beaming with all the affection I can muster, all the true sweet regard for my friendly fellow man, I spin around out of his way and tag him again with the dagger, plugging the blade deep in his left kidney.

Howling, he stumbles into the thick-trunked oak that was just at my back. He takes it headfirst and bounces off, weaving drunkenly in the mud.

"Friend warrior." This is how I finish him, all sweetness and light. Without the *slightest* shred of darkness in my heart. "You are like unto the finest flower in the brightest sunbeam on the loveliest day in all the year." Darting to one side, I duck down and recover the sword I dropped earlier in this battle—dearest Eros. "God bless you for bringing such *joy* to my life."

With that, I swing the sword up, then down and through his neck with a perfect, practiced stroke.

So good am I at this that not a *trace* of hatred or savage satisfaction punctuates the moment when his head separates from his shoulders and plops into the muck.

Breathing hard, I scan my surroundings. I see the bodies of the three men I've killed, sprawled in various bloody contortions...and the body of Vicka, my partner on the road until now, whom they killed before I could kill them first.

That is what love can accomplish. Its power is arrayed around me for all to behold.

Moving swiftly lest another patrol comes my way too soon, I secure my beaten black body armor, then retrieve and put on my battered helmet with the old red-white-and-blue banner etched into the hard plastic. I retrieve my motorbike, too...but the front tire has been slashed, and it won't start. I guess I can't complain; it's over a century old, and I've gotten a lot of use out of it until now.

"Go with God, fair machine." I drop it in the muck, grab my dagger from the dead man's kidney, and set off at a brisk jog through the woods. The autumn sun is closing in on the horizon, and I need to make my destination by nightfall.

Everything is riding on the completion of my mission. All my people down in Burytown are counting on me to succeed.

Though it is hard to imagine I *can* succeed this time. The killing of men and women has always come easy to me. It is *that* very inclination that could make this new mission such a challenge.

Heart pounding, I run through the mud, brush, and leaves, ever up along the steep contour of the mountainside. This part of what was once known as the state of Pennsylvania is full of such mountains—the *Alleghenies*, as we call them yet today. They have been my home for all five and twenty years of my life, and navigating them is second nature to me.

Reading the wind and the angle of the sun, I know I'm not far from my goal. In spite of the best efforts of my attackers, I will reach my destination, though what happens after that, I cannot say.

Finally, I burst from the woods and find myself at the edge of the old road. I also find myself face to face with two men in camouflage body armor, wielding six-guns.

Slowly, I take off the helmet. "Greetings to you both."

"Hail and well met, good stranger!" The one doing the talking has the biggest, friendliest smile...and the steadiest grip on his revolver. "State your name and purpose, that we may love you all the better!"

Instinctively, I meet his gaze with the most genuine grin I can muster. "I am Sir Gardner Schell of Burytown," I tell them. "I have come to meet my bride."

Expected as I am, the sentinels holster their guns and lead me through the barricades blocking the road. On the other side, my destination awaits—a place I've only visited a handful of times, though Burytown lies but seven miles to the west of it.

The building looks for all the world like an old ocean liner (the kind I've seen only in photos), complete with decks, portholes, and a pair of big smokestacks on the roof, angled toward the stern. It is as if, by some miracle, a seagoing vessel has been stranded in the heights of a mountain range, along the curve of a once-great highway that has seen better days.

GRAND VIEW SHIP HOTEL. That's the old name of it, painted in big black letters on the side of the ship facing the road. *SEE 3 STATES AND 7 COUNTIES.* That's painted on the prow. Armor plating has been added all around, but those words out of history remain.

The *real* name, the one it's known by now, is not painted anywhere. But ask anyone within fifty miles of here if they know of Kendall's Keep, and they will point you right to it. Everyone who uses this stretch of road—known in olden times as the Highway of Lincoln—must pay a toll to Kendall's men to pass this point.

"What took you so long?" Lord Rubicon Kendall strides out of the keep in a white sea captain's uniform, looking hale and hearty and overly friendly. A sword hangs at either hip, plus a long rifle at his back, and rightly so; his clan is at war. "You were expected *this morning,* good sir knight."

"If not for the *second* ambush, I most certainly would have been here sooner. And Vicka, my late retainer, as well." I point at the path that I traveled up the slope. "The *Loved Ones* grow ever bolder, my Lord."

Rubicon grins through his neatly trimmed ebony mustache and goatee. "It is a delight we have in common, yes? Your people down in Burytown have been *especially* showered with their affections, have they not?"

"Such a blessing." I say it stiffly, though I manage a smile. The siege of Burytown is my whole reason for being here. An alliance with Rubicon's clan would give us the punch we need to break the siege and lay our friends the Loved Ones to rest for good.

Though such an alliance does not come without a price.

"I am in your hands, my Lord." I bow my head and spread my arms. "Assuming our pact yet stands."

"It does. My Lady Kendall, God rest her soul, had people in Burytown. I am only too happy to offer you this chance." He lays a hand on my shoulder. "*If* you are ready for the challenge, Sir Gardner."

"I would not be here if I were not."

"Well said." Rubicon nods sagely, peering into my eyes with the focus of a hawk. "And would you accept the guidance of an advisor in this quest of yours? He was of much help when *I* was in your shoes."

"Thank you, my Lord, but that won't be necessary."

Rubicon cocks his head to one side, looking amused. "May he provide a *benediction*, at least?"

Before I can answer, an old man rises on the main deck on the second level of the ship/keep and clears his throat. "Let us pray," he calls down to us. Like Rubicon, he wears a uniform, though the pieces don't go together well: white cap, black jacket, red ascot, lemon trousers.

Confidentially, Rubicon leans over and whispers to me. "Bon Cloister up there will perform the ceremony, you know. *If* there *is* one."

"In the century since the Great Collapse," says Cloister, "only *love* has sustained we few survivors. As this young knight stands on the precipice of the greatest struggle of all—holy wedlock—we pray that he may turn to *another* face of love and do what we all know he *must* do to succeed."

"Amen." Grinning, Rubicon smacks me on the back.

"Times a million," says Cloister as he digs out a pipe and lights it with a hellaciously long furnace match.

"Here we are." Rubicon leads me past armed guards into the keep, then down a short hallway. "Have a seat in the Coral Room, Sir Gardner."

We enter a room with turquoise walls and red-rimmed portholes. A polished wooden bar occupies most of one side, with a black-cushioned elbow rest and pink-upholstered barstools with backs. Dusty glasses and bottles line shelves behind the bar, glinting in the last flickers of daylight slipping in from the windows in the dining room next door.

I sit on a long red bench against the opposite wall. A knight must *never* sit with his back to the door, as I have learned the hard way.

Just then, I hear footsteps—hard shoes descending a staircase.

"Here she comes." Rubicon smiles and bounces on the balls of his feet. "Good luck to you." He winks and whispers that last.

My heart beats fast as the footsteps approach down the hallway. I have fought a thousand battles, but this is new ground for me.

"Sir Gardner." Rubicon steps aside and gestures at the doorway. "I introduce my daughter, Listy Kendall."

I rise as she enters the room. Never in my life have I seen anyone so *beautiful*.

Listy curtsies. "Sir Gardner." She is in her early twenties, with all the firmness of youth in her pale, porcelain skin. Loose, dark curls frame an oval face with lively eyes, delicate nose, and full red lips. I can see from the fall of her long, creamy gown that her body is perfectly sculpted, bust and hips swelling pleasingly above and below a slender waist.

I manage a bow, but words fail me. Entranced, I can but stare as she watches and waits, smiling.

Rubicon raises an eyebrow and gestures at the bar. "Perhaps you might like a drink, Sir Gardner?"

His question barely registers. I am spellbound.

"My father has pledged my hand to you, good knight," says Listy. "It might do us well to converse upon this betrothal, don't you think?"

Her voice, as soft and flowing as the song of a meadowlark, freezes me further. I am drawn to her, mesmerized as I have never been before—yet locked down as if shackled and gagged. A man of action I have always been, but now I am turned to stone.

And none of it makes any sense to me.

"Ha. I wondered if this might happen." Rubicon walks over and squeezes my shoulder. "Perhaps some time with Bon Cloister might not be a bad idea *after* all, sir knight."

Fresh air does me some good. As I stand at the railing of the keep's main deck and watch the sun set, my wits slowly return to me.

Without invitation, Bon Cloister shuffles over to stand beside me, lighting a fresh pipeful of tobacco. Up close, I see how withered he is, how ancient in his shabby hodge-podge uniform.

"What is the Story of Love, Sir Gardner?" He puffs twice on the pipe, then exhales sweet cherry-smelling smoke from his nose. "Tell me how love as we know it came to be."

Everyone knows this story, but I humor him. I'm embarrassed about what happened in the Coral Room and eager to make things right.

"One of the plagues of the Great Collapse in the Twenty-First Century was *The Commandment*," I tell him. "Scientists unleashed a contagion to rewrite human DNA and bring about peace on Earth."

"How so?"

"People became physically unable to harm others out of hatred or anger. This was in fulfillment of Jesus Christ's commandment to love thy neighbor as thyself."

"Indeed." Smoke from Cloister's pipe drifts out over the vast landscape sprawling beyond the mountain. The setting sun casts blazing light over the acres of trees in their red, gold, and orange autumn finery. "And how did that work out when the *other* plagues struck, and civilization *collapsed?*"

"It made it nearly impossible to fight for survival."

Cloister smiles. "And so we learned to fight—to *kill* if need be— the only way we *could*. With *love* in our hearts." He pulls the pipe from his mouth. "And we got very *good* at it, didn't we? The love-that-kills?"

I nod.

"*But!*" Cloister jabs the pipe stem at me. "What happens when we get so *good* at it, we forget what it's like to feel the *love-that-cherishes?* For some, especially the more...*accomplished* warriors, like yourself... this can sometimes lead to profound...*disharmonies.*"

"The love-that-cherishes?" I scowl.

"Caring for someone so much that we *don't* want to damage or murder them," says Cloister. "Feeling an attraction so *real* and *profound* that we want to join with the other person in a multitude of ways."

The song of the katydids buzzing in the trees makes more sense to me than what he's saying. "Is that even possible?" I ask.

Cloister narrows his eyes. "Do you *want* it to be?"

I think of my people in Burytown, who are depending on me. I think also of that beautiful girl in the Coral Room, and the way she seemed to glow when I gazed at her. "Yes." I whisper the word. "But how?"

"Righteous discipline." Cloister clenches his right hand. "And self-control. You must reach deep within yourself and change the love-that-kills to the love-that-cherishes...but *only* for this one person, your bride. For all others, especially those who threaten kith or kin..." He unclenches his hand and draws the edge of it across his throat like the blade of a knife.

Frustrated, I close my eyes and clench my teeth. I feel like going over the rail and running off into the night with Eros in hand, ready to love all comers. That, at least, would not be like the great unknown I now face.

"So many feelings..." I grip the rail hard. "What if I can't *master* them, Bon?"

"Then your bargain with Lord Kendall will never be consummated." Cloister puts the pipe back in his mouth and puffs on it. "For neither he nor Listy herself shall brook a union where there is no *true* affection."

"Damn." I toss my head as if I'm trying to wake myself from a terrible dream. "I don't even know where to start."

"There are some mental drills that might help." Cloister pats me on the back. "Perhaps we can get you ready for tomorrow morning."

"What's happening tomorrow morning?"

"Your first date," says Cloister. "Also, if all goes well, your marriage proposal."

I wake, as always, before dawn, springing to full alertness with all the force of old habits. Sleeping too soundly or late can get you killed in the field, after all.

I wash up in a basin of tepid water in my room, then dry and dress. Looking out the window, I see it's still dark outside...but won't be for long. I am early for this morning's meeting, which is just how I like to be.

In this, Listy Kendall and I have something in common. When I arrive on the main deck, she is waiting there already, setting up an easel and palette of paints by the light of an oil lamp.

"Good morning," she says, waving a brush in my direction. "I trust you slept well, Sir Gardner?"

My heart races, and words catch in my throat. She looks as lovely as she did when we first met, in the Coral Room...and I feel just as frozen, just as shackled by conflicting emotions.

But then I run one of the exercises Cloister taught me, repeating these words in my head: *Kindness is not always hatred. Hatred is not always kindness.*

Something about that simple repetition weakens the bonds just enough for me to speak. "Yes, I did sleep well." It isn't much, but I consider it a victory.

"Glad to hear it." She strokes a rich red base on the canvas as the sky begins to brighten. "You don't mind if I paint, do you? It's going to be such a lovely autumn morning."

"Not at all." I can barely force out the words. The way her lacy white blouse clings to her breasts, and her black britches hug the curves of her hips and bottom, I have trouble focusing on the conversation at hand.

"So, Sir Gardner." Listy swirls in white with the red, stirring it into a deep pink color. "What hobbies do *you* have?"

C-Love, not K-Love. That's another exercise Cloister taught me. *C-Love, not K-Love,* as in *the love-that-cherishes,* not *the love-that-kills.*

"Well..." I fight for focus. "I sharpen my *blades* in my spare time. And train younger knights in battlefield techniques."

"Sounds more like *work* to me." Listy tips her head and gives me a funny look out of the corner of her eye. "Do you ever court *maidens*, I wonder?"

I feel myself blush. *C-Love, not K-Love. C-Love, not K-Love.* "I, uh... no, I..." In spite of the mantra, my brain locks up, and my voice trails off.

"Oh, look." Listy pauses in dabbing at the canvas and gazes out at the scenery, mouth open in wonder. "Come here, Sir Gardner."

I step up beside her, following her gaze with my own. The sky, by now, is fairly bright, so the vast gulf below is awash in predawn light —but it appears not at all as it did the evening before. Everywhere I look, instead of swaths of colorful trees and distant green fields, I see an expanse of mist blanketing everything.

"I love when it's like this." Her voice is low and soft. "My grand-father used to say it was like an ocean of cloud out there. He half-expected to see a dolphin jump out of it, he said." She bumps my arm with her elbow. "Not that he was *biased*, living in a ship on the mountain and all."

"Three states, seven counties." Lost in the view, I get my voice back. "It's as if they've disappeared."

"They're still out there. They always are." Her elbow nudges my arm again. "You just can't *see* them."

Staring into that milky abyss, I let my imagination run away with me—something I rarely do. "It's more like Heaven than an ocean," I say, though I've only ever seen photos of oceans or paintings of Heaven.

When a bird pops out of the mist nearby, it startles me back to reality. I become fully aware of Listy's body next to mine, her elbow against my arm...and that triggers the kind of reaction I had before.

Even as it happens, I hate myself for it. Burytown is in dire need; am I so *damaged* that I can't at least *bluff* my way through the one chance I have to *save* it?

Yes, apparently.

Stumbling back from the railing, I knock over a chair and almost fall. Listy turns, a look of pity on her face that somehow makes it all the worse.

"S-sorry..." All my life, love has been a weapon. Feeling it has always been a pretext, a preamble to some kind or other of blood-bath. Thinking of it now *not* as a means to murder feels *wrong...confusing.*

Yet it's *there*...a *whisper* of that *other* love that Cloister talked about. And the more I feel it, *the more I don't know what to do with it.*

Listy seems to have no such difficulty—unless, of course, she isn't feeling C-Love toward me in the first place. She seems perfectly comfortable in all our interactions, even as I find myself intensely off-balance.

I'm sweating as if I'm in a fight, and my belly's full of butterflies. I wish I'd never come here, opening myself up to all this confusion- - even if staying home would have meant certain death without the alliance I'd hoped to find.

Time is running out for that home of mine...though just how quickly, I only now discover.

The door to the deck flies open, and a dark-skinned woman stalks through, heaving for breath. She is a woman I *know*, a messenger from Burytown called Polly Sullivan.

"Sir Gardner!" She gasps out the words. "I bring word of Bury-town! Its downfall is *imminent.* This very day, your precious *home* shall fall to the *wolves* at its doorstep."

I slide Eros down into his scabbard with the scrape of metal against metal. I do the same for the rest of my blades, slipping them into their various sheaths with familiar, practiced ease.

Standing in the middle of my room, I take a deep breath and release it. Everything is in its place again, and the world makes sense. My course is clear and straight, and my heart is filled with so much *love* for those who threaten my home.

Nodding to myself, I snatch my helmet from a hook on the wall, then storm out of the room and down the stairs. Lord Kendall, Bon Cloister, and Listy wait at the bottom, between me and the exit.

"Ho, sir knight." Rubicon raises both hands as if to hold me back. "We have heard with deep regret the terrible news from Burytown."

"Save your regret for the Loved Ones," I tell him. "For I go now to shower them with my deepest affection."

"Of course," says Rubicon. "You have concluded your business with us in full, then? Shall I signal my man-at-arms to rally the forces we have pledged you?"

I spare a glance at Listy, who bears a troubled look on her face. There is a pull deep within me, a gravity catching at my heart—but other powers overwhelm it.

"Good sir, the people of Burytown shall humbly welcome any and all forces pledged to act in their interest. But it is not true that our business is concluded." I bow my head. "I have yet to fulfill the terms of our pact."

"And *will* you?" asks Rubicon.

I feel Listy's frown upon me as I speak. "If Burytown's state is as dire as Polly Sullivan reports, I cannot promise anything. My own future might be exceedingly brief."

"Then, regrettably, I cannot offer aid," says Rubicon.

"Father!" snaps Listy.

Rubicon slashes his hand through the air. "We risk *much,* sending so large a force away from our own battlements. We risk this very *keep* and all who *depend* on it. We cannot—*will* not—take that risk without a *pact.*"

"But *I* am the *currency* in this pact, am I not?" says Listy. "Have I *no say* in this..."

Rubicon cuts her off. "The pact is *everything.* In this world, *bargains* are how we *survive.*" He shakes his head at Listy, then me. "Let me ask you this, Sir Gardner. Is there *no* possibility of forging a love-that-cherishes between the two of you?"

"I can perform a ceremony here on the spot," says Cloister. "A bond of wedlock so hastily conceived shall be *no* less legitimate."

I look at each of them in turn, considering. Again, when my eyes meet hers, I feel that pull, like the current of a river...but then that *other* force rises up and blots it out. K-Love wins out, as well it should. My people *need* me.

"It is not fair to the people of Burytown to linger one moment more as their home falls to invaders," I say. "And it is not fair to *you* to take your hand in wedlock if I might make of you a widow before this day is done." I bow to Listy. "As much as I might wish it could be otherwise."

"But you are *more* likely to live another day with Lord Kendall's forces at your back," says Cloister.

"And what kind of man would I *be* if I married this woman to save my own *neck?*" Impulsively, I reach for Listy's hand and kiss it. "That does not sound to me like anything *close* to a love-that-cherishes."

I let go of her hand...yet my next words are intended only for *her* ears. "Farewell. Perhaps we shall meet again in that heavenly ocean of mist."

With that, I square my shoulders, push past Lord Kendall, and march outside into the late morning sunlight. Polly, who's been waiting, kickstarts her motorbike and revs it loudly as I don my helmet and climb on behind her.

Then, in a cloud of dust and gravel, we spin around and fly down the highway away from Kendall's Keep.

It surprises me how much I think of Listy as we ride down the mountain. The memory of kissing her hand stays with me, as does the memory of gazing into the mist by her side with her elbow resting against my arm.

But when the time comes to banish her from my thoughts, I do. The field of battle, as I understand all too well, is no place for thoughts of C-Love...only K.

Polly and I dismount and stow the bike a mile back from Burytown, then travel the rest on foot. The sounds of the fight reach us as we hurry through the woods—the clash and clang of steel, the scattered blasts of pistols and rifles, the screams of the wounded and dying.

Then the fight itself reaches us, too. Within sight of the rooftops of town, we are set upon by a trio of Loved Ones, soaked in gore and whipped into a frenzy.

"I *love* you!" A red-bearded warrior leads the ambush, swinging a blood-smeared ax overhead. "I will *show* you *how much!*"

Adrenaline burns in my bloodstream as I slip Eros from his scabbard and stand ready to meet the charge. "*Come* then, brother, and let us *see* who has the *most* love to *give!*"

They attack us like men possessed, half-crazed with K-Love stoked to extreme levels by relentless bloodletting on the field of battle. But Polly and I are possessed by a love that's as strong or stronger and untainted by corrupt motives. Our unwavering brand of love, born of devotion to home and clan, can carry the day against even the longest odds.

Though even as loving as we are, the odds we now face are long indeed. After ending the first three fighters with great love and swordsmanship, Polly and I push closer to the heart of the battle— just in time to see a horde of Loved Ones break through the line of defenders at the edge of Burytown.

People we know go down fighting as the invaders pile on. Every one of our noble warriors smiles with no less loving kindness even as blades, bullets, and war hammers put them to rout.

It is now that I think of Listy once more, for I realize I shall never see her again. With the perimeter breached and our forces so clearly outnumbered, Burytown has not long to live.

Smoke fills the air as flaming arrows set fire to rooftops. Men and women on horseback and motorbikes tear through gaps in the line, escorted by slavering hounds. It is the end of the world, *my* world, and all the smiles and proclamations of love make it all the more hellish.

Doomed as our home may be, Polly and I charge into the fray with smiles and swords flashing.

K-Love, not C-Love. K-Love, not C-Love. Eros swirls and whizzes in my good right hand, slipping through one throat after another. In my good left hand, a dagger jabs and slashes, cutting faces, hearts, and guts like the fang of a dragon.

No mercy is shown, not a whit...though even as my blades sow mayhem, I feel only deep-down love for every soul I maim or kill.

I am, in these moments, perfection—my focus diamond-hard, my killing exquisite, my love unblemished. Dancing from one fighter to the next, leaving geysers of blood in my wake, I am like a holy angel, beaming and unstoppable.

But for every man or woman who falls before me, another three or four or more pile in. For every blow or cut that I deflect, another flurry rains down on me.

I swear I will fight to the last, but the outcome is set in stone now. The end is near.

Polly and I fight back to back, swords and daggers in constant motion—until suddenly, she is gone. Turning in my murderous gyre, I see her dragged under the bloodthirsty tide, and I move to save her.

But at that moment, someone gets in a lucky shot across my back with a crowbar, and I drop. Keeping hold of my blades, I twist, blindly sweeping Eros in a futile swath that catches nothing.

When I hit the ground, the horde closes in around me. *Love you love you love you,* chant dozens of voices overflowing with eager and deeply sincere affection.

I see the crowbar and other bludgeoning weapons hoisted over-head, ready to crash upon me like a landslide. Holding fast to the handles of my blades, I ready myself for one final fusillade to finish the day, one last statement to cast upon the canvas of this terrible work.

"I love you!" I howl the words at the top of my lungs. *"I love you from the bottom of my heart!"*

It is then that I hear a salvo of gunshots crackling nearby. Men topple around me like rotten fruit, dropping their bludgeons.

More clamor then—a thunder of footfalls, a clatter of blades. More gunshots and the twanging of bowstrings, the sizzle and *thunk* of arrows. More men and women fall, and the rest erupt in panic.

Seizing the opportunity, I leap to my feet and pick up where I left off, slashing and stabbing in every direction. As Loved Ones fumble and scatter, I clear them like chaff.

A giant of a man, bald as a pumpkin and bedecked in blood, refuses to panic and swats the helmet right off my head. I answer with a knife through his windpipe...just as a sword thrusts through his heart from behind.

He topples as both blades withdraw—and I see whose sword joined mine in stopping the menace.

It was *hers*. "Good Sir Gardner!" None other than *Listy Kendall* grins back at me from the visor of a white helmet. "Fancy meeting *you* here." Laughing, she wipes the blood from her sword against the hip of her white body armor.

My heart hammers in my chest at the sight of her. I am so caught up in her beauty and the shock of seeing her that I forget to lose the power of speech. "You *came?*" Looking around, I see men and women wearing the coat of arms of Kendall's Keep (in patches or tattoos) plowing through the invaders of Burytown. "But what of the *pact?*"

Listy narrows her eyes and lifts her chin. "Wedded or no, I will *never* stand idly by so long as there is something I can do to save good folk like the people of Burytown."

In that instant, I get a shiver, a frisson of electric joy. I want nothing more than to wrap her in my arms and never let go.

Because she *came*. Because she's *fighting* on behalf of my people for no other reason than because it's *right*. Because she's so *beautiful* and *thoughtful* and *capable* and *confident,* and I *want* her with every fiber of my *being.*

Is *this* what Cloister was talking about? The love-that-cherishes? *An attraction so real and profound that we want to join with the other person in a multitude of ways?*

"I suppose the pact is *moot*, then? Since Burytown got the help it needed without the two of us submitting to wedlock?" As Listy says it, a bruiser roars forth, and she dispatches him with a flick of her sword.

"Actually, I've been thinking." Lifting Listy's visor, I lean in and kiss her gently on the lips. "Perhaps we might discuss *another* pact?"

Her eyes lock with mine, and she kisses me back—not gently. "Perhaps."

Then, whirling, she takes up the fight again, swinging her sword with all the nimble grace with which she paints an ocean of mist on a canvas.

Smiling, I fell an attacker of my own, dropping him dead with a heart full of love—but for *once*, it is *not* the love-that-kills.

EVERY DAY NEW, BRIGHT AND BEAUTIFUL

ANNIE REED

Annie Reed has had stories appearing in eighteen volumes of Fiction River *with more appearances to come. Her award-winning story "The Color of Guilt," chosen as one of* The Best Crime and Mystery Stories 2016, *originally appeared in* Fiction River: Hidden in Crime. *One of the founding members of the* Uncollected Anthology, *a series of themed urban fantasy stories published three times a year, Annie's stories also frequently appear in* Pulphouse Fiction Magazine. *Her novels range from* Pretty Little Horses *and* Paper Bullets *featuring Northern Nevada private investigator Abby Maxon, to* Faster, *a superhero origin tale. A northern Nevada resident herself, Annie can be found on the web at www.annie-reed.com and on Facebook as annie.reed.142.*

The beautiful and touching story touches upon a quiet, gentle, and patient lifelong love, which I feel is an excellent way to finish off this anthology. As Annie says about this tale, "it's a hard thing to watch a loved one lose themselves as age and disease steal their memories." Annie has experienced that herself more than once. So many of us have, and can relate to the pain and angst that it causes. But what about the patience and endurance that is also required?

"I realized," Annie continues, "that while I've written lots of stories about love, I've never written about the kind of courageous love it takes to endure one partner's loss of who and what they are."

"But are those things truly lost?" Annie asks. "Or are they discovered all over again each new day? And what if those discoveries came with joy instead of sorrow?"

A stranger found Marnie in the sun room on Saturday.

"Hello, sweetheart," he said with a smile.

Marnie turned her attention away from watching bright yellow birds flitting around the blossoming trees beyond the big picture windows. She could imagine how wonderful the flowering trees must smell, could almost feel the warm breeze that fluttered their leaves and sent blossom petals drifting down to the lush green grass below.

"Look at the birds!" she said to the stranger. "Aren't they beautiful? Yellow is my favorite color, did you know?"

"I seem to remember you told me that," the stranger said.

"They look so soft," Marnie said. "Have you ever held a bird?"

He sat down in a chair near where she sat in her wheelchair. "No, I haven't," he said.

She might have, once upon a time. Although not in her hand but on her finger. Little scaly stick toes grasping her forefinger like a branch. The bird weighed nearly nothing, light as a marshmallow, its little head cocked to one side, its belly sky-blue, its wings and the back of its head black-and-white striped like a zebra.

Had it talked to her? Or had it chattered to itself with its head inside a porcelain feed cup in its cage? Happy bird sounds echoing through her room while the sun streamed through her window.

Was that a memory or something she'd dreamed about?

Was there a difference?

The stranger had faded blue eyes the color of the feathers on the bird's belly. Wispy white hair frizzed around his head. He held a brown fedora in one large-knuckled hand. With the other he rubbed his knee. His smile had dimmed, like a cloud had passed over his own personal sun, so Marnie gifted him with a brilliant smile of her own.

"I had pudding for breakfast today," she said. "Can you imagine that? Isn't that just the best thing, to have pudding for breakfast? Pudding is one of my favorite things to eat."

"Mine, too," he said. "I like chocolate pudding the best."

"Do you have it for breakfast?"

"Sometimes. Maybe not as much as I should. My wife never let me have pudding in the morning. She always wanted me to have oatmeal."

The stranger wore a simple gold ring on his left hand. Marnie was glad he had a wife. People shouldn't be alone.

His wedding ring looked scuffed and old. His hands looked scuffed and old, too, with faded scars on the backs that crisscrossed each other like washed-out lines of chalk on a sidewalk.

That reminded her of...

"I used to play hopscotch," she said, catching the memory and holding tight.

What fun that had been! Jumping over squares to land *smack!* right in the middle of the one on the other side. The exhilaration she felt when her feet landed firmly inside the lines of that next square.

That had to be a memory, not a dream, didn't it? She could almost taste chalk dust in the air as the heat from the concrete came up through the soles of her tennis shoes and her nose itched from the smell of freshly mown grass.

The neighbor's dog, a big black Lab, had barked at Marnie and her friends as it ran back and forth behind a chain-link fence in their front yard, defending its territory from invaders playing on the sidewalk right in front of the fence. She'd been frightened of the dog at first until she realized it just wanted to play with them. She always brought it a treat after that.

One memory led to the next.

Rolling down that sidewalk on skates. Jumping over a rope her friends twirled around her, sometimes two ropes at once, jumping double-time, her hair flying around her as she laughed even when she messed up and came down on the ropes.

"I played hopscotch and jump rope and roller skates," she said.

Or did she just imagine she had? Even now the memory of hopscotch, so clear just a moment ago, had begun to fade into a dream.

"Did you ever play hopscotch?" she asked.

He shook his head. "Back in my day, boys didn't play hopscotch. Or jump rope, unless they were training to be fighters."

"Oh, is that what you were? A fighter?"

That sounded so interesting. She wondered what it would feel like, stepping into a ring, hands wrapped up in gloves so big they looked like cartoon hands. Knowing you had the strength to go with those gloves. To dance around the ring on legs so muscular your feet felt like springs.

"No, sweetheart," the stranger said. "I was never a fighter."

"Then you must be a lover," she said. "Isn't that the saying? A lover not a fighter?"

At least, she thought that was the saying, but it had an odd effect on the stranger. His eyes grew shiny bright, and he squeezed his knee so tight the knuckles on his hand turned white.

Maybe she'd said it wrong and he didn't want to tell her.

When he spoke again, his voice was rougher than before.

"That is what they say."

She'd been right, but she didn't feel as relieved as she should have. Something niggled at her mind from deep inside, down in that place she thought of as a deep, bottomless lake where the memories of her life before the sun room and the birds beyond the picture windows hid from her. A place that was the opposite in all ways from the bright world outside.

She didn't want to think about that place. The world was full of beautiful things, and she'd rather look at them than think about that dark, bottomless lake. So she turned away from the stranger to look outside.

A new bird had flown into the tree, this one with a brown back and a rusty-red breast.

"A robin," she said. "The first robin I've seen this spring!" She didn't know if that was true, but she thought it might be. "I love the spring. It's my favorite time of the year. Everything's so bright and new. Much better than winter. I don't like the cold. It makes my legs ache."

She wasn't sure of that either, but it sounded right as she said it.

She smoothed the afghan over her legs. It was just the right size to fit her wheelchair, crocheted with yarns of gold and green and yellow, just like a warm spring day. Had she made it? Her fingers traced the lines of the yarn, and she thought she recognized the pattern and the stitches necessary to make it, but she wasn't sure. All she knew right now was that the afghan kept her legs warm.

She could just imagine sitting outside beneath the flowering trees with the afghan tucked around her lap, the sun shining down on her head and the birds flittering around her, chattering to themselves. Maybe she could do that later. Ask the woman in the white shirt who'd helped her take a shower that morning to wheel her outside so she could sit in the sun.

"Wouldn't that be wonderful?" Marnie said. "Sitting in the sun and listening to the birds?"

Something bubbled up from the bottomless lake in her mind. A memory of lying on a blanket on the beach, the sun baking her back while gentle waves broke on the shoreline and gulls circled overhead, always on the lookout for abandoned food. Children were playing nearby, laughing and shouting and splashing in the waves. Good rock music played on someone's transistor radio, and the breeze brought the smell of beer and hamburgers charring on a portable grill. Someone was rubbing coconut-scented suntan lotion on her back with large, gentle hands.

She closed her eyes, reveling in the memory of that long-ago beach and the utter joy of sharing the experience with the only man she'd ever loved. Surely this was a memory, not a dream.

Marnie dozed off as she imagined those large, gentle hands rubbing the sore muscles in her back.

Gradually the place where she lived intruded on her dream. The cries of seagulls became the squeaks of crepe-soled shoes on linoleum. The splashing laughter of children playing in the waves turned into the sounds of dishes being scraped and washed in the kitchen. The low rumble of a motorboat engine turned into a moan coming from one of the other rooms in this house where people like Marnie lived.

She jerked awake with a start. Where was she? She'd been on a beach just a moment ago, hadn't she?

No. She was sitting in her wheelchair, looking through the window at the birds.

Had she been talking to someone? Or had that been part of the dream, too?

Across the room, a young woman dressed all in white was

pushing an elderly man in a wheelchair in front of another picture window.

That wasn't the man she'd been talking to. She remembered a hat, a battered brown fedora.

"If I go outside today," she said, "I'll need a hat."

Maybe the man she'd been talking to would let her borrow his.

She turned to ask him, but he was gone.

A stranger found Marnie in the common room on Monday.

"Hello, sweetheart," he said with a smile.

She was sitting in her wheelchair in front of the room's single large television. He grunted as he sat down on the sofa next to her wheelchair.

"Are you here to watch my favorite show with me?" she asked.

"I suppose I am."

He held a brown fedora in his hands. The hat had seen better days if the scuffed brim was any indication.

Like the stranger himself. His large hands were scarred, the blunt fingernails yellowed with age. He had kind-looking blue eyes and wispy white hair, and he wore a wedding ring that looked a lot like the ring Marnie wore on her left hand.

The woman who'd helped Marnie shower that morning had made her take the ring off so that it couldn't slip off. The ring was too big, the woman had said, but Marnie's finger had felt naked without it. She'd slipped the ring back on as soon as she could.

She played with the ring now, twisting it around her finger as she tried to reach for a memory that felt important. Something to do with the rings? But the memory slipped beneath the dark surface of the lake in her mind where most of the memories of her life hid, out of reach.

A woman in white sat at a small desk off to the side of the television room near another stranger, this one in a wheelchair like Marnie. The woman was small with long black hair, a round face, and dark, happy eyes. She nodded at the stranger who sat next to Marnie.

"Good to see you today," she said. "You want water? Or maybe iced tea?"

He shook his head. "No, thank you. I'm fine."

"The tea here is very good," Marnie said. At least she thought it was. "You should have some."

"I'm good," he said. "What are you watching?"

"It's a very good show," she said. "My favorite. This man"—she pointed at a gray-haired man on the screen, very distinguished looking in a black woolen overcoat—"he has to get to his grand-daughter's school even though the police are trying to stop him."

On the small flat-screen television, the man was making his way on foot through a snowstorm.

"Maybe when he gets there, they can build a snowman or make snow angels," she said. "A big one for him and a little one for her."

Marnie didn't know how she knew about snow angels. Had she made one herself? Flopped down on her back on snow so cold it took her breath away, but she didn't mind because scissoring her legs and flapping her arms like wings was just so much fun?

"Did you ever make snow angels with your children?" she asked the stranger.

His smile stayed fixed in place but the lines around his eyes grew deeper. More pronounced.

"My wife and I were never blessed with children." His eyes brightened. "But we made snow angels once on vacation. It wasn't supposed to snow, but we woke up to a world covered in white. She insisted that we go and play outside."

That sounded like so much fun!

"You must have enjoyed yourselves so much," Marnie said.

"Marnie," the woman in white said from her desk. "Don't you remember—"

The stranger on the sofa next to Marnie held up his hand with his index finger raised. His smile was gone and his eyes were icy blue and cold.

Marnie shivered and turned her head to look at the woman in white. She had as stern a look on her face as the stranger.

"You know what her doctor says," the woman said. "We are to—"

"No." The stranger almost sounded angry. "We've talked about this."

"She will get worse if we don't—"

"I won't have you distress her over things beyond her control. Leave it alone."

The woman in white looked like she wanted to say more, but she didn't.

Marnie didn't like this. She didn't know who they were talking about, but she didn't like that they were angry.

What if they were talking about her?

"Did I do something wrong?" she asked.

She didn't know what she could have done wrong. Was it something she'd said? She couldn't remember what they'd been talking about. Angels? The program on the television?

Why couldn't she remember?

"No, sweetheart," the stranger said. He smiled at her, a gentle smile that took the worry away. "I promise you, you didn't do a single thing wrong."

He had trouble getting the last few words out, like something had gone wrong with his voice.

Marnie had heard his voice before, she was sure of it. In a hospital room? Was that it?

A cold room with icy white walls and a steady beeping sound. Pressure around her upper arm as a machine hissed. Something taped to the end of one of her fingers. Tubes draped around her face that hissed air up her nose. Feeling like a trapped animal while someone reassured her over and over again that everything would be all right.

Had that been a dream?

No. The room and the walls and the pressure of the cuff on her arm had to be a memory. Who in her right mind would dream of a thing like that?

"I was in a hospital," she said.

"Yes," the stranger said.

"And you were there."

"I'll always be there," he said.

"Every day?" she asked.

"For you?" His smile came back all the way. "Every single new day of your life."

Marnie's husband found her sitting in her wheelchair beneath a flowering plum tree in the backyard on Wednesday afternoon.

"Hello, sweetheart!" she said, holding up her arms for a hug.

He stood still and blinked at her, and for a moment she wasn't sure if he would hug her or not. Then a huge smile lit up his lined face, and he leaned down and hugged her hard.

"Oof!" Marnie patted him on the back. "You act like you haven't seen me in ages."

He drew in a sharp breath through his nose, then straightened up. His faded blue eyes were shiny bright. "Just happy to see my girl."

She eyed the flyaway wisps of his white hair. "You need a haircut, you old hippie."

She'd started to call him that when his hair had first turned silver. It had been longer in those days, but she'd kept it up even after his scalp took up more real estate on his head than his hair.

He sat down on a wooden bench next to her wheelchair. Overhead the sun shone bright out of a mostly cloudless sky. Bright yellow birds flitted around a tall elm in the yard next door, chattering at each other and teasing the dog that lived in the house next to the group home where Marnie lived.

She couldn't quite remember how she got here or why she needed a wheelchair. Those memories were stuck beneath a dark cloud somewhere in the back of her mind, but she didn't want to think about that. Her husband had come to visit, the day was beautiful and bright, and the sun felt wonderful on her old bones.

"You're going to need a hat if you sit out here much longer," he said. "Want mine?"

"That old thing?" she said with a smile.

She reached over and plucked his fedora out of his hands. He'd worn that hat at their wedding, much to her mother's chagrin. But my, how he'd cut such a handsome figure.

She plopped the fedora on her own head. It was much too big for her, but she pushed it to the side at what she imagined was a rakish angle.

"How do I look?" she asked.

"Beautiful," he said.

She took one of his big, strong hands in hers. His hands still bore the scars of the hard work he'd done on the assembly lines before the factory had shut down.

"Do you remember the first time we held hands?" she asked.

"I do. We were in the backyard at your parents' house, sitting on the swings. Your dad was mowing the front lawn and your mother was inside making dinner."

"And you...you had..."

She frowned as the memory seemed to skip just beyond her reach. The sunlight seemed to dim a bit like the edge of a cloud had touched the sun.

"I reached over and took your hand," he said. "And you wrapped your fingers around mine, but you really wrapped them around my heart."

Marnie cocked her head, trying to remember. The fedora slipped off and landed on the afghan covering her lap.

"I did?"

He squeezed her hand. "You did. And the best thing was, we never let go. Not even when your mother came out to get us for dinner."

She squeezed his hand back. It felt right holding his hand, although she didn't quite know why.

"We're going to have roast turkey and stuffing and gravy for dinner," she said. "Would you like to stay? Do you like turkey?"

He looked at her for a long moment. She couldn't quite make out the expression in his eyes. Maybe he didn't like turkey and didn't know how to tell her. She liked turkey quite a lot, especially with stuffing and gravy.

Finally he sighed and smiled at her. "Turkey dinner it is," he said. "With my best girl. Sounds like a date."

Marnie smiled back.

He was such a nice man.

A stranger found Marnie in the sun room on Friday morning.

"Hello, sweetheart," he said with a smile.

She was sitting in her wheelchair in front of the picture window. Sunlight fell on the afghan on her lap, warming her legs nicely.

She'd been having such marvelous dreams this morning. Walking in the sunlight on an old country road, the dirt crunching beneath her sandals. She'd held a wide-brimmed straw hat in one hand and the large, gentle hand of the man walking beside her with the other. Crickets chirped in the high grass in the fields on either side of the road, and up ahead blackbirds squabbled over a mud puddle in the road.

She'd felt so warm and comfortable in that dream. Had it been a memory instead of a dream? She couldn't tell, and really, what did it matter?

Dream or memory, either one made her feel good.

She turned her head and looked at the stranger who didn't seem like a stranger. He grunted as he sat down on a chair near her wheelchair. Wispy white hair peeked out from beneath his well-worn fedora, and he was smiling at her.

She reached out for his hand. "Will you watch the birds with me?" she asked.

He took her small hand in his large one and squeezed lightly. "It would be my honor."

She threaded her fingers through his like they'd always fit together just so.

She sighed a happy sigh and turned her attention back to the world beyond the big picture window where bright yellow birds flitted through the branches of a blossoming tree and somewhere, Marnie was sure of it, a young girl held the hand of the man she loved while walking down a country road on a warm spring day.

ABOUT THE EDITOR

Mark Leslie is a writer, editor, and bookseller from Waterloo, Ontario.

Mark published his first short story, "The Progressive Sidetrack," in 1992 and has since published stories in various magazines and anthologies, including the story "Impressions in the Snow" in *Fiction River: Sparks*, edited by Rebecca Moesta.

Mark has edited the anthologies *North of Infinity II, Campus Chills*, and *Tesseracts Sixteen: Parnassus Unbound*.

Mark's fiction titles include *One Hand Screaming, Evasion, A Canadian Werewolf in New York* and *I, Death*. He also writes nonfiction explorations of the paranormal for Dundurn, a Toronto-based publisher. They include *Haunted Hamilton, Spooky Sudbury, Tomes of Terror, Creepy Capital*, and *Haunted Hospitals*.

Between 2011 and 2017, Mark worked as the Director of Self-Publishing and Author Relations for Kobo where he was the driving force behind the creation of Kobo Writing Life, a free and easy to use author/small-publisher friendly platform designed to publish directly to Kobo's global catalog in 190 countries.

When he's not writing, or trying to overcome his addiction to alliteration in true ghost story book titles, Mark attaches "Lefebvre" back onto his name and works as a professional speaker, and a book nerd with a passion for craft beer.

Special offer—only from Kobo!

Reread your favorite stories anytime with a free ebook
edition of *Fiction River: Feel the Love* from Kobo.

Just go to kobo.com, add the book to your cart,
and enter FEELTHELOVE in the promo code field
on the checkout screen.

ACKNOWLEDGMENTS

Thank you to the following wonderful people who supported the 2018 *Fiction River* Kickstarter Subscription Drive·

AJ Lemke
Alexandra Brandt
Andrew Rees
Angela Penrose
aniket gore
Annie Reed
Bill
Bonnie Elizabeth
Brian D Lambert
C.A. Rowland
Camille R. Lofters
Carolyn Ivy Stein
Caryl Giles
Céline Malgen
Chrissy Wissler
Christel Adina Loar
Darren Blake

David Hendrickson
David Macfarlane
Denise Gaskins
Diana Deverell
Dorothy Fuhrmann
Felicia Fredlund
Francelia Belton
Francesca Jourdan
Frederic Lambert
Gary A. Leicht
Gavran
GMarkC
Harley Christensen
Helen Katsinis
Howard Blakeslee
J.A. Marlow
J.R. Murdock
Jamie Curierre
Jamie Ferguson
Jim Gotaas
Jim Ryals
Joe Cron
Johanna Rothman
John Lorentz & Ruth Sachter
Karen L. Durst
Kari Kilgore and Jason Adams
Kate Pavelle
Katharina Gerlach
Keith West
Ken Talley
LC
Linda Maye Adams
Lotus Goldstein
Louisa Swann
Lynda Martinez Foley

M. Louisa Locke

M.G. Herron

Maralee Nelder

Marian Goldeen

Mark Kuhn

Marla Bracken

Marnilo Cardenas

Mary Jo Rabe

Mary Kennedy

Mervi Hamalainen

Mike Nisivoccia

Naomi Gray

Neil Flinchbaugh

Nic Cain

Peter Sartucci

Pierre L'Allier

R.J.H.

Rebecca M. Senese

Rhel

Rich Kacy

Risa Scranton

Rob Voss

Sharon Kae Reamer

Simon Horvat

Stephannie Tallent

Steve Perry

Terry Mixon

The 6th JM

William Hall

FICTION RIVER: YEAR SIX

Feel the Love
Edited by Mark Leslie

Stolen
Edited by Leah Cutter

Doorways to Enchantment
Edited by Dayle A. Dermatis

Superstitious
Edited by Mark Leslie

Unlikely Heroines
Edited by Allyson Longueira

Chances
Edited by Denise Little

A subscription to *Fiction River* saves you money and ensures that you receive the very best short fiction from some of today's best authors. Subscriptions are available in electronic and trade paper formats and begin with the very next volume. Don't wait! Subscribe today at www.FictionRiver.com.

Missed a previously published volume? No problem. Buy individual volumes anytime from your favorite bookseller.

Unnatural Worlds
Edited by Dean Wesley Smith & Kristine Kathryn Rusch

How to Save the World
Edited by John Helfers

Time Streams
Edited by Dean Wesley Smith

Christmas Ghosts
Edited by Kristine Grayson

Hex in the City
Edited by Kerrie L. Hughes

Moonscapes
Edited by Dean Wesley Smith

Special Edition: Crime
Edited by Kristine Kathryn Rusch

Fantasy Adrift
Edited by Kristine Kathryn Rusch

Universe Between
Edited by Dean Wesley Smith

Fantastic Detectives
Edited by Kristine Kathryn Rusch

Past Crime
Edited by Kristine Kathryn Rusch

Pulse Pounders
Edited by Kevin J. Anderson

Risk Takers
Edited by Dean Wesley Smith

Alchemy & Steam
Edited by Kerrie L. Hughes

Valor
Edited by Lee Allred

Recycled Pulp
Edited by John Helfers

Hidden in Crime
Edited by Kristine Kathryn Rusch

Sparks
Edited by Rebecca Moesta

Visions of the Apocalypse
Edited by John Helfers

Haunted
Edited by Kerrie L. Hughes

Last Stand
Edited by Dean Wesley Smith & Felicia Fredlund

Tavern Tales
Edited by Kerrie L. Hughes

No Humans Allowed
Edited by John Helfers

Editor's Choice
Edited by Mark Leslie

Pulse Pounders: Adrenaline
Edited by Kevin J. Anderson

Feel the Fear
Edited by Mark Leslie

Superpowers
Edited by Rebecca Moesta

Justice
Edited by Kristine Kathryn Rusch

Wishes
Edited by Rebecca Moesta

Pulse Pounders: Countdown
Edited by Kevin J. Anderson

Hard Choices
Edited by Dean Wesley Smith

FICTION RIVER PRESENTS

Fiction River's line of reprint anthologies,
edited by Allyson Longueira.

Fiction River has published more than 400 amazing stories by more than 100 talented authors since its inception, from *New York Times* bestsellers to debut authors. So, WMG Publishing decided to start bringing back some of the earlier stories in new compilations.

Debut Authors
The Unexpected
Darker Realms
Racing the Clock
Legacies
Readers' Choice
Writers Without Borders

To learn more or to pick up your copy today, go to FictionRiver.com.

PULPHOUSE FICTION MAGAZINE

Pulphouse Fiction Magazine is returning twenty years after its last issue. The first issue came out in January 2018, and the magazine will be quarterly, with about 70,000 words of short fiction every issue. This reincarnation mixes some of the stories from the old *Pulphouse* days with brand-new fiction. The magazine has an attitude, as did the first run. No genre limitations, but high-quality writing and strangeness.

For more information or to subscribe, go to
www.pulphousemagazine.com.

Made in the USA
San Bernardino, CA
12 February 2019